Finding Junie Kim

ALSO BY ELLEN OH

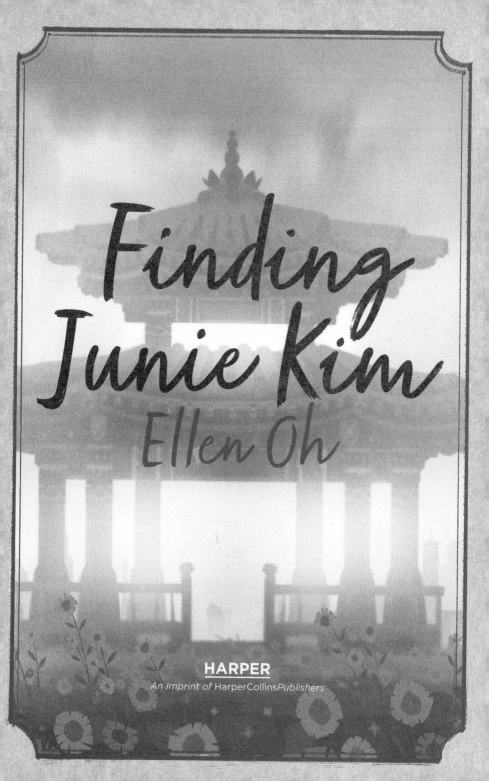

Finding Junie Kim

Ellen Oh

HARPER
An Imprint of HarperCollins Publishers

Library of Congress Control Number: 2020950993

ISBN 978-0-06-298798-3

Typography by Joel Tippie

21 22 23 24 25   PC/LSCH   10 9 8 7 6 5 4 3

❖

First Edition

This book is dedicated to my mom and dad
and all the survivors of the Korean War.
May it no longer be the Forgotten War.

BOOK I

Junie

Chapter 1

AUGUST IS STILL THE SUMMERTIME. So why do we have to go back to school? Shouldn't school start in September, when the summer is actually over? I don't get it. It's literally only a week away.

"Junie, hurry up or you'll miss the bus!"

The first day of school and I'm already filled with that horrible empty-stomach crampy feeling of dread.

"Junie!"

I can hear the slight annoyance in my mom's voice and yet I'm still frozen in place in my room, staring at my schoolbag. It's a brand-new messenger bag, dark gray with bright red straps, just like I wanted. But it also means going back to the terrible place.

Middle school.

"Junie Kim!"

"I'm coming!"

Grabbing my bag, I force myself to walk downstairs to the kitchen, where my mom is waiting. On the table is a peanut-butter-and-jelly waffle sandwich and a tall glass of milk. It's what I call my power breakfast, and it's my favorite. But today the thought of eating it makes my throat close up.

"You're gonna have to wolf that down fast, honey."

I shake my head. "I'm not hungry."

"Eat a little anyway," she says, pushing me into my seat. "You need to eat breakfast to get through the day."

She packs my lunch sack into my schoolbag and picks up a big stack of files. My mom is a lawyer with the Department of Justice. It sounds really cool, but it keeps her really busy. That's not as cool.

"Mom, can't you drive me to school today? I don't mind if I'm there early."

She shakes her head regretfully. "I'm sorry, honey, but I have a meeting and I have to run now. Otherwise I'll be late."

There will be no escaping hell this morning.

It's the worst thing in the world that my best friends don't live near me, and therefore I have no one to ride the bus with. It would make the trip bearable. At least last year my older brother was on the bus with me. But now he's going to high school. I'll be all alone with the current worst person of Livingston Middle School.

The walk to the bus stop is only a few blocks from my house, but it reminds me of a nightmare I always have. It starts with a scary chase sequence and ends with me falling off a building, where the fall feels like an intense forever as I scream and scream and then I finally jerk awake. The problem with the falling nightmare is that even after waking up, I'm still scared, as if there's more to come. That's what it feels like reaching the bus stop. I don't know what else is coming, but I know it will be bad.

"Hey, it's the North Korean commie!"

Taking the middle-school bus every morning means listening to Tobias Rodney Thornton, the resident bully, spew racist hate at the only Asian student on the bus. That would be me. Junie Kim. I'm not the only nonwhite kid on the bus. But Tobias doesn't mess with the Black or Latino boys, at least on the bus. Because there are more than one of them.

Tobias is nothing but a bully and a coward, just like his older brother, Satan. Actually, his real name is Samuel Austin Thornton, but Satan suits him better.

Nobody likes either of the Thornton brothers. They're both big and mean and don't care about what other people think of them. And Tobias is five foot ten and probably like two hundred pounds, so he could pummel anyone's opinions into the sidewalk.

As long as I've had to deal with him, I've only ever seen him show two emotions: angry and more angry.

This morning he looks like he's his normal mean.

"Commie!" he spits out as I scurry as far away from him as I can. The bus stop is on the corner of the local park, so there's a lot of space for all of us to spread out. It's one of the biggest stops, with anywhere from fifteen to twenty kids waiting every day. Since Tobias has planted himself on the grassy corner of the park, I rush over to the end of the sidewalk and stand next to a No Parking sign. I pray under my breath that he stays on the park side, but today is not my lucky day.

"Can't you hear me talking to you, dog eater?"

I hunch up like a sad turtle and try to ignore him, but he's now throwing sticks and dirt at me.

I look around, hoping something else will grab his attention.

Megan and her little clique huddle together, as far away from me as possible. We haven't gotten along since I won first place for the sixth-grade essay contest and she got second. She's never forgiven me for doing better in an English class when I was "foreign," and she was American. Truth is, even though I was born and raised here, I'll never be truly American to her.

I'm friendlier with some of the boys, but right now everyone is just trying to avoid Tobias's attention, and since he's focused on me, they're all earnestly avoiding my eyes.

Everyone's too afraid of him to stick up for me. I am overwhelmed with this weird feeling that is sadness, but in a way I've never felt before. It feels like hopelessness. It feels like this is the rest of my life.

The bus pulls up and I rush over to it. Since we're the first stop, it's completely empty. Even though it isn't cool to sit in the front, I make sure to sit near the bus driver. Tobias is mean but not stupid. Our bus driver is not the friendliest man. He is no-nonsense and does not like troublemakers. He keeps the rowdier kids in line by standing up and glaring. Since he looks like he wrestles alligators for fun, it's very effective.

The bus has a hierarchy to it. All the sixth graders have to sit in the front of the bus, while all the eighth graders lord it over everyone else in the back. Seventh graders sit in the middle or as close to the back as the eighth graders will allow. Since Tobias has claimed the back of the bus as his domain, I stay as far away from him as I can. In fact, I'd sit on top of the bus if I could, to avoid breathing the same air as him. While there's only a few stops after ours, it always feels like the longest ride.

Livingston Middle School is a big, boxy red building that looks like a prison. We pull into the school parking lot and immediately notice that there are several police cars in front of the building. Usually there's at least one police car every morning. But four of them? Something must be up.

Inside, everyone is speaking in hushed tones. The teachers don't say good morning. They all look so serious.

The pale-yellow hallways are crowded with students, which is unusual. Sixth graders head straight to the cafeteria and seventh and eighth graders are supposed to line up in the gym before first period. But it looks like no one is in the gym. In the crowd I spot my best friends, Patrice and Amy. I weave over to them and see that Amy is crying and Patrice looks ready to hit something or someone. This is not surprising, because they are usually opposites in almost all ways. Patrice is model beautiful and always wears her thick black hair slicked back and pulled tight into a low ponytail. Her dark brown skin is absolutely flawless. Meanwhile, Amy has bushy, curly blond hair that springs out everywhere and a ghostly-white complexion that shows her multitude of freckles.

"What's wrong?"

"Junie! Someone sprayed swastikas and racist graffiti all over the gym walls!" Patrice says angrily.

My mouth drops open in shock. "Did you see it?"

Patrice shakes her head. "They won't let any of us in since the police are here. But everyone's talking about it. It was targeting Blacks, Jews, and Asians."

"That's literally the three of us!" Amy suddenly looks really scared. "Do you think it was meant for us?"

Patrice bites her lip. "It's not like we're the only ones . . ."

"Does anyone know what it actually said?" I ask.

"I think only the teachers know for sure," Patrice says. "And they're taking it really seriously."

"I don't want to see it," Amy replies. "Just hearing about it is awful. Who would hate us that much?"

We glance down the hallway where we see all the head administrators hovering around the gym doors. The morning bell rings, and the hallway fills with moving bodies. It's loud, but not the normal boisterousness of a middle-school morning.

Patrice and I walk to English together while Amy leaves for her math class. None of us talk; we just wave. I feel lethargic and tired and I'm not even in first period yet. I look over at Patrice, who is walking quietly next to me, her eyebrows furrowed. I can feel the intensity of her emotions radiating from her. I rub her shoulder, and she gives me the saddest smile. In class we sit at our seats and are immediately surrounded by classmates.

"Did you hear what it said?"

"Who could it be?"

"Was it someone from our school?"

I don't know how to respond, so I stay quiet, but I can see Patrice trying to hold back her temper.

Second bell rings, and Ms. Simon tells everyone to take their seats.

Suddenly, the PA system crackles, and we hear the principal's voice over the loudspeaker.

"Good morning. This is Principal Sumner, and I am very sorry to have to start this day, our first day back to school, with such terrible news. Hateful racist and anti-Semitic graffiti was found in our gym. Hate has no place in this school, and we denounce this terrible criminal act. Our school is a place where all must feel free to learn, free of fear and hate. We must remind ourselves that our community stands for welcoming everyone, and it is our responsibility to provide a safe and welcoming environment. There is much work that we need to do, and there is healing that our community will need. An email has been sent to all parents this morning, and counselors will be available to speak with any student who needs their services.

"Due to this criminal act, our beautiful gym has been defaced. Therefore, all gym activities will be held outside today. Rest assured that we are taking this incident very seriously and will investigate this matter thoroughly with the Montgomery County police, and appropriate action will be taken against the perpetrators. We encourage anyone with information to come and talk to staff. This horrible act is not representative of our school and our student body and will not be tolerated."

When he signs off, the classroom erupts in conversation.

Ms. Simon claps her hands several times to get our attention. "I know it's hard to concentrate right now, but we do have a lesson to get through."

Roland Mathers, who is kind of a know-it-all and talks like he's forty, raises his hand and starts to speak even before she calls on him. "Ms. Simon, can you at least tell us exactly what was written on the walls? I think we should know what the vandals said about our community and if any of us might be in danger."

Ms. Simon purses her lips. "I can't tell you the exact nature of what was said, but I can tell you there were no direct threats. Just hateful words specifically aimed at the

Black, Jewish, and Asian communities."

Patrice's hand shoots up in the air. "But Ms. Simon, doesn't the very fact that racist and anti-Semitic words were used make it a threat?"

I tense up at her question. This is our first day with Ms. Simon, who is a middle-aged white lady, and I worry that she might be the type who doesn't get it.

Ms. Simon nods. "You're absolutely right, and I apologize. While no specific threats of harm were written, the very nature of the words themselves was meant to cause fear and intimidation. It is in fact a hate crime, which is why the police are involved. I know it's frightening, but I assure you that the administration and the police are going to make sure that these perpetrators, whoever they are, are caught and punished."

I can see Patrice is as relieved as I am to hear Ms. Simon speak so forcefully and call it a hate crime. She seems like a good teacher, one who really cares.

It's hard to focus on classes after that. I keep wondering what exactly was written on the walls. How bad was it? In the hallways, nobody can talk about anything else, and rumors are all over the place. I hear bits and pieces as I walk by groups of students. Some are clearly shocked and afraid, while others are excited by the most interesting thing to happen in Livingston in a long time.

"I heard there were KKK symbols and that it said to deport all immigrants."

"They said the handwriting looked like it had to be a student."

"Well, it can't be someone who goes here because they broke in late at night, and who would want to come back to school if they didn't have to?"

"I don't believe it. It's all fake news. . . ."

Ugh, I really hate the term *fake news*. I whip my head around to see who made the last comment and am not surprised to see it's one of the obnoxious boys wearing a red *Make America Great Again* hat. It was my mom who explained to me that the slogan was about exclusion and not inclusion. Who they didn't want in this country, in order to make it a world they wanted. It's why it hurts so much to see those hats. It makes me feel unwelcome in my own birthplace, and the country of my parents. The hats remind me of all the people who will never accept me as a real American.

Patrice grabs my hand, and I turn to see the anger tightening her lips into a straight line.

The boy knows we've heard him, and he starts following us and chanting "Fake news! Fake news!" and his friends laugh like hyenas. I'm clenching my teeth so hard I can feel my jaw hurt.

Patrice spins around and looks the boy dead in the eye.

"Piss off," she says without raising her voice, but her eyes shoot lasers. The boy raises his hands in surrender, smirks, and turns away.

I wish I was more like Patrice. She's not afraid to confront people, and she never looks foolish doing so.

"I hate the fake newsers," Patrice says. "They do it deliberately. By denying it, they can pretend it doesn't exist. No racism. No global warming. No refugees dying. It's all about denying the truth."

I look at Patrice in awe. Sometimes she sounds so much older than she really is.

She catches me looking and gives me a small smile. "I'm repeating what my parents say."

"I know," I reply. "But it still sounds right when you say it."

Our cafeteria is on the second floor and always feels way overcrowded and noisy. It has an unusual L shape, making it hard to navigate due to the crush of students. We head for our usual table in the far right corner, but have to pass the annoying popular kids' table. They're mostly white except for Esther Song, the only other Korean girl at our school, who never acknowledges my existence. She's one of those Asians who ignores all other Asians because they remind them that they aren't actually white. My mom says it's internalized racism: when racism messes with you so much you hate who you are and wish you were white.

"Hey, Patrice, I bet you did all that vandalism just so you could say racism is still real. Help! I'm Black and a girl and I'm being oppressed!"

Stu Papadopolis is a smirky, two-faced weasel. But he's also popular because he's rich, and some girls think he's good-looking, which I personally don't get. He reminds me of a beady-eyed rat. And he wears so much cologne I literally gag whenever I'm near him. I want to arrest him for air pollution.

Patrice is glaring at him so hard her nostrils are flaring. "Stu, you are such a racist."

He rolls his eyes dramatically, sending his idiot goons into hysterics. "See what I mean? She's always screaming racism! News flash, Patrice, not everything is about race."

"Only a privileged white guy would say that," Patrice snaps at him.

"Now that's racist and sexist!" Stu howls loudly. "I'm gonna report you to the administration. Oh, wait a minute. Nobody cares about white males anymore. Because we have 'privilege.'" He uses finger quotes. "Right. We're the ones that are really being discriminated against."

Patrice is shaking with rage, and I'm so angry I just want to rip Stu's head bald.

"You're a horrible, nasty troll," I shout at him.

"Shut up, Kim Jong Un. Why don't you go back to your own Communist country?"

"This is my country! I was born here!" I'm so angry I can't help but stumble over my words.

"Says who?"

"Says my birth certificate!"

"Pffft, fake news! You can get fake birth certificates from China."

Before I can say another word, Patrice is pulling me away.

"Come on, Junie, don't talk to him. You'll just get frustrated by his stupidness."

I glare at Esther as I leave, but she avoids my eyes even as she laughs with the others. What a traitor. I can't believe she doesn't see how racist all her friends are. Or maybe she does and just doesn't care. None of them do. I see it in the faces of kids who are rolling their eyes and laughing about the vandalism. What Patrice and I find so horrifying is just a big joke to them.

Patrice and I cling to each other as we speed over to our table. There's not a lot of students of color at Livingston Middle School, but it's true that we tend to stick together. Patrice says we need to be our own support group because of how openly racist a lot of kids have been ever since the presidential election.

As we sit down next to Amy, I'm reminded again how she is the only white girl at our table.

"Stu Papadopolis is such a jerk!" Patrice says as she plops down on the bench.

"Him and his goon squad are jerks," Hena replies. "Every time they walk by me, they whisper 'terrorist.' I hate them." Hena is Pakistani American, with the most gorgeous set of long black curls that I've ever seen on a human.

Lila and Marisol nod fiercely. "Ugh, they think they're so hilarious. Like calling us burrito and taco and telling us to go back to Mexico," Lila says. "They're so brainless they think that South America means Mexico." Lila is Peruvian

American and Marisol is Cuban American, and they are literally the best of friends. They do everything together and are as close as sisters and as opposite as sugar is to salt. Lila is short and brown, a bubbly fast-talker who always has a bright smile for everyone. Marisol is blond and fair and moody. But somehow their differences don't matter when they can unite in their shared hatred of Stu Papadopolis and his gang of evil trolls.

"And they're getting worse. They love standing in front of doors to block us and calling themselves the wall," Marisol chimes in. "And if we get mad, they tell us to chill out and take a joke. It's not funny."

"Ugh, they're horrible," Patrice says.

Then Lila and Marisol call them a bad word in Spanish that sends everyone into giggles. Even I can't help but smile. I love the way curse words sound in different languages, but Spanish is my favorite. It is so emphatic.

"I want to put some dog pee in his fancy Hydro Flask." Marisol smirks.

They all laugh again, but it reminds me of my morning. "He and Tobias Thornton are the worst," I say.

"Isn't he that eighth grader who looks like he's thirty?"

I nod morosely while the others laugh. Tobias is so awful I don't even find jokes about him funny.

"Is he still picking on you?" Amy asks. "His brother used to make my brother Aaron's life a living hell. That's why Aaron went to a private high school."

"Does he like it there?"

"Yeah," Amy replies. "My parents asked if I want to go there after middle school. After today, I wonder if I should."

If only I could run away from Tobias too. But my mom always says that running away never solves anything. You have to confront your problems head-on. But what if you're really scared that your problem is going to physically hurt you?

"Guys, what are we gonna do about this school?" Patrice asks in a serious tone.

"What do you mean?" Amy asks. We all look at Patrice in confusion.

"The graffiti and the everyday racism. We have to do something."

"But what can we do?" We all end up bombarding Patrice with the same question.

She gnaws on her lower lip, something she does when she is thinking hard. "We need to protest! Make people take notice of us," she says.

I'm shaking my head. "What will that do? What will it change? They'll just laugh at us."

Patrice bangs her hand on the table, making all of us jump. "So?!" she says loudly. "They laugh at us anyway. Let's do something to make them realize how wrong they are!"

Amy, Hena, and Lila are nodding their heads.

"Instead of a protest, why don't we organize an event? Something that makes people think and talk and learn," Hena says.

"And force them to listen to us!" Lila says as she claps her hands enthusiastically. I don't know what it is about Lila and clapping. If she ever wants to play an instrument, I would vote for cymbals. She'd be a natural.

I can't help but roll my eyes over their excitement. I definitely don't want any part of this.

Patrice slaps my arm lightly. "I saw that, Junie. Stop being so negative."

"I'm not being negative; I'm being realistic. Nothing we do is ever going to change their minds, so why even bother?"

Marisol is the only one who agrees with me. "Yeah. It's not like we have any power. We can't make them listen to us. They already treat us like trash. It would probably just make everything worse."

I'm about to agree with Marisol, but I see the look in Patrice's eyes and I stop. I can feel a headache beginning in my left temple.

"That's not a reason not to do anything! What happened today is really bad. Aren't you scared? This is how some of the students here think! We have to change that. Let's get the administration to make them listen to us!" Patrice is really fired up.

Amy agrees, but that's no surprise. Amy always agrees with Patrice. "Patrice is right! We can't do nothing! I'm in!"

"Me too!" Hena and Lila both say.

Lila stares at Marisol, who rolls her eyes but then nods in agreement.

My head is beginning to pound, and my insides are rolling like I'm a can of soda that's been all shook up. All the stress of the day is starting to get to me, and I'm suddenly so irritated with the world.

"Junie, stop shaking your head! We can do this!" Patrice snaps at me.

I should shut up—in my gut I know I should. But I don't seem to have any control over my mouth. "It's a whole lot of work for what's going to be the biggest waste of time," I say.

Patrice gives me a look that makes my heart wither. There's something so adult about it, as if I am some terrible disappointment to her.

"Then don't do anything, Junie," she says. "We'll do it without you. We don't need your negativity dragging us down."

Her words cut deep, leaving me bleeding internally. But instead of addressing the pain, I get angry.

"Fine, go ahead and do your stupid protest that nobody gives a crap about!"

I grab my lunch bag, stuff all my wrappers in it, and head out of the cafeteria. The others are calling my name and asking me to stay, but I ignore them. I can feel angry tears burning the backs of my eyes, and I don't want anyone to see me cry. I just want to go home and crawl into my bed and never see anyone again.

Chapter 2

NOT HAVING ANY HOMEWORK MEANS I can do whatever I want. For me, that means drawing. I do little doodles all over any paper I can get my hands on, sometimes even on my arms. A lot of times, I let my feelings out in my doodles. I've been doodling all the bad things that happened today. My favorite drawing is of the morning. I drew myself as a sad turtle with its head pulled halfway into its shell as it stood waiting for the bus. Behind the turtle, I drew Tobias as a big ugly pig in clothing that's too tight, with a mean expression on his piggy face.

When my parents come home, they rush my brother and me to get ready to go to dinner at my grandparents' house. My grandparents live fifteen minutes away in Rockville, which is the city right next to us. I always thought that was weird. If they were so close, why weren't they in the same town? But that's Maryland for you. If you drive for a little while in any direction you hit another city. My parents don't even work in Maryland; they have to commute to Washington, DC. But they ride the Metro train into the city. Although I don't get why they have to drive to the Metro, instead of just driving to work. Adults are weird.

When we arrive, the house is full of guests. It's a mix of my grandparents' old friends and some new members of Grandma's church group. I just bow my head and smile. The Korean words flow right over me, familiar and yet incomprehensible. Only bits and pieces make any sense to me. Like the words I've heard enough to understand.

Mostly just "How've you been?" "How was school?" "You got so big!" and "Did you eat?"

Since there are no other kids, my brother and I are stuck eating with all the adults in the dining room. We're crammed in between my parents and my grandparents on one side of the table. It's really boring, because they speak mostly in Korean. But at least the food is delicious. My grandma is the best cook. My mom always says that if Grandma opened a restaurant, it would be crowded every single day. But instead she's a real estate broker and is always busy driving clients all over the place. Grandpa used to work at a small import/export company until he retired a few years ago. Now he spends most of his time gardening, reading, and writing articles that he submits to the Korean newspapers. He's also disabled due to arthritis in his spine. So he has to use a cane when he goes outside, and he can't walk for too long. My mom says it must be so frustrating because my grandfather used to be such an active man, but he never lets it bother him. He is always happy and positive.

The dining table is covered with dumplings, and all types of meat and vegetable jeon, which is basically fried yummy stuff, and then all sorts of noodles and side dishes and the absolute staple of every Korean household, kimchee. But the highlight is the huge platter of galbi jjim, which is my favorite. It is braised short ribs that have been stewed in a delicious marinade until the meat falls off the bones. I am drooling. Grandma fills my plate up with all my favorite foods and a big dollop of white rice, and I dive right in.

Grandpa nudges me and asks, "How was school today?"

I make a sour face as I shovel a large bite of rice and meat into my mouth.

Grandpa chuckles and lightly pinches my cheek before turning back to the conversation.

My dad starts telling a story in English, and everyone is laughing. This really bugs me because for nearly an hour the conversation was all in Korean. Why can't they talk in English all the time so I can understand everything?

"That reminds me of when I was living in Korea and I'd been playing basketball. So I'm in sweats and a T-shirt and I stop by this little grocery store to buy rice, and I ask the ahjumma for bap. And she starts yelling at me! I'm so confused. I think maybe she's low on rice or something. So then

I say, 'No, just a little bit,' and she grabs a broom and chases me out."

Everyone is really laughing, and I don't get it.

"Why did she get so mad?" I ask.

"Because 'bap' means cooked rice. And it also means food," my grandfather tells me. "She thought your dad was a beggar asking for free food. What he should have said was 'sal,' which is the word for uncooked rice."

I shake my head. "Korean is hard."

My grandfather ruffles my hair. "But you should learn it anyway."

After a while, the talk turns to politics, which always happens with adult conversations these days. It's like they can't help themselves.

One of the adults I don't know is commenting on how much he likes the president because of his tax cuts. He and his wife are probably in their late twenties or early thirties. They have that *I like money* look. They're also second-generation Korean American, like my parents, because their English is definitely better than their Korean.

I glance over at my mom and I see that my dad has a tight grip on her hand, as if to say *Chama*. It's a Korean word that they use a lot. It means to endure and suffer through it. My grandfather says that it's something Koreans have had to do historically, because Korea was invaded so many times. I think that's so sad.

The guy is still going on about how much he likes the new

government, and his wife agrees and says, "It's nice to keep more of our money instead of giving it all out in welfare and handouts to illegal immigrants. We work really hard for everything we earn. Why should we have to support people who are too lazy to work themselves, or who come here illegally to take advantage of our economy?"

I can't help it—I let out a loud gasp.

Oh, no she didn't.

My brother, who is usually oblivious to everything, coughs and wheezes, as if he is choking on something. I can feel myself gawking at them like they've sprung horns and tails. I don't have to look at my parents to know that they're angry; I can literally feel it in the air. This electric energy of discomfort. But before anyone can say anything, my grandfather clears his throat, folds his hands together on top of the table, and leans forward to speak.

"Oh, what a terrible thing it would be if all Christians thought like that," he says in his serious voice. "How sad Jesus would be to hear such an un-Christian sentiment."

I can see the smug, self-righteous expressions on their faces change to shock and bewilderment.

"Let's not forget Acts 20:35. 'In all things I have shown you that by working hard in this way we must help the weak and remember the words of the Lord Jesus, how he himself said, "It is more blessed to give than to receive."'"

The couple looks very uncomfortable now as all the others around them are nodding their heads. I'm biting my lip to keep from smiling at how nicely my grandfather is reprimanding them.

"You say that you admire our new president, but I can't help but wonder what Jesus would think of him? After all, Jesus believed in helping the poor, the weak, the sick, the downtrodden, the hungry, whoever they were. He never said, 'I shall help those in need, but only if they are legal immigrants.' He loved everyone."

I nod my head vigorously. Even though my mom is Christian, my father grew up Buddhist, and so my parents didn't force religion on either me or my brother. But we know a lot about Christianity from our grandparents. And what I've learned from them is that Jesus loved and believed in helping everyone.

"However, he was Jesus and we are not. We are not perfect. We are all human with flaws. But what we can hope for is to better ourselves, be the best Christians that we can be, and always ask ourselves, what would Jesus do?"

Glancing over at my parents, I can see my dad's dimple twitching, which means he's trying not to laugh, and my mom is smiling widely.

The couple are now bowing and apologizing. Grandpa smiles at them. "No need to apologize. It is a good reminder to all of us that we must strive to better ourselves always."

Since it's a school night, we end up leaving before the others. In the car, my brother starts to snicker.

"Oh man, Grandpa really humiliated those people!" Justin crows.

Mom makes a disapproving sound. "Your grandpa would never do that."

My dad laughs. "But you have to admit that your father is the master of putting people in their place in the nicest possible manner."

"True, but it only works when the people have a conscience," my mom says.

I sit back in my seat and wonder if Grandpa would be able to put the bullies at school in their place also. Would his way work on them? Should I mention this to Patrice and the others?

I don't think so. Grandpa's way works because he is able to subtly shame people with their own words. The bullies have no shame. And besides, Patrice is mad at me. For some reason, I'm mad also. But I can't explain why. I feel betrayed and alone and so angry. Yes, the graffiti is a terrible way to start the year, but I have to deal with Tobias every single day on the bus by myself. Last year, Justin would at least take the bus with me whenever he didn't have practice or workouts. And he had to deal with Satan, who really hates my brother.

It was a tough time last year. Satan would antagonize Justin, Justin would ignore him, Tobias would come after me, Justin would defend me, Satan would come after Justin, and around we would go again. This year both Justin and Satan go to high school together. But Justin is a jock and pretty popular. So Satan leaves him alone now. Lucky him.

By the time we get home, I'm feeling depressed about taking the bus again. Inside, my parents call us into the living room and ask how our day was. My brother replies by asking them for money. They go back and forth as they try to get more than nods and grunts from him. Justin was never one for talking in detail.

When they're finally too frustrated to ask him any more questions, they turn to me.

"It was okay," I respond. "I like most of my teachers. They all seem nice."

My mom looks relieved and smiles happily.

I don't think my parents have seen the email yet, because they haven't said anything to me about the graffiti. And I'm glad. I don't really want to talk about it. But I don't want to ride the bus in the morning.

"Mom, Dad, can one of you give me a ride to school in the morning? I really hate taking the bus."

I see Justin look up from his cell phone and give me the once-over.

Dad pats my back. "I can't because I have to be at work real early the next few weeks."

My dad is an auditor for a big accounting firm. To be honest, I don't know what he actually does, but it all sounds complicated and boring.

"Oh, honey, it really is so much more convenient if you take the bus," Mom replies. "The bus stop is so close, and drop-off is such a pain at your school. And just that extra fifteen minutes to drop you off means traffic gets so much worse."

"Okay, Mom." I sigh. "I'm going to bed, then."

Justin gets up and pats me on the shoulder before brushing past me up the stairs. I guess that's his way of sympathizing with me. We've never told our parents about the bullying. I know that for my brother, it's because he hates when Mom comes to school. As a lawyer, Mom is a bit overprotective and aggressive. In third grade, Justin brought in a plane to school for career day and said he wanted to be a pilot when he grew up. One of the kids at his table made slanted eyes at Justin and told him Asians couldn't fly planes because their eyes were too small to see well. When Mom found out, she made the administration call the other parents in and apologize. Justin hated it, because she caused such a huge scene. Ever since then, he's never told her about any of his problems. I guess he rubbed off on me too. Even after an entire year of bullying by the Thornton brothers, we never told our parents. We just dealt with it. We did that Korean thing. Chama. Endure. Suffer. But now I have to do it alone. And I don't know if I can.

Chapter
3

MY MOM WAKES ME UP earlier than usual the next morning with a serious expression on her face.

"Junie, why didn't you tell me about the racist graffiti?"

She must have finally read the email from school.

I rub my eyes. "They said they were sending all parents a letter about it," I reply. "I figured you'd read it."

She's stroking my hair and leans down to give me a hug. "That must have been awful to hear about it," she says. "Do you want to talk about it?"

"Not really." I don't want to talk about it because I'll have to talk about Patrice and the fight, and I'm not ready. It hurts too much.

Mom is looking at me with that gaze that makes me squirm with guilt. But she doesn't push it. Instead, she nods and gets up.

"Okay then, why don't you get up now and I'll drop you off at school. If you don't mind being a little early."

I bolt out of bed. "I don't mind at all!" Anything to avoid Tobias.

When I come down for breakfast, I marvel at the spread of food on the table. Mom must have been really upset about the email. Breakfast is the only meal she can actually cook. She admits that it's because everything but the eggs comes premade, so it's hard for her to mess it up. Justin is polishing off a plate of eggs, sausage, and hash browns. As I sit down, he grabs two large biscuits and starts slathering jam on them. There's only two left.

"Don't you have to leave for the bus now?" I ask pointedly.

He looks at his phone. "I still got time." His bus comes twenty minutes before mine.

I hurriedly grab the last two biscuits and put them on my place mat. They're the buttery kind with lots of layers. I open one up and peel off thin slices to eat. The biscuits are still hot and so soft. My mom brings me a plate of food, and I am content.

"Justin, you really need to go now," Mom says.

He shoves one biscuit into his mouth, wraps the other one in a napkin, grabs his bag, and waves goodbye.

I'm dipping my biscuit in the gooey center of my sunny-side-up egg when Mom sits down with her cup of tea.

"How are Patrice and Amy doing? They must have been pretty upset about the graffiti."

Thinking of them and the graffiti brings the fight back into my mind. The eggs no longer look as appetizing as they did a second ago. I force myself to eat them anyway.

"Yeah, they were really upset."

"The principal says they are going to have a parents' meeting Friday night with updates from the police," she says. "I'll be pressuring them to have some kind of schoolwide discussion on diversity and the dangers of hate speech like this."

My stomach is now gurgling, and I've completely lost my appetite. I smile weakly at my mom and tell her my stomach is a bit upset and I have to go to the bathroom. She looks troubled, but she lets me go.

Mom drops me off at school but doesn't push me on anything else. It's early and the buses haven't arrived yet. They must have painted over the gym fast because it's open again and I'm one of only a handful of students in there. I sit on the bleachers near our normal meeting place. Amy arrives first.

"Junie! You're here early. You okay?"

I shrug.

"You know, I wish your dad would let you get a smartphone. We were texting last night, and it would've been good for you to have been on it. We were talking about Patrice's idea."

This past summer was when most of my friends got smartphones. They've been texting and using social media apps. Meanwhile the only way I can talk with them is to actually call them from my home phone or use email. But let's be real, no middle schooler uses email. However, my dad doesn't believe middle schoolers should have phones. Justin got one only because he was starting high school. But knowing they were texting all night makes me feel more isolated than ever. There are five of them. Couldn't one of them have called me last night? Was I not worth talking to?

"I have a phone at home," I respond in a low voice. "You could have called me."

"Oh, it's much easier to text, Junie." Amy isn't really listening to me. "You've just got to convince your parents to get one for you."

My lack of a cell phone makes me an inconvenience. Too much of a pain to call me. That's all my friendship means to them.

"Well, it's good I can't text. It's a stupid idea anyway." I can feel how petty I'm being, and I know it isn't right to be like that, but I just can't help it.

"Don't say that, Junie," Amy says gently. "You don't know how upset Patrice was. It was really scary to think that we go to school with people who hate us all so much they're willing to vandalize the school. She's right. We can't just do nothing."

I am the nothing they couldn't bother to call.

"As if anything we do would make any difference at all," I say abruptly. I really don't want to talk about this anymore.

"That's a terrible attitude to have."

"You know it's the truth."

"No, it's not true!"

I look up in surprise to see Patrice and the others have arrived. Patrice stands in front of me, her arms folded as she glares.

"Junie, you've been so negative about everything for a while now," Patrice says. "You're always shooting down anything we want to do. I'm sick of it. This time it's too important, and I'm not going to deal with your negativity. If you can't be supportive, then I can't be your friend anymore."

I'm not the only one shocked by her words.

"Patrice, that's way harsh," Hena says.

"No, it's not! Junie's been a bummer all summer. She barely hung out with us, and when she did, she was nothing but negative and depressing. And don't act like I'm the only one who thinks so. We all agreed we were tired of her attitude."

I can barely hear any of their words anymore because my heart is beating so loud in my ears. This is what they talk about when I'm not with them. How much of a pain I am. My chest hurts and I feel like crying. I have to get away from them. I grab my bag and walk out of the gym. A teacher stops me to ask me where I'm going. I can't see who it is because now the tears are flowing and I'm sobbing. The next thing I know I'm in the counseling services waiting area. I'm not a fan of coming here, even though it has comfy sofas and tables where you can sit and work.

Ms. Blair has been my counselor since last year. She has

these warm brown eyes that make you believe she really cares. She's all about talking through your feelings, which is why I avoid her at all costs. I don't like talking to adults in general. And I definitely don't want to talk about my emotions with them. She takes me to her office and seats me at the round table in front of her desk. It's a bit dark and has no windows, but the walls are covered with colorful artwork.

"Can you tell me what's wrong, Junie?"

"I'm fine," I respond. No, I'm not. I'm hurting. But I'm not going to tell her that.

"Is it because of the graffiti incident? Has that made you feel bad?"

"Yeah, that's it." That's better than her digging into my emotions.

"Do you want to talk about it?"

I shake my head vigorously. "I'm fine now," I say. "I think I just needed to cry it out. Can I go to class now?"

Oh wait, Patrice is in my first period with me. I don't want to see her. I deflate. Maybe it would be better to stay in the counselor's office. I rub my eyes. It's hard to keep them open. I'm just so tired. I want to sleep forever.

"Actually, would it be all right if I stayed here instead?" I ask. "All that crying wiped me out."

Ms. Blair's eyes are so sympathetic that I feel the urge to cry again, so I look down at my hands. I start picking at a scab from a cut I got a few days ago. I pick at it so hard it starts to bleed.

Ms. Blair pulls my hands away and wipes away the blood before cleaning it and putting a bandage on it.

"Do you think you might be willing to tell me why you cried?"

I keep staring at my hands. "I don't really know."

"Well, if you ever feel like talking, my door is always open."

I nod, even though I know I'll never come and talk to her.

"If you want, you can put your head down on the table and rest until second period."

Without a word, my head sinks down on the conference table and I close my eyes. I just want to sleep. The next thing I hear is the second-period bell. I jump up to my feet and thank Ms. Blair before dashing out of her office.

In fourth-period social studies class, Mrs. Medina gives us a new assignment. Everyone groans dramatically, but she claps her hands to quiet the class down.

"We're going to do a little project that I like to call living history. Where we study the different generations that make up our society." Mrs. Medina beams at us. She's tall and attractive with cool black eyeglasses that make her look smart but in a posh way. "You guys are Gen Z, born between 1997 and 2012. Before you are the millennials, also known as Gen Y, who were born between 1981 and 1996. Then there are the Gen Xers, 1965 to 1980. But this project is not going to be about X, Y, or Z. Instead, this project will focus on one of the older generations."

Mrs. Medina puts up a graphic on the Promethean board. It says:

The Greatest Generation—1901 to 1927
The Silent Generation—1928 to 1945
The Baby Boomers—1946 to 1964

"These are the three older generations," Mrs. Medina continues. "The greatest generation suffered through the Great Depression and fought in World War II, while the silent generation were children of the Great Depression and fought in the Korean War. The baby boomers were called that because of the increase in births after World War II. Their war was Vietnam. Each of these generations were deeply affected by the war of their time."

Mrs. Medina comes to stand in front of us again.

"Your project is to interview someone from the silent or boomer generation and get some interesting highlights of their life story. The list of questions will be posted online, and this will be your end-of-the-semester project, so you have a lot of time to finish it. You guys complain, but you actually might enjoy it!"

They all groan again, but I'm too miserable to care.

After class is lunch period. I have no intention of going to the cafeteria, so I wait until everyone leaves and then I walk over to Mrs. Medina's desk. Her knowing eyes are watching me over the top of her black frames.

"Junie, you're always so polite," she says with a kind smile. "Too polite. You patiently wait and let everyone cut ahead of you instead of pushing yourself forward."

"It's okay. I didn't mind waiting. Besides, now I don't have to worry about anyone waiting after me, and I can have more time with you." This was what I'd planned. I could ask questions without anyone else around and avoid my friends.

Mrs. Medina laughs. "Smart thinking! What did you want to ask me?"

I chew on my lip. I had been beating myself up trying to come up with a question to ask her.

"Why does it have to be from the silent or boomer generation?" I ask. "My parents are pretty interesting. But they are Gen X, I think."

Mrs. Medina tilts her head to the side as she listens to me, her hands clasped on the desk. "This is a good question, Junie," she responds. "And yes, I definitely want you to interview someone from an older generation than your parents'. You see, the silent and boomer generations are old now. In fact, we are losing many from the silent generation. I think it is so important to record their stories before they are all gone."

It strikes me that the silent generation is my grandparents, and the idea of losing them causes a painful twisting in my heart.

"My grandparents are from that generation," I say. "I

don't think I know a lot of their stories. But I do know they lived through the Korean War."

"They sound like the perfect people to interview for this project!" Mrs. Medina says.

The word *record* is stuck in my head.

"Mrs. Medina," I ask abruptly. "Would it be all right to do a video presentation of my interview?"

Her face brightens in delight. "That would be marvelous, Junie! Not just for this project, but for your own family history. I'm sure your parents would love it also."

I spend the rest of lunch talking to Mrs. Medina about oral history projects and good questions, and then I wander over to my next class before the bell rings. I make it through the rest of the day without seeing or talking to any of my friends. But the truth is, none of them made much of an effort to see me either.

Maybe I didn't even need to try to avoid them.

I put on my headphones but keep the music off as I join the crowds headed out of school. It's a chaotic mess as new sixth graders try to figure out where to go and seventh and eighth graders push each other around. I keep my head down as I walk to my bus line. From the corner of my eye I can see Hena, Lila, and Marisol lining up for their buses. They look really serious. I hurry past, but they're too busy talking to spot me. At my line, I hang back, avoiding Tobias, who is busy picking on some unlucky sixth graders. The bus arrives quickly and everyone boards. Sitting in the front means I'm the first one out at my bus stop. But before I leave, I hear the kids behind me talking about more graffiti.

"They found more racist graffiti in the boys' bathroom."

"That's gotta be a student."

"What a jerk."

It's such a horrible feeling to know that you go to school with people who hate you for something you can't ever change.

As I walk home, I try my best not to think about how horrible my day was. But it's like my mind is on autoplay, and all it does is show me a highlight reel of all the bad. The sharp pain I have inside me is now just a heavy sense of sadness that aches low in my chest. It's not a new sensation. I've had it on and off since last year. It's become a familiar pain. It tells me I'm all alone.

Chapter 4

I'M SO TIRED WHEN I get home that I lie down on the couch in the living room and I doze off. The sound of the front door slamming wakes me up.

Sitting up, I see my brother throw his bag on the floor and head to the kitchen. Rubbing the sleep from my eyes I follow him. He pours himself a bowl of Frosted Flakes and milk and begins munching. It looks so good I make my own bowl.

"How's it?" he asks through a mouthful of cereal.

"Sucks," I reply.

Justin nods. "High school's a little better."

"I don't believe you," I say.

"No, seriously. It's so big, you can easily avoid anyone you hate."

My friends did a pretty good job of avoiding me today. The thought turns my cereal flavorless. I finish it anyway as

I watch Justin eat a second bowl of cereal, this time of Cocoa Krispies.

"You smell bad," I tell him.

"Coach made us do suicides during practice." He raises his arm and fans his underarm odor toward me.

I gag but also sympathize. I've seen my brother's soccer drills. The suicide sprints are definitely the worst. I wouldn't last a minute.

"Go shower before you kill me," I say as I lean as far away from him as I can.

Being with Justin helps push back the creeping sadness. It's still there, but now I can feel other things, like annoyance at my brother, who is sticking his gross armpit right in my face.

"Get away from me, you pig!" I shove him hard.

Justin laughs and walks over to the fridge to grab some Gatorade.

"Is Tobias still bothering you?" he asks after a long chug.

I pause for a moment. "No more than usual." I guess that's true, even though it doesn't feel it.

Justin scowls, making him look pretty intimidating. Over the summer, he got a lot bigger and taller. Now he looks like he goes to high school. I admit that he is pretty good-looking for a brother, although I would never tell him. He already has a mammoth ego.

"You want me to meet you at the bus stop and talk to him?" He cracks his knuckles like he's some tough thug instead of my dorky older brother. "I don't have practice on Friday."

"Nah, don't make a big deal about it. I'm fine," I respond. Which is a lie. I'm far from fine, but I'm not about to tell Justin that. He takes his position as the oldest pretty seriously and believes in looking out for his little sister, even though I'm as tall as he is. Also, he never told our parents about the bullying when it involved him. But now that it's just me, he might rat me out. I don't want to worry my parents. I've never given them any trouble. They love saying that to everyone. I'd like to keep it that way.

Justin finishes his drink and bonks me lightly on my head with his fist. "Suit yourself," he says, walking toward the stairs. "But let me know if you need me."

I rub my head and grumble, but it feels good to know my brother has my back. It sucks not having him on the bus ride.

"Hey, Justin," I call out. "Before you shower, you want to shoot some hoops?"

He comes running back with a big smile. "Winner gets dishes?"

"First to ten, spot me three points?" I ask.

"Cool."

During dinner, Justin is still complaining about my win.

"I'm never spotting you points again, Junie. You're such a cheat!"

"I won ten to five," I reply. "The three points didn't make a difference."

Justin is glaring at me over his spaghetti. "You cheated. You took advantage of me being tired, and you cheated."

I smile evilly. "That's on you. You didn't have to agree. But now you got dish duty." I giggle at my little rhyme as he snarls at me.

I shake a lot of parmesan cheese on my pasta. "Mmmm, cheese. But that means you gotta scrub extra hard to get the sticky off."

Justin groans. "Dad, why'd you have to make spaghetti tonight? I hate washing the pots!"

Our dad puts so much cheese into his meat sauce that it leaves a hard, sticky residue on everything. It's why I didn't let Justin have a rematch. Mom was coming home late, so I knew Dad was cooking today.

"Stop complaining and eat your broccoli," Dad says. "It's trash and recycle day, so Junie, you get to handle that tonight."

"Yes, Dad."

Even though Justin's upset, it doesn't stop him from eating a gigantic serving.

"Junie, can you get me a glass of water with lots of ice?" Dad asks.

I walk into the kitchen and I spot the sink piled high with pots and dishes. I'm a bit shocked at how bad it is, even more than usual. The big difference between how my mom cooks and how my dad does is that my mom cleans as she cooks, while my dad uses everything he can get his hands on and leaves a wreck. I kind of feel sorry for Justin, but not bad enough to switch. I fill up a glass and bring it back to my dad.

"So how was school?" he asks.

Neither Justin nor I reply. Both of us dig into our food as if someone is going to snatch it away from us.

Dad sighs and decides to start on Justin first. As I listen to Dad probe and Justin grunt in response, I can feel my mood change. I don't want him to ask me about school and friends or anything. I don't want to talk about how much of a loser I feel like.

Before Dad can ask me questions, I finish my food off and ask to be excused.

"Don't you want any dessert?"

"No, thanks," I reply. "I'm pretty tired. I'll take the trash and stuff out, then go to bed."

My dad looks surprised. I'm usually a late-night person. They have to tell me to go to sleep all the time.

"Don't you want to wait up for Mom?" he asks.

"I'll try," I answer, and pick up my dishes to take to the kitchen. I leave them by the side of the full sink, grab the trash and recyclables, and dash off.

I know Justin's seen the sink when I hear him yell, "I'm not washing all of this!"

In my room, I find myself staring at the phone. All my friends have cell phones, and yet none of them have called me. I pick up my sketchbook and I draw a picture of my friends laughing together as they all huddle around their cell phones. Behind them, I draw a small Junie holding a banana instead of a phone, a black cloud raining on her head.

Bitterness eats away at my insides, turning the food in my stomach into lead. Giving me indigestion. I wish my mom was here. She'd give me some gross medicine and stay by my side until I fall asleep. The sadness is back in full force. It's so overwhelming that it makes it hard for me to move. I walk slowly to the bathroom to brush my teeth. It feels like ages before I'm changed and in bed. I'm so tired now. Even if I wanted to stay up to see my mom, I can't keep my eyes open.

Mom drives me to school in the morning, but I make her wait until right before the bell rings. That way I can head straight to class. It's now been two days since the fight, and no one seems to care enough to come and talk to me. I've moved officially into anger now. If they can't be bothered to talk to me, then I don't want anything to do with them.

There's another principal's announcement about the graffiti in the boys' bathroom. More promises that they will find the perpetrator.

Meanwhile Patrice and I ignore each other in class. I refuse to look at her, bolting out of the room before she's even gathered her things together. I spend lunch period in the counselor's office pretending that the racist graffiti is still upsetting me, which is sort of true. It's the reason for my fight with my friends. Ms. Blair seems very concerned, and I try to smile and pretend that I'm all right. I don't want her calling my parents. Mostly, she leaves me alone. Lets me sit and eat my lunch at the table in her office. I take out my small sketchpad and doodle. The bell rings and I gather my things to head to fifth period.

Ms. Blair stands up to check on me one last time.

"I'm feeling fine, Ms. Blair," I say with a smile. "I promise."

She doesn't look like she believes me. Stepping closer, she takes my hands and pats them gently. "Junie, you can come and talk to me about anything, not just about the graffiti. You can talk to me about classes, schoolwork, friends. I'm here for you. Please come anytime. My office is always available."

I don't know why, but her words make me tear up, and I have to take several moments trying not to cry. I swallow over and over before I finally can speak.

"Thanks, Ms. Blair." My voice is hoarse and rough from all the tears I swallowed back.

The rest of my periods drag painfully long. I keep my head down and my earbuds in so if I see any of my friends, I can pretend not to see or hear them. But the first time I think I hear my name called in the hallways, I immediately glance around. I don't see anyone.

It's not until the end of the day that I finally see any of them. I spot all of them together, looking happy and laughing, not missing me at all. It stops me in my tracks, and for a moment, I can feel my heart breaking. I slow down, not wanting to run into any of them. It isn't until they all scatter that I start walking again.

My anger is completely gone, but the sadness is back. Actually, it never left. At this moment, surrounded by so many people, I feel utterly alone. There is this constricting pain in my throat. It's so tight.

When I get to my bus line, I notice that the bus is late. I see Tobias standing head and shoulders above all the other kids. I don't want to see him or even hear him breathe. I'm not ready for his bullying. I'm never ready, but especially now when I feel like my world is falling apart. I don't know what to do. I catch my breath in short little pants. I feel heavy. Each step is harder to take. My heart hurts. I'm too young to have a heart attack, right?

Tobias sees me coming, and I can see the sneer on his pale brutish face.

"Hey, it's the communist pig!"

I wish the bus would come already, but our driver must be running late today. All the other buses are loading up except for us.

Tobias is now standing in front of me.

"Is it true you people eat nasty rotted food that smells like garbage? Is that why you smell? Huh?"

He is poking me hard in the shoulder. I walk away but he keeps following me and poking me.

"There's a missing-dog poster in our neighborhood. You

guys ate it, right? You dog eaters."

I'm shaking with rage now. And he's hurting me. He pokes me again, and this time I slap his hand away.

"Don't touch me."

"Or what, commie?"

I don't reply. He goes to poke me again, but I swerve out of the way and he misses. Some people giggle, and I can see the rage in his face. At that moment, the bus pulls up. Tobias shoves me hard to get to the bus and I go flying onto the ground, landing painfully on my hands and knees. I can feel the tears overwhelm me. There's no way I'll let any of them see me cry. I turn away from the line of kids getting on the bus. I'd rather walk the two miles home.

There's not a lot of people on the sidewalks by the time I start walking through the suburban neighborhood my school is in. The buses are all gone, and so are all the cars picking up students. I take the long way around school to avoid seeing any teachers or staff who are now starting to head home.

I've never actually walked home before. But I head toward the main street, which I recognize from my bus route. I've stared out the window of my bus enough to know the way. What would normally be a ten-minute ride is going to take an hour because I'm limping badly. The pain in my knees makes every step seem like my legs are on fire.

My thoughts are a jumbled mess. Anger, hatred, sadness, fear, and disappointment. I spiral through all of them. But the thought that stays with me the most is seeing my friends together and how they've clearly forgotten me. That they've decided I'm no longer worthy. Is that why Tobias picks on me? Because I'm a loser with no friends?

My chest is now hurting more than my knees. It feels like a heavy weight is crushing me, but it's all internal.

Patrice is my oldest friend. We met in kindergarten. I miss those days.

I was a very shy and quiet child who barely talked to anyone. During recess, I always envied all the other kids who could climb to the top of the jungle gym. It was very high, and I was too scared to even try. But one day I got the courage and I made it all the way to the top. Except when I looked down, I got scared again and I froze. Being shy, I didn't cry out for help. It was Patrice who saw I was stuck and climbed up to show me the way down. Ever since, we've been best friends.

Patrice is an only child, and we shared everything together and learned all about each other's favorite foods, books, movies, and hobbies. Not that we had the same taste. She loves romance and I prefer action movies. She doesn't like spicy food, and I'm Korean so I'll try to put Tabasco on almost everything. And yet we were still as tight as friends could be. We had sleepovers and summer camps and have been there for each other through appendicitis (Patrice) and a broken leg (me).

The only thing we didn't do together was ballet. Patrice is an amazing ballet dancer. She's been dancing since she was three. I love watching her dance, but it's not my thing. I like art. She can't even draw a straight line. It never mattered before.

Amy transferred in third grade and was as shy and quiet as I was. It was Patrice who befriended her, and we soon became the best of friends. Amy's a dancer also, and she signed up for the same ballet classes that Patrice was taking. Even though they spent more time together because of it, Patrice and I were still the closest. I always knew I came first.

Until we started middle school.

Livingston Middle School has kids from three different elementary schools. It's where we met Hena, Lila, and Marisol and formed our own little clique. Six new friends all hanging together. But in the process, I've slowly been pushed away from my closest friend.

I dash away a tear that slips out. Everything hurts. I feel like I've been walking for hours. My slow pace has finally brought me to the park near the bus stop. I see a bunch of kids hanging out at the swing set, and I immediately cross the street. I don't want to see anyone from school. I cut through the parking lot of the townhome complex and come out closer to my block.

Sometimes I hate my house and my neighborhood. I wish I could live near Patrice; then maybe we'd still be close. If only I lived there, then I could get rides to school with Patrice like Amy does sometimes. I could walk home with Patrice and hang out at her house after school. I wouldn't have to leave as soon as my parents came to get me. I could stay over and walk the two blocks between Patrice's and Amy's houses.

I don't blame Amy. I really like her, and she's been a good friend to me. It's not her fault that she has become a more convenient friend for Patrice. It's my fault for not trying harder, not fighting to keep my place in the friendship. I have no one to blame but myself.

By the time I get home, I'm hurting bad. The house is empty. Justin has soccer practice, and my parents are at work. I drop my bag and head to the bathroom. My palms are completely scratched up and bloody, and my knees are even worse. I guess that's the problem with the ripped-jeans style. No protection for your knees.

I wash the blood away and realize that there are shards of glass in my knees that I wasn't even aware of. Now that I can see them, the pain is so much worse. I try to pick out the pieces, but they're in too deep. I need tweezers. I wish my mom were here. She'd know what to do. She'd take away the pain. But she isn't here. I'm all alone.

I'm frustrated and tired and so very sad. I know I can't leave glass shards in my cuts. I sit down and pull out everything I see. It takes a long time, and by the time I'm done, my knees throb so viciously, I can't stop the tears.

I hobble to the kitchen and pull out the medicine box. I need something to make the pain go away. All I want is to stop hurting. I reach for a bottle of ibuprofen and I shake some out. They pour out into my hand. Ten or more of the little brown pills. I'm staring at them. How many do I have to take to stop feeling so bad? What would happen if I took all of them?

I just stand there, holding this handful of pills and thinking of everything that has happened, and the pain in my heart overwhelms me. Right now, right at this moment, I can't take it anymore. I don't want to feel this sadness. Why does this hurt more than my messed up knees?

I roll the pills around in my palm. How many will stop the pain forever? Five? Ten? How many is enough? I pour the whole bottle into my hand. There's now a huge mound of medicine that is slowly starting to overflow. The tiny balls spill onto the ground, one by one. I can hear the light tapping as they hit the tile floor.

I'm mesmerized by the pile of little round pills. Maybe this is the answer to all my problems. No more Tobias. No more school. No more loneliness. What's the use of being here anymore if it hurts so much? When my friends don't care about me anymore? I've fought with Patrice in the past, but we always made up in the same day. But over the summer there were weeks when we didn't talk to each other. She took an elite ballet program with Amy. It would've been weird if they hadn't gotten closer. But I thought going back to school would be different, but it's not. It's infinitely worse.

No one will even miss me. I just want to sleep and never wake up. Never have to feel this horrible pain again. Never have to worry about taking the bus or being bullied or dealing with racism or losing my friends. That last thought sends this sharp stabbing pain into my heart. My friends don't want to be friends anymore.

I stare at the pills and my hand trembles. More and more pills fall down, pinging one by one as they bounce on the floor. I hear myself sob. I'm scared. I'm so scared of my own thoughts and feelings. I let my hand fall, and I hear the cascade of pills as they drop and roll everywhere. Exhaustion hits hard and suddenly. My eyelids are so heavy, and I'm tempted to just lie down on the floor. Instead, I force myself to go up to my room. I don't even bother to change out of my dirty, blood-covered clothing. I just climb into bed and sleep.

Chapter 5

I'M AT A THERAPIST'S OFFICE. Both my parents have taken off from work to be here with me. Apparently, Ms. Blair had called my mom to tell her she was concerned about my well-being. When my mom came home and saw all the pills spilled next to my bag, she freaked out. She woke me up in a panic and was about to call an ambulance when I told her I hadn't taken any pills. But I admitted to her that I'd thought about it. And that's why we're here. At a therapist's office. Actually, this is the second therapist we are seeing. I didn't like the first one at all. She made me feel even more depressed than I already was.

Yesterday, we spent the morning and early afternoon in doctor's offices. First, they took me to my pediatrician, Dr. Rose. She's been taking care of me since I was a baby and I really like her. She knows me pretty well and got me to tell her a little about what was going on. After drawing my blood and doing a full physical exam, she advised my parents to take me to see a psychiatrist and also a therapist. My mom is a very solution-oriented person. She immediately had four appointments set up for me.

The psychiatrist was this old guy who smelled weird and had a blinding white smile. I didn't like him. He asked a lot of questions, which I responded to with one-word answers, partly because I wanted him to stop smiling at me. At the end he diagnosed me with "major depressive disorder with suicidal ideation." He said a lot of words I didn't understand but that made my mom cry, and then gave me a prescription for antidepressants. Because I wouldn't talk, he advised my parents to get me into therapy right away.

Mom, being Mom, had already beaten him to it. She'd scheduled two appointments for the next day and took down more names of therapists that he recommended. I was just relieved that I wouldn't have to go to school.

Afterward, my parents took me out to lunch. We went to my favorite restaurant, a little Japanese café that has a Maneki-neko statue. It's this cute cat that waves its left paw up and down. I once asked Ms. Tomoko, our waitress, why it waved, and she explained that Maneki-neko means "beckoning cat," and waving the left paw means it's inviting customers into the restaurant. Ms. Tomoko has been taking care of us since I was a baby. She treats me more like I'm her granddaughter than a customer. And she loves my art. I've been drawing pictures at every meal there all my life. In fact, they have one of my drawings of their cat on the wall right behind the cash register.

Today, I wasn't very hungry, but I ordered their delicious miso ramen and fried pork cutlets called tonkatsu. I didn't want Ms. Tomoko to worry, so I forced myself to eat.

"Junie, do you want to have your friends come over?" my dad asked.

I shook my head and slowly slurped a ramen noodle.

"Did something happen with your friends?" Mom asked. "I noticed they didn't come over this summer as much as they used to. But I thought it was because you were all in different summer camps."

I separated out the bean sprouts and seaweed from my noodles, making a pile on the side of my bowl. I stared intensely at the shiny circle of oil in the middle of my broth.

"Do you want me to call Patrice's and Amy's moms and schedule something for you girls this weekend?"

Carefully, I put my chopsticks down and folded my hands in my lap.

"Please don't, Mom."

"Did something happen? Did you guys have a falling-out? What about Hena and the others? Lila and Marisol, right?"

"They're all still friends," I said quietly. "Just not with me."

"Why not with you? What's going on? Why are they still friends but not with you?"

I could see my dad trying to calm Mom down, but she was

upset, which for some reason made me really mad.

"Well, they all have cell phones and can text each other and have group chats," I snapped at her. "What did you expect would happen?"

"That's it? They're not friends with you because you don't have a cell phone?" Dad asked in surprise.

I had a headache and I didn't want to talk anymore. I just wanted to go home and sleep.

"Please, let me go home," I begged. "I don't feel well. I just want to get out of here."

At home, I went straight to bed and slept through dinner. I was surprised they let me sleep.

This morning, Justin woke me up before he left for school.

"Why didn't you tell me you were having a hard time?" he asked.

Sitting up in bed, I rubbed my eyes. "I don't know."

He gave me a serious look. "Don't do that again," he said. "I'm your Oppa. I'm supposed to look out for you."

I snorted at him saying *Oppa*. He has never wanted me to use the Korean word for big brother. "We're in America," he'd say. "Call me by my name."

It would feel odd to call him that now.

"You're missing school to meet with therapists today, huh?" Justin asked.

I nodded.

"Good luck." He handed me a small box of my favorite chocolates and waved goodbye.

I was touched and surprised. Justin is the black hole of food in the family. I'm amazed he had the willpower not to eat them all. Instead, I enjoyed every bite and went back to sleep.

Then Mom woke me at ten to eat breakfast and head to the first therapist. The one I didn't like. She was older, with dyed red hair that made her pale skin look sickly white. She smiled a lot, but her eyes were dead-fish cold.

After the appointment, my parents took me to my favorite burger place. I wished I could tell them not to bother. They could have just made me a peanut-butter-and-jelly sandwich and I wouldn't have cared. I've lost my sense of taste and my appetite. As we waited for our food, my mom pulled out a cell phone box and passed it to me. I stared at it blankly.

"Had we known that you would be left out of your friend group, we would have gotten you a cell phone earlier, Junie," my mom said.

This is my mom's solution-based thinking. *Junie is depressed. Junie lost her friends. Solution—get Junie a cell phone.*

I pushed the box back. "I don't want it."

"But why?"

I have no one to call. No one to text. If anything, the cell phone made me more aware of my loneliness. I blinked back tears. Why am I always crying?

"It's okay, Junie," my dad said. "We'll hold on to it until you're ready."

My burger and fries arrived with a chocolate milkshake,

but the food just didn't appeal to me. Even the smell of it made me want to gag. I gulped down the milkshake, because it was cold and sweet and the only thing I could really taste. It's funny how I can only taste the sweet things when I'm feeling so sad and bitter.

Now I'm at the second therapist's office. She's part of a group called Barton & Associates that have offices in a townhouse. The building is cute on the outside and warm and cozy on the inside, with bright lighting and fun posters on the walls. There's one family waiting inside the waiting area, but otherwise it's quiet. After a few minutes, the therapist comes out. She's a very kind-looking woman with long, curly brown hair and a warm smile that crinkles her eyes.

"Hi, Junie. I'm Rachel. How about we come into my office with your parents and just get to know each other a little bit?"

I follow her into her office. It's big with pale-yellow walls that have really pretty watercolor paintings and a comfy blue sofa. There's a large coffee table that has all these cool things on it. An Etch A Sketch, a block puzzle, a Rubik's Cube, a small sand-raking garden, putty, and so much more. She sees my attention is caught by the Rubik's Cube, and she places it in my hands.

"I can never get more than one side done," she says. "Maybe you'll be better than I am."

She begins to chat with my parents, and I mostly tune

out. It's the fourth time I've had to sit through my childhood medical history and my current issues. Every so often, Rachel directs a question or comment to me. I just nod, shake my head, or shrug. I have no words to contribute in this discussion. I don't want to be here. I play with the putty or stare up at the pretty watercolor painting.

"Junie, I want you and your parents to know that anything you tell me in therapy is confidential," Rachel says. "I will not share anything you say with your parents unless you expressly agree that I can or if you say something that makes me believe you are in danger."

I'm mildly interested to hear this, especially because I can see my mom is not that happy about it.

"I want to explain what we do here in this practice," Rachel continues. "When I work with clients, I like to teach them about mindfulness and emotion regulation."

I just stare at her blankly. None of this makes any sense to me.

"Mindfulness is the ability to be in control of your mind. To be present in the now without judgment or overthinking. It's just the act of being. And emotion regulation is a skill set that helps you to be in charge of yourself during periods of high emotions."

I nod. It sounds good, I guess.

"Now, let's send your parents out so we can get to know each other."

After my parents leave, Rachel shows me a binder filled

with pages of different kinds of furniture sets clipped out of magazines.

"I'm thinking of redoing my bedroom and need some advice. I've been told I have horrible taste, and I really want something modern. Since you are an artist, I'd love to hear your thoughts. What do you think of my choices?"

It's so unexpected that I look out of pure curiosity. She shows me a wide range of photos of rooms ranging from fancy to simple, elaborate to plain, ugly to beautiful.

"I kind of like this one, but I'm just not sure about it," she says, pointing to a hideous mess of a room that's as far from modern as you can imagine. I think I once saw a room like this in the Metropolitan Museum of Art in New York. It's all dark colors and busy patterns. It doesn't look like it would suit Rachel. But I don't want to hurt her feelings.

"That's nice but not really that modern," I say carefully. "I think these choices over here would fit more what you said you were looking for."

I point to a set of photos of rooms I like. They're very clean and bright with sleek and simple furniture. When I grow up, I'd love a room like that.

Rachel nods and proceeds to admire the three choices I've set aside, asking me questions about what details I like and if my room is like this.

I laugh. "I think my mom had a fairy-tale princess crisis when she had me," I say. "My room is purple, and my bed has a big white canopy on it."

"That sounds really lovely. Don't you like it?"

I grimace. "I'd rather have my brother's room. Although he's filthy. But his room is just a room, not some Disney Princess fairy-tale suite."

"Have you ever thought to tell your parents how you feel and ask them to change your room? You're older, and the style might not suit your current maturity level."

"Yeah, you're right, but my mom always talks about how much she wanted a room like mine when she was little but never got it. I don't want to hurt her feelings."

"That's very sweet. But I have a feeling your mom won't be as hurt as you might think," Rachel says. "Do you always tend to keep your thoughts and emotions to yourself?"

I think about it. "Yeah, I guess so."

She pauses as she takes some notes in a leather journal that looks very professional. "Do you have difficulty talking about your feelings?"

Yes, definitely yes. I nod.

"Do you ever feel overwhelmed by your feelings?"

Absolutely. I nod again.

"When you get angry, do you let your emotions out, or do you let them simmer internally?"

"That depends," I say. "Sometimes I'm so mad I yell at people. But other times I run away."

"Tell me about a time you ran away."

And just like that, I find myself telling her all about the graffiti and the fight with my friends. For the first time, I tell someone what's hurting me, and I cry almost the entire time. When we're done, I am so relieved. I feel as if a heavy weight has just gotten a little bit lighter. My burden is still there, but now I've shared it with someone, and it feels good. Maybe this therapy thing might be good for me. I don't know, but I'm willing to give it a try.

Chapter 6

I WAS ONLY IN SCHOOL three days this week, and I'm already feeling anxious about going back. I'm in my bed, staring up at the canopy and wondering how mad my mom would be if I tore all the sheer white fabric off. I don't mind the light purple walls, but the flowy, white fabric tied in bows is too much. But then I think about what Rachel said. That she was sure Mom would understand. I stand up on my bed and start to reach for the fabric, but I'm too short. At that moment, my mom knocks and walks in. She has a glass of water and my bottle of antidepressants.

"Honey, I . . . what are you doing?" she asks.

Sheepishly I sit down on the edge of my bed. "I really don't like all the fabric hanging down. It isn't my style."

Mom sits next to me and gives me a side hug. "You know what? I always thought I wanted one of these beds when I was young, but I know what you mean. It's not really my style either! I'll take them off for you today."

There is this little glow of happiness I feel at her words, and I find myself smiling at my mom. She passes me a pill and the glass of water and I take it quickly.

"How soon will the medicine help me, Mom?" I ask.

"The doctor said it takes a few days to a week to get into your system," she replies.

"Do you think it will work?" I look at her skeptically. I don't know how a pill can help me feel better.

My mom holds my hand. "I don't know for sure, but I don't think it will hurt," she says. "But I think the biggest help will be your therapy. I'm so glad you like Rachel."

I nod. I don't know if medicine will help, but I think talking with Rachel has already started helping me.

"Junie, I'm sorry to do this, but I have to go into the office this weekend, and Dad has to take Justin to a few games today. I don't want to leave you alone. Is it okay if I take you to Grandma and Grandpa's house?"

I hesitate. "Did you tell them?" I ask.

"Oh no, I just said you've not been feeling well." Mom pats my hair. "Junie, we won't share your private business. It's up to you whether or not you want to tell Grandma and Grandpa."

"Okay then," I say, although I really don't want to go anywhere.

* * *

We pull up to their cute little house. It's literally the type that every little kid draws, a square with a triangle roof. I always think of it as the house the three bears lived in when Goldilocks broke in. Seriously, that girl was a total crook. Imagine breaking into someone's house, eating all their food, breaking all their furniture, and then sleeping in their bed. I always thought the story would have been better if the hungry bears had eaten Goldilocks for dinner.

My grandparents' house has red brick and bright white trim and a pretty garden full of flowers because they love gardening. Their backyard is full of vegetables that they grow and send to us to eat.

Mom drops me off and waits for me to knock on the door. When Grandma lets me in, Mom waves goodbye and takes off. Once I'm inside, Grandma immediately urges me to the dining table, where soup, rice, and a lot of banchan, Korean side dishes, are set out for one person.

"You must be hungry. Eat first."

This is what Grandma says whenever she sees me. I always wonder if my face looks like I'm constantly starving.

The dining room is nice and bright and has wallpaper with fruit designs. When I was little, I saw the Willy Wonka movie and decided to lick the cherries on the wall. I tried several of them before realizing they didn't actually taste like cherries. I can still see little scrapes from where I nibbled at it.

As I sit at the table in front of Grandma's delicious food, Grandpa plops down next to me.

"Can I have some too?"

"What is this, your second breakfast?" Grandma questions him.

"Seeing Junie eat makes me hungry again." He smiles at me.

Grandma shakes her head and brings Grandpa some soup and rice also. She then fills the banchan plates with more of my favorites.

"Otherwise, your Grandpa will eat them all, and what will my poor Junie eat?"

She gives me a kiss on the cheek, puts on her jacket, and grabs her bag.

"It's Saturday, so I have a lot of appointments today! Lots of houses to show!" She waves goodbye and runs out the door. Grandma is always busy. My mom says Grandma was always like that. She doesn't understand the art of doing nothing. Even when she rests, she is doing something. She and Grandpa are so different. Grandma's hair is still black with some graying at her temples. I'm pretty sure she dyes it regularly but leaves some gray to make it look more realistic. I wish I could tell her that the black dye she uses is not very natural looking. Meanwhile Grandpa has a shock of snow-white hair. I think Grandpa looks handsome and dignified.

As the door closes behind her, Grandpa and I look at each other and then start eating with gusto.

"I love Korean breakfast," I say around a mouthful of rice

and kimchee. "Rice is my favorite. I would eat it three times a day every day."

"Spoken like a true Korean," Grandpa responds approvingly. He leans forward. "Although I only eat like this when you come over," he says confidingly. "Usually breakfast is bread and jam with my coffee."

"Yeah, but you love bread and jam," I say. "It's your favorite."

He nods. "I didn't have it when I was your age. The first time I had bread and jam wasn't until I was in college."

I can feel my eyes widen at the thought of not having bread and jam. It was unthinkable. But then I couldn't imagine growing up during wartime.

"What about peanut butter?" I ask with my mouth full.

"Never ate it until I came to America," he replies. He is wrapping rice and little anchovies in my favorite kim, little flat squares of salty, crispy seaweed, and says "ah" to me. I swallow quickly and open wide so he can pop it into my mouth.

After breakfast I help Grandpa clear the table and wash up. He makes me a cup of hot chocolate with little marshmallows, and then we go sit in the cozy living room. There are several watercolor copies of famous paintings hanging on the walls. They were all painted by my grandfather when he retired. My favorite is of a vase of sunflowers by Claude Monet. I saw the original in New York when my mom took me to the Metropolitan Museum of Art. I like my grandpa's better.

When he's not gardening, Grandpa likes to re-create his favorite paintings from the Metropolitan Museum and the Smithsonian American Art Museum. He is an amazing artist. They look like the originals, but different in a way that is so clearly my grandfather's style. Light and vibrant. Looking at his art makes me happy. I hope to one day be as good as he is. My mom says she's jealous that all the artistic talent skipped her generation and manifested in me.

Grandpa sits in his big brown comfy armchair that doesn't match the fancy yellow-striped sofa set that Grandma picked out. But the armchair suits Grandpa and is way more comfortable than the elegant-but-hard-as-a-rock sofa I'm sitting on.

"Tell me, how's school?" Grandpa asks as he settles into his seat.

I blow on my cocoa and sip up the melted goodness of the marshmallows before I respond. "It sucks."

"What's the matter?"

I don't even know where to start. Talking about it at the therapist's wore me out, so I just focus on my hot chocolate.

My grandpa pulls out a bag of walnuts and proceeds to crack them open. I don't like the taste of walnuts, but I find myself fascinated by the methodical cracking. My grandpa hums slightly as he gathers a pile of nuts. It's all very calming for some reason. It's so hypnotizing that I find myself speaking without even realizing it.

"They found racist graffiti all over the walls of the gym

and the boys' bathroom," I finally say. "There were swastikas and lots of racist stuff."

Grandpa makes a tutting sound with his tongue. "Aigo," he says. "That's terrible. Especially in a middle school. Who can it be?"

I shake my head. "Nobody knows."

"Against Asians too?"

"Yeah. It was even in the newspaper—didn't you see it?"

Adjusting his glasses, Grandpa peers at me in concern.

"It seems like every week there is some kind of terrible racist incident happening in this country. What did your mom and dad say?"

"They're upset. Because it was inside the school, not outside. There's going to be a parents' meeting next week about it at school."

"You think a student could have done something like that?"

My thoughts immediately go to Tobias, and I nod firmly. I wouldn't put it past him to do something just like that.

"That's just terrible," Grandpa says. "What a sad life to think of other people in such demeaning ways."

"Racists are the worst," I say. "But it's not like there's anything we can do about it."

"That's not true! Why do you say that?"

"Because they hate us," I answer. "They just hate us for not being like them. Talking to them is a waste of time. They will never change."

70

Grandpa seems surprised at my words. "Do you really believe people can't change?"

I can feel my depression creeping up on me, weighing me down with heaviness.

"Bad people are always bad." I think of Tobias and his brother and Stu Papadopolis and his friend group. They probably don't think they are bad people, but their actions make them bad.

Grandpa lets out a long "hmmm." I feel like he is judging me, and I'm hurt. It's like talking to Patrice again. I let out a big sigh, not because I'm frustrated but because it's hard to put into words how I feel. But I want Grandpa to understand.

"Sometimes good people do bad things," Grandpa says. "We are human; we make mistakes."

"No, bad people are always bad. And racists are evil."

"So much fatalism." Grandpa is shaking his head at me. "What happened, dear one? Who is hurting my beautiful granddaughter?"

I'm tired of talking. So I do what I always do when my parents pressure me: I become silent. My depression makes it easy. My parents have learned to leave me alone when I don't want to talk. But the one thing about my grandfather is that he is the most patient man in the world. And awkward silences don't bother him. He just sits and waits for me.

I don't even know how long we are quiet. But I find it harder to sit through. Here, in my grandparents' house, I can't run to my room. I can't escape his kind but penetrating eyes. So instead, I keep my eyes down on my now-cold cocoa.

Grandpa suddenly stands up and comes to sit next to me. He pulls me close and pats me on my back as if to say, *There, there. It's all going to be okay.* I can smell peppermint and his spicy aftershave lotion. I want to remember this scent. This is what my grandfather smells like.

I struggle to fight back my tears, swallowing hard against the lump in my throat but losing the battle. Once again, I am crying as I tell him all about the bullying I've dealt with for over a year, how sad and alone I've felt. I tell him how I've lost all my friends because I refused to join their activist crusade. I tell him what I've been unwilling to share with my own parents.

"Why don't you tell your parents?" he asks me.

I shake my head hard. "Please don't tell them. I don't want them to go to school and make a big deal about it. It will make everything worse."

"Your parents would be so sad to know this," he says. "And this is a terrible burden for you to handle by yourself."

"I'm seeing a therapist now. Let me talk to her first."

"But what will you do? How will you handle your bully?" Grandpa asks in concern.

"Nothing. I'm just going to ignore him. He'll get tired eventually."

That isn't true. They never got tired of bullying me and my brother last year.

Grandpa is quiet for a long moment, but then he gets up and goes into the kitchen. I can see him rustling around in the pantry, and then I hear the popping in the microwave. Several minutes later he comes back with a big bowl of popcorn.

"Eat this while I tell you a story," he says as he sits back in his armchair again. "Once there was a widow who was bringing food home to her children when she ran into a tiger who said, 'Give me some of your food and I won't eat you.' So the woman did that. But the tiger kept following, and he kept saying, 'Give me some of your food and I won't eat you.' So she kept giving the tiger all her food, until finally she had no more food. And then the tiger ate her. Your bully is the tiger, and if you don't fight back, he will never stop."

"But the bully is bigger and stronger. I may get eaten anyway."

Grandpa leans forward and taps the tip of my nose gently.

"Let me tell you the rest of the story. After the tiger ate up the widow, he dressed in her clothing and went to her house to eat up her children. But the children saw the tiger's tail and they ran up the tree, and the tiger tried to climb the tree, so the children prayed for help, and then a rope came down from heaven. Then they climbed into the sky to become the sun and moon. The tiger then also prayed for a rope, and he got one too. But it was a rotted one, and so as he climbed it, it broke and he fell. The end."

I don't get it. "So what does that mean for me?"

"Sometimes you must ask for help, Junie."

I feel myself scowling. Grandpa's stories always have morals, but this one I don't want to hear.

"Sometimes asking for help makes things worse," I respond.

"But you should ask anyway."

It isn't that easy.

"Everything's different now, Grandpa, ever since the election. People don't even try to hide their racism."

Grandpa is silent again. He stares at me with so much sadness that I can feel the tears prick the backs of my eyes again. His silence has always been part of his conversation.

"Why are you looking at me like that?"

"Because you are right, and it breaks my heart. I thought I had left this behind when we moved to America."

"Left what behind?"

"This deep, hateful division caused by conflicting ideologies."

I'm so confused. What racism problems could Korea have? I ask him that, and he shakes his head at me.

"I'm talking about the ideologies that split Korea into North and South," he says.

"Oh, you mean the Korean War."

Grandpa shakes his head again. "Korea was divided before the war. I've told you about when Korea was occupied by Japan and we almost lost our culture and our language."

I nod vigorously. After my grandpa had told me about

the occupation, I read a book called *When My Name Was Keoko*. It was written by one of my favorite authors, Linda Sue Park. Not only is she a great writer, but she's Korean American, which makes me really happy. But it was a pretty sad story, about one family's struggle against the oppressive Japanese regime.

"After the Japanese lost World War II and their control over Korea was ended, Korea was then occupied by the Soviet Union in the North and the Americans in the South. It was the Americans and the Soviets that divided Korea in half."

"But why?"

Grandpa tilts his head to the side and pulls at his ear before making a sound that is very Korean for *I'm not sure* or *I don't know*. Adult Koreans always make this sound. It's done with a slight grimace as they suck air through their teeth, which makes an interesting hiss.

"It would be so much easier if I could explain it to you in Korean." He smiles. "The simple explanation is that neither the Soviets nor the Americans wanted Korea to fall to the other side."

I can feel my eyebrows furrowing. "But what did Koreans want?"

"All Koreans have ever wanted was to be united again into one country," he says. "But the Soviets supported Kim Il Sung, the North Korean dictator, while the Americans helped elect Syngman Rhee, the corrupt South Korean president. And the

Korean people suffered the most."

I don't really understand the politics of it all. And I don't know how it relates to what is happening in my school. My confusion must show on my face.

"Okay, let's talk about ice cream. What is your favorite flavor?" Grandpa asks me.

"Chocolate."

"Mine is strawberry. Now what if I said all people who like chocolate are horrible people and we should get rid of chocolate forever?"

"That's just ridiculous."

"That's how extremism can seem. It looks ridiculous to us, but when people believe in something fervently, it can be dangerous. And during the Korean War, it was a clash of western democracy against Communism, with each side trying to kill off anyone who opposed them. It's how over two million civilians were killed by their own government, solely for believing in the wrong ideology."

The two-million-people-killed statistic shocks me. How could a government be responsible for killing so many of its own people?

"Do you remember the Korean War, Grandpa?" I ask.

Grandpa nods. "I was twelve years old when it started."

I'm a bit startled to realize that he was the same age as I am now. The idea of living through an actual war is not something I've ever thought about. That my grandfather had to is both fascinating and horrifying.

"Your grandma was ten," he continues. "I had it easy compared to her."

"Why? What happened to Grandma?"

"That's not my story to tell. One day you should ask her about it."

I'm very curious now and wish Grandma was home so I could ask her.

"But tell me your story, Grandpa! What was it like growing up during wartime?"

He glances at me, his head tilted to the side as he gives me a slight smile. "It's a long story. Are you sure you want to hear it?"

I nod enthusiastically, eager to hear Grandpa share his wartime experiences. It's shocking to think that he lived through such a terrible war. I just can't imagine anything like it.

Grandpa leans forward and rests his elbows on his knees. "To know about the Korean War, you must also know about the history of Korea."

"Gah! Not another history lesson!" I moan. I hate history. It's my least favorite subject.

Grandpa waits patiently through my whining. When I am done, he begins.

"I was very young during the Japanese occupation. But one of my earliest memories was watching my parents crying tears of joy as they set fire to the Japanese flag that used to hang in front of our door. They thought it meant we were finally free. Instead, millions more Koreans died because of a country torn in two, caught between foreign powers and corrupt governments. But the absolute worst of it was seeing your own countrymen turn on each other. Commit the most horrible deeds, all in the name of nationalism."

Perking up, I listen intently. This kind of history lesson I don't mind.

"What's nationalism?" I ask.

"It's pride in your country, but with the belief that it is better than other nations," Grandpa explains. "Like how Japan has always believed in its superiority over all others. It was why they thought nothing of colonizing Korea and taking all of its resources and sending them to Japan while leaving Koreans to starve. In Korea, nationalism pitted north against south."

Grandpa is no longer smiling. "I have never understood what would cause people to turn on each other. Turn on their neighbors. People they've known for generations. The only thing that made sense is that the entire nation of Koreans had suffered from years of trauma. They call it PTSD, right?"

"Yeah, we learned that in school. Post-traumatic stress disorder. It's what a lot of the veterans have after coming home from war. But how can a whole nation have it?"

Grandpa steeples his hands and gazes at something above my shoulder. "I'm not a medical professional, but I do know that Koreans as a whole have suffered deeply. The Japanese occupation was brutal. At the same time, there are many bad people in the world. Corrupt leaders and policemen. They do bad things because they have evil in their hearts. It's easier to understand why they do terrible things if they are themselves terrible people. But when ordinary citizens turn on each other, it doesn't make sense. That's why I like to believe they all suffered from trauma."

"Did you have trauma, too, Grandpa?"

"Oh yes," he replies, as his eyes stare off somewhere behind me. "I don't think anyone survived the war without being traumatized by it. But still, I was one of the lucky ones."

BOOK II

Doha

June 28, 1950

Chapter 7

IN THE HEAT OF THE summer, the boys jumped into the large pond. Shirtless and with hair shaved short to prevent lice, they scampered and wrestled and searched for frogs in the mud. Far away in the mountains behind them, the rapid-fire *rat-a-tat-tat* of machine guns echoed loudly.

The boys froze, tilting their heads toward the shooting, listening intently, before turning back to their play as the sounds faded. But one boy stood still, pensively staring up at the lush green mountains that surrounded them. He could make out the flash of the artillery that left small plumes of smoke in its wake.

"What's the matter, Doha?"

"I heard the Reds came for Sunjin's hyung during the middle of the night," Doha answered. He was upset because he liked Sunjin's big brother a lot.

"But Sunjin's father is dead! I thought they weren't supposed to take the head of the household!" Minki shouted angrily.

Kitae made a derisive grunt. "The Reds don't care about nothing but themselves and their stupid Communism."

"Poor Sunjin," Minki sighed.

"It'll be a lot worse for his hyung. He'll be stuck in the mountains eating nothing but weeds." Kitae shook his head. "My dad said they'll all be dead by winter."

"Your dad's been saying that every year," Minki retorted. "They're still up there, ain't they?"

The Communist guerrillas had a terrible habit of raiding the village for food during the night and kidnapping young men to join their ranks. Then when morning came, the police would come around interrogating all the villagers about Communist activities. Recently, things were getting more and more violent. Some of the guerrillas were actual North Korean soldiers who crossed over to recruit, mostly kidnap, young South Korean men. Others were locals who professed themselves to be Communists and denounced the Americans' involvement in their government.

Doha finally turned away. "Wonder if Sunjin's hyung is up there now."

"Probably," Minki said as he wiped the sweat from his face with his dirty arm. "Although this is pretty close to town for them. Usually they go to mountains near the sea. But they know what they're doing. The guerrillas have been hiding in the mountains since the Japanese were in charge. They'll be fine."

"Not this time," Kitae cut in. "The ROKA is going to set the mountains on fire and burn them out."

The Republic of Korea Army was only a few years old. Doha's father had explained that the ROKA had formed after the Japanese lost the big war, and was currently being trained by American soldiers who had come to help liberate Korea.

"Burn them out? That's terrible," Doha said.

"No, it's not. It's great news!" The tallest and biggest of the boys nodded fiercely. "They need to get rid of every last one of those filthy Communist scum."

Gunwoo's voice was fierce with anger that Doha understood. Gunwoo's family had escaped from the North and lost many members to the Russians and North Korea's KPA, Korean People's Army.

"But Sunjin's hyung . . ."

"He's a Red now. He deserves what he gets," Gunwoo said fiercely.

"It's not like he wanted to be one," Doha pointed out. "He didn't have a choice."

"Then he should have run away," Gunwoo replied.

Doha meant to argue more, but the other boys started making shushing sounds. "It's Sunjin," Kitae whispered. "He's coming."

Down the dirt path, they could see a skinny boy followed

by several young girls who seemed to be comforting him.

"Hey, Sunjin! You okay?" Minki called out.

The skinny boy arrived and plopped down on the rocky shore. His eyes were swollen from crying. The girls hovered around him before they were chased away by the splashing of the other boys.

Even as the girls screamed and scampered away, hurling insults back at the boys, Sunjin sat staring at his feet. All the boys except Gunwoo circled around him.

Doha sat next to Sunjin and put an awkward arm around his shoulders. Kitae and Minki crouched close by, looking uncomfortable. But Gunwoo stayed out near the reeds, holding his net over the water.

"Is your mom gonna be okay?" Kitae asked. "How is she going to survive without your hyung around?"

Doha shot Kitae a sharp look while Minki shoved Kitae so hard he fell over.

"Don't worry, Sunjin," Doha said. "You know our families will help you."

Sunjin let out a shuddering breath. "My mom says she is going to have to do wash and sewing again. Can you tell your moms? Sewing would be better because of her bad back."

"Of course! I'll tell my dad right away," Doha responded eagerly. "His clinic always has so much to sew, and my grandmother can't do too much because her eyesight has gotten bad."

Doha didn't know if what he was saying was true, but he

knew that his father would help his friend's family. Before he could say anything else to reassure his friend, he noticed Sunjin shrinking, his unhappiness palpable. Sunjin and his brother had been very protective of their mother. She'd fallen off a ladder trying to thatch their roof with yellow rice straw and had broken her back. That had been six years ago, the same year the Japanese had killed Sunjin's father for being a resistance fighter.

Realizing how awful this must feel for his friend, Doha bit back his words. He could see that the others were just as awkward and uncomfortable around their friend. Unlike the girls, they didn't have the right words of comfort.

With a nudge of his elbow, Doha said, "It's blazing hot. Let's go jump in the water."

As Minki and Kitae eagerly agreed, Doha seized his friend and shoved him into the pond, whereupon the others promptly splashed him with water.

"Argh! You dirty cockroaches! I'll get you!" Sunjin yelled as he vigorously splashed the others.

Doha was relieved to see his friend smile but couldn't help noticing that Gunwoo stayed away. It troubled him.

Chapter 8

BACK IN TOWN, DOHA SEPARATED from the others and headed farther into the village. His neighborhood was a series of walls surrounding a narrow dirt path that turned into a long and winding road from the main street. Modest white outside walls crowned with slanting tile decorations gave no hint of the elaborate courtyards and inner living quarters that were hidden like pearls in their oyster shells. Doha's own courtyard was lush, with pink peonies and golden forsythias, magnolia and plum trees, and azalea bushes that bloomed to a man's height.

His family lived close to his father's medical clinic. There were only two small hospitals in Seosan, his father's and one on the other side of town, near the ocean. His father, Dr. Han, had a reputation for being a warm and excellent medical doctor. He was well respected in the area, and sometimes people even came to his clinic with nonmedical questions. His father never charged them for advice. Which of course was why they kept coming back.

"Eomma! I'm hungry! Give me food," Doha shouted as he burst into the outer courtyard of his family home.

His mother and older sister, Yuni, immediately hushed him. They were sitting with his grandmother on the elevated wooden porch that framed the outside of their house. Bean sprouts were spread on newspapers in front of them, but they were largely ignored. Doha was shocked to see so many people standing inside his courtyard. Most of them he recognized from town. Local government workers, farmers, and merchants. There must have been fifty people packed into their outer courtyard. But what were they all doing here at dinnertime?

Mr. Choi, the village leader, and a few of the elders sat with Doha's father on the elevated porch at the other end of the L-shaped house. People were listening to them talking about the loss of the old ways in the changing world. Doha wasn't that interested and was about to go back out when Police Chief Song entered the courtyard and headed straight for Doha's father. A long, whispered conversation ensued before the police chief addressed the crowd.

"The Commies have invaded. They took over Seoul. President Rhee has left Seoul and is now in Daejeon," Police Chief Song announced. "I heard word that there are thousands of refugees from the North who are heading south. The trains are packed full and the roads are clogged with refugees."

The response was immediate distress as people shouted in alarm. Daejeon was a city almost 150 kilometers south of Seoul and 100 kilometers southeast of Seosan. Doha remembered going there by train once when he was very young.

"Rhee abandoned Seoul!"

"What will happen to us?"

"They will kill us all!"

Chief Song waved his arm for quiet. "One at a time, please!"

"Are the refugees coming here?" a merchant lady asked.

Doha thought that was an odd question to ask first. Shouldn't they be more concerned about the approaching war?

"We barely have enough food to feed our residents. What are we going to do if a lot of outsiders come here?"

"Well, they are heading south. Some might come here, but most are heading as far south as they can, probably all the way to Busan, since it's the biggest city and has an American military base nearby," Chief Song replied.

Doha's eyes widened. Busan was on the southeastern coast, a diagonal line across Korea from Seosan.

"Do we need to go to Busan?" Farmer Jung asked. He was a red-faced, blustery man who intimidated Doha. He had the biggest farm because he'd rushed to take over Japanese properties as soon as they were forced to leave Korea after World

War II. "I can't leave the farm, but maybe I should send my family to safety."

"We should be fine here, but we have to stop the refugees from coming."

Everyone started talking all at once, people worrying about whether they had to leave town. Whether it was safe for them to stay. How close the fighting was. How they could stop refugees from coming.

Doha was troubled by all that he heard. If people were fleeing war, shouldn't his village help them?

"If a lot of refugees come, we won't be able to feed everyone this winter," another farmer was saying. "We hardly had enough last year."

That bothered Doha. In all his life, he had never worried about running out of food. But as he saw the sober faces of the adults, he was reminded of how his mother would always send baskets of food to Sunjin's family and others. It was a moment that made him deeply aware of how lucky he was that his father was a doctor. How privileged he was. He suddenly wanted to be with his family. Looking around, he caught his grandmother's eye. She waved him over.

"Halmoni," he said as he hugged her.

"Aigo, my little puppy," Halmoni cooed. She pushed aside the cloth sitting on top of a basket of roasted ears of corn and passed him some.

But he'd lost his appetite. Talk of war and the Commies scared him. Realizing that others had suffered from hunger when he had so much pricked at his conscience.

"What about the Commies? When will they come here?" one of the shop owners asked.

"They're already here!" someone else shouted. "They're in the mountains during the day and come down to steal from us during the night."

Chief Song cleared his throat. "Listen, those are mostly local Reds. The North Korean Army isn't here yet."

"Maybe we need to leave also! Head south for now." Doha recognized his teacher, Mrs. Lee, speaking.

"We should be safe here," her husband responded.

"I don't know about that," Chief Song interrupted. "They've been evacuating villages in the line of fire."

"But we're not in the path. We'll be safe," someone was saying. "We're far enough west."

"What does that have to do with anything?"

"The Commies will head south. They'll bypass us."

"How do you know?"

"That's why the Communists have been getting bolder. They tried to break into the prison house and release the Communist leaders."

"Communist leaders? Nonsense. They're not leaders of anything! They're just poor farmers listening to that Communist garbage. Especially old Moon. He's just a drunkard. He's no more a Communist leader than your ancient granny. Chief Song, you should release those poor wretches and let them go home." Doha recognized the speaker as one of the shop owners from the marketplace.

Police Chief Song ran a hand through his thick, graying hair. "It's not like I want to arrest them," he said. "I know they're harmless, but I have no choice! We have orders to round up all local Communists and Communist sympathizers. But it won't be our problem much longer."

"Why's that?"

"The army's sending soldiers to gather all the prisoners together," he said. "It's better that way. I've not felt good about this whole situation."

"Is the army going to protect us?" someone shouted out, but Doha couldn't see who it was.

Chief Song shook his head. "They want all our young policemen to join the war effort and leave town."

There was a loud commotion in response. "What about us?"

"Who's going to save us from the Commies?"

"Our army will protect us," a villager said.

Someone laughed derisively. Doha thought he was someone who worked in the local government office.

"That's a joke! Our army is too inexperienced and seriously underpowered! The Soviets gave the KPA two hundred tanks while ROKA has none! They're a joke! No wonder they took Seoul so quickly!"

Before the man could continue, the village leader, Mr. Choi, stood up to speak. "That's enough! No need to scare anyone unnecessarily. I have heard the Americans are sending troops."

Another wave of loud relief as everyone processed this new information.

"The Americans will fight; that's what's going to happen. You saw what they did to Japan in the big war. Got them out of our country for good! They'll flatten those Commies in no time." Doha wasn't surprised to see that it was Gunwoo's father who spoke so passionately. Doha knew him to be a huge fan of Americans, although his admiration was solely based on the fact that they resoundingly beat the Imperial Japanese Army. Like most Koreans, Gunwoo's father despised the Japanese.

At his words, there was an immediate clamor of loud voices arguing for and against the likelihood of a swift and easy Communist defeat in the hands of American military might. As voices were raised and emotions became heated, the argument began to spiral out of control.

"Seonsaengnim, please speak up!" someone called out to Doha's father. When Doha was small, he always thought seonsaengnim only meant schoolteacher, but it actually meant someone with a higher educational degree. So doctors were also called Seonsaengnim, as a form of respect. Doha once asked his father why that was and his father had said, "Because doctors are also teachers. We teach people to take better care of themselves." That made a lot of sense to Doha.

The room abruptly went quiet in deference as Dr. Han slowly rose to his feet.

"I will not lie; I am deeply concerned," he said. "We are once again relying on a foreign country to help save us. But this time, against our own fellow Koreans. This doesn't feel right. Our leader is a corrupt dictator in the pocket of the Americans, and the North follows a Soviet puppet who calls himself 'the Great Leader.' Who is protecting us? Who really cares about our people?"

There were murmurs of agreement among the crowd.

Doha's father shook his head grimly. "First we were oppressed by the Japanese; now we are caught between Russia and China on one side, and the Americans on the other. When will free Koreans control our own destiny?"

A wave of voices erupted from the crowd; it was hard to make out who was yelling what.

"We'll never be free if the Communists take over!"

"China wants to control Korea again! The only way to save our country is to fight!"

"But the army is conscripting all our young men."

"And if they don't enlist, they'll be taken by the Communists anyway," Mr. Choi said grimly. "Look what happened to Widow Song's oldest son. They didn't even care that he is the only source of income for his disabled mother and little brother; they wanted his youth and his strength. They are bad men who only care about their ideology!"

They were talking about Sunjin's hyung. Doha turned to his grandmother and asked quietly, "Halmoni, will they take me and Sunjin, too?"

Halmoni wrapped her arms tight around Doha's shoulders. "No," she whispered only for him to hear. "Thank the heavens my precious boy is too young."

But then her sorrowful gaze turned to Doha's maternal aunt and uncle. Doha could see they were standing next to each other, his aunt's hands wrapped tight around her husband's arm. Recently married, his new uncle was a schoolteacher.

"They have no choice. It's the Communists or the ROKA. And no self-respecting Korean should ever willingly join the Communists," Mr. Choi said sternly. His eyes also turned to Doha's uncle.

Dr. Han sighed and walked over to Doha's uncle and gently patted him on his shoulders.

Doha's uncle bowed. "I'll do my duty, of course. There's no way I'll join the Commies."

There were murmurs of concern and sympathy among the crowd, all of whom had attended their spring wedding. Doha could see how pale his aunt was as she clung tightly to her husband. He wondered how soon his uncle would have to leave to join the ROKA.

With a sad nod, Dr. Han faced the crowd again. "We Koreans have a long history of surviving against many invasions. We are survivors. We survived forty-five years of oppressive Japanese rule as they tried to systematically destroy our culture, our language, and break our spirit. But they couldn't, because we are resilient. And we are also fighters. We kept our language and our heritage even under pain of death. That is who we are. We are stubborn and proud. Whatever happens next, we will fight, and we will survive. But remember, to do so, we must look out for one another, take care of our neighbors. We survive not individually, but as a community. That is our strength."

He gave the crowd a slight bow and walked over to escort the elders out. This was the signal for everyone to head home. As they filed through the outer doorway, they thanked Doha's parents for their hospitality.

When everyone had left, his mother and sister went back to picking off the tails of all the bean sprouts. They sat on the outer wooden floors, each with one leg hanging over in identical fashion as they laughed together. Since Yuni had turned fifteen this year, they looked more like sisters than mother and daughter. Doha's father said they were the most beautiful women in all of Korea, which made Doha roll his eyes. But he had to admit his mom and sister were both very pretty.

"Doha," Yuni called to him, "come help us."

Shaking his head, Doha shimmied over to where his father was getting ready to return to his medical clinic to check on his patients. Quietly, he grabbed hold of his father's hand and looked admiringly at his serious face.

His father smiled down at him and gripped his hand tight.

"Doha, are you coming to help me at the clinic tonight for a little while?"

He nodded. He'd rather go to the clinic than snap bean

sprouts at home. Also, he had a lot to think about from his father's speech.

Junie

"Grandpa, your dad was really cool, huh?" I ask in admiration.

Grandpa smiles. "He was my hero."

Chapter 9

AT THE CLINIC, DR. HAN was greeted immediately by Nurse Pak, a recent graduate of a nursing high school, who was training with Head Nurse Cha.

"Seonsaengnim, I was ready to go to your house," she said with a bow. "An emergency just came in."

As she spoke, she urged Dr. Han toward the back of the clinic. Several people were in the waiting room. They all bowed and greeted him as he walked through. Doha saw his friend Minki sitting in the waiting room with his older brother. They both looked tired and worried.

"Minki!" Doha called out as he approached his friends. "What are you doing here? I thought your parents didn't trust doctors. Are you sick?"

His friend shook his head. "It's my little sister Mija. She was not feeling well for several days. Nothing the shaman did was working; she was just getting sicker. So I begged my mom to come here."

"That's terrible!" Doha looked to see where his father was talking with the head nurse, Nurse Cha. "Let me find out what they think is wrong."

He went over to his father's side as Nurse Cha was explaining what she'd diagnosed. Nurse Cha had been educated by American missionary nurses in Seoul. Dr. Han always said Nurse Cha should have been a doctor, she was so good at medicine.

"Seonsaengnim, Mrs. Jeong is in the exam room with her youngest. She's slipping in and out of consciousness and burning with fever. She's favoring her lower right side. I think it's appendicitis, but she's in a very bad way."

"If that's true, we'll need to put her on antibiotics right away," Dr. Han replied. "How is our current supply?"

Nurse Cha made an unhappy noise. "Very low. I'm not sure I even have enough for Mija."

His father headed into the main medical room where several small beds were set up. On one of the beds lay a very still figure of a small child. Doha peered into the room and saw that it was little Mija. She was terribly pale except for two bright spots of color high on her cheeks. She was unnaturally still for a kid who was constantly on the move.

"Please, Seonsaengnim, save my baby!" Mrs. Jeong sat, holding tightly to her daughter's hand.

For a moment, Doha could see an angry, almost anguished

expression on his father's face as he turned away from Mrs. Jeong and rubbed his eyes.

"Mrs. Jeong, I'm going to do my best, but we don't have much time now. If only you had brought her to me earlier, before her appendix ruptured. But now the infection has spread, and she's gone septic. We must operate right away."

"Seonsaengnim, what does that mean?"

Dr. Han didn't answer her, concentrating on getting Mija into the small operating room in the back of the clinic.

"Seonsaengnim!"

Nurse Cha intercepted her, not letting her enter the room.

"Mija is fighting a very dangerous infection and she has to have surgery if there is any chance of saving her. Please, wait outside with your children," Nurse Cha said. Spotting Doha, she waved him over. "Doha, take Mija's mother out to the waiting room."

With a bow, Doha led the anxious woman to where his friend Minki and his brother were sitting.

"What's wrong with her, Doha? Did your father say?"

"It's a really dangerous infection. She is in surgery now."

"Will it save her?"

Doha wanted to say of course his father could save her. But he'd seen the anguish on his father's face; he knew that Mrs. Jeong had waited too long before bringing Mija to the clinic. There was no way to know what would happen.

"I don't know, Minki," Doha answered quietly. "She's very sick."

An hour passed in agonizing slowness as Doha sat with Minki's family. They were too worried to talk, so all Doha could do was keep them company. Suddenly, he felt his stomach give a painful rumble and remembered he hadn't eaten any dinner. He thought of the corn his grandmother had been going to give him. Hopping to his feet, he told Minki he would be right back. Running home, he asked his grandmother for some corn, and she gave him four ears wrapped in a white cloth. He carried it to the clinic only to see Nurse Cha take Mija's mother to the operating room. The next moment, he heard a heartbreaking scream and then the loud wailing of Mrs. Jeong. Minki and his brother rushed out to her.

Doha's heart sank. He followed behind, dragging his feet, afraid to see what his heart already knew. Inside, Minki and his brother were crying and hugging their mother, who was pressing her face against Mija's. He watched as Mrs. Jeong flung her body over her daughter's, pushing Mija's pale hand over the side of the table, where it hung limply. Doha dropped his bundle of corn in shock. As a doctor's son, he should've been used to death. But this was the first time he'd seen the death of a child. A child who was a friend.

"Doha, let's give them some privacy," Nurse Cha said. She picked up the now-dirty corn, wrapped it up, and gently led Doha away.

She took him to his father's office and left to return to the front desk. Doha watched as his father sat slumped low in his chair, his eyes closed.

"Abeoji, are you all right?" Doha asked.

Dr. Han opened his eyes and pulled Doha into a tight embrace. Doha could feel wetness through his shirt and realized his father was crying. Once again Doha found himself frozen in shock. He'd never seen his father cry before. It was in that moment that the weight of what he'd seen hit him like a kick in the stomach. Mija was dead. He would never see her chasing after Minki or hear her infectious laughter as she shouted, "Oppa! Catch me!"

He felt the burning sting of tears in the backs of his eyes. This pain was real, and Doha didn't know what to do about it.

His father pulled away and wiped his eyes. "You should go home, Doha. You must be exhausted."

"Aren't you coming too?"

"I can't. I have to stay here for Mija's family," his father replied. "If only Mija's mother had brought her to me even a few hours earlier, she could have lived. If only they didn't believe in shamanism more than medicine." He stared off at the horizon.

There was a bleakness in his father's eyes that weighed heavily on Doha's heart. He knew how deeply his father cared for all his patients.

"I'm sorry, Appa."

Dr. Han stretched and got to his feet. "Let's get you home and in bed. It's getting late."

With a steady hand on Doha's back, father and son walked out of the office, past the family weeping in the operating room, and to the front desk where Nurse Cha was sitting.

"Good night, son!"

Doha waved and walked out the front door. As he stepped out onto the road to his house, he could hear the loud engine noise of approaching vehicles. He watched as three military trucks drove past him to the front of the clinic and stopped abruptly, kicking up a huge cloud of dust. They were Republic of Korea Army.

Doha coughed and watched as a ROKA soldier in a dark olive-green uniform jumped down and strode into the clinic. Within a minute, he returned with Doha's father and the two nurses. Another soldier climbed out of the lead truck and bowed to them. Doha was too far away to hear, but the soldier looked and acted like an officer. He could see he was right when the man began shouting orders and the soldiers in the trucks sprang into action. There was a commotion at the back of the truck. Doha could hear moaning as they began carrying injured men on stretchers into the clinic. They carried in ten injured soldiers. Doha inched closer to peer around the truck and was alarmed to see how badly hurt the men were. Some were missing limbs, and one had his face completely wrapped in bloody bandages.

After the last of the wounded were transported in, the commanding officer saluted Dr. Han, and then with one last bow, he and all his men boarded the trucks and drove off again.

Doha stood staring at the line of trucks driving away. If

they were dropping off wounded here, then the fighting must be close. Doha was chilled by the thought, worried for his family and friends.

Junie

"Grandpa, why did Mija's mom not believe in doctors? I don't understand. Why did they go to a shaman? What could a shaman do?"

"Back then, many superstitious people believed that you got sick because of evil spirits," Grandpa says. "They didn't trust modern medicines. They relied on folk remedies, herbs, and offerings to shaman. It was around that time that Korean medicine modernized. A lot of Korean doctors would get American medical school training and return to Korea. But even now you will find people who would rather pay money to ward off evil spirits than go to the hospital."

"Poor Mija." I sigh.

Chapter 10

"THE COMMIES ARE COMING! The Commies are coming!"

Doha sat up in shock to see his friend Kitae running into his courtyard to scream the news. He'd been lying on the cool bamboo mat of his living room with the sliding doors open to allow the warm breeze to circulate through the house.

"Eh, what?" Doha asked in confusion. "From the mountains?"

His friend had to stop to catch his breath. Kitae's missing front teeth caused him to sound like a breathy whistle as he struggled for air.

"No, North Koreans! The KPA are marching into Seosan," he wheezed. "Saw them with my own eyes. Must warn everyone!"

"Did you go to the clinic?" Doha asked urgently "The ROKA soldiers are there! The ones who arrived a few weeks ago."

Kitae's eyes grew big. "I'll go warn them!"

As Kitae ran off, Doha got up to follow him.

"Where do you think you're going? Lie down right now," his grandma scolded. "You're still sick."

"But Halmoni! I have to go to the clinic and warn Abeoji!"

His grandmother grabbed him by his shoulders and pushed him back on the mat.

"You have to lie down and not worry about the clinic," she retorted. "Kitae will take care of it just fine."

Reluctantly lying down, Doha frowned. "But the soldiers. They'll be captured by the enemy."

Halmoni brushed his hair gently to the side as she wiped down his face with a cold wet towel. "And your father will do what he can to help them," she said gently. "You've had a fever for two days now, so you're not going anywhere until you're all better."

Worrying about the ROKA soldiers had strained him, and Doha fell into a feverish sleep. When he woke up, his fever had finally broken. Feeling strong enough to eat, he sat up to see his grandmother setting the low dining table with food for his sister, who'd just returned from the clinic.

"Doha, you woke up? Come eat," his grandmother said.

Doha sat up and slid over to the table, where his sister was picking at her food. "Noona, what happened to the soldiers? Did Kitae come and warn you?"

Yuni's pretty face paled as she blinked back tears.

"What's the matter, my precious granddaughter? What worry is keeping you from eating?" Halmoni asked.

"We didn't have much time before the Reds arrived," she said in a shaky voice.

Doha was hit with uneasiness. "But the ROKA soldiers! What happened to them?" Doha asked.

Tears suddenly coursed down Yuni's face. She dashed them away with the backs of her hands and took in a shuddering breath. "We had no way of hiding them; the Reds came too quickly," Yuni recounted in a quiet voice. "They had wounded also and demanded that they get immediate care. When they brought them in, they searched the clinic and found the ROKA soldiers on the second floor. They took them all away, even the ones too sick to be moved. And they were so brutal. Abeoji tried to stop them and they put a bayonet to his throat. Then the officer in charge held a gun to Nurse Pak's head and said, 'We need a doctor, but do we really need two nurses?'"

"Is she okay?" Halmoni asked in concern.

Yuni nodded. "Eomeoni explained that given the number of wounded that needed care, even two nurses were not enough. So they let Nurse Pak go, but I've never been so scared in my life."

"What did they do with the soldiers?" Doha asked.

Yuni shook her head. "I don't know."

"Aigo! Aigo! Aigo!" Halmoni was beside herself with shock. "Those poor, unfortunate boys!"

Halmoni had helped the nurses at the clinic with a few of the young soldiers. She'd been upset to see that many were no more than teenagers. All she could talk about was how they were too young to be at war.

"What's going to happen to them?" Doha asked. "They won't really kill them, will they?"

His sister looked at him with eyes wide with fright. They'd heard so many horrifying stories about North Korean cruelty. Doha feared he already knew the answer to his question.

Late that night, Doha's father finally came home. The hot night had kept Doha twisting and turning. He decided he'd go see his father. But as he approached the living room, he heard his father talking about what had happened earlier that day with Halmoni and Doha's mother. Knowing that they would probably stop the conversation if he appeared, Doha decided to eavesdrop on them.

"What's happening? Has all of Korea fallen to the Reds?" Halmoni asked.

"From what I've heard, the North Koreans have captured Daejeon, and President Rhee and his government have fled to Busan."

"Spineless cowards," Halmoni spat out. She'd always hated Rhee, calling him a fake Korean and an evil man. "What about those young soldier boys?"

There was a long pause, and then Doha could hear the exhaustion and anger in his father's voice. "They took them."

"Those boys were still really sick!" Halmoni said. "How could they move them out of the hospital? Where did they take them? They're too sick to go to prison!"

"They're not in prison," Dr. Han said.

"Then where are they?"

Someone was crying. Doha peeked around the doorway to see his mother sobbing into her hands.

Halmoni was wiping the tears from her face. "Don't tell me they killed them?"

Doha could hear the pain in his father's voice. "They took them near Buchunsan and buried them alive."

Doha covered his mouth tightly to keep from making a sound. Buchunsan was a small mountain on the other side of town. He couldn't believe what he'd just heard. He'd been talking to one of the soldiers every day. A nice guy from Seoul. He'd been telling Doha all about Seoul and what it was like in the biggest city in Korea.

"Aigo, aigo," his grandmother cried over and over again.

She was gently patting Doha's mother, who was doubled over in tears. His father sat with his head bowed. His hands, clenched into tight fists, were shaking slightly.

"Ideology will kill us all."

Junie

"I don't understand, Grandpa," I say in shock. "Why did they kill the soldiers? They were wounded. They couldn't fight! Weren't they supposed to be prisoners of war or something?"

Grandpa nods. "That's because the North Koreans did not consider South Korean soldiers to be prisoners of war, protected under the Geneva Convention. Instead, they

110

considered them to be fellow citizens who were committing war crimes."

I'm so horrified I sit staring at my grandpa for several minutes.

"Junie, you want me to stop now?"

"No, no! Please don't stop."

Chapter 11

"DOHA! HELP ME, PLEASE!"

Doha was sitting on the wooden porch of his house with his sister, eating corn, when his friend Gunwoo ran into their courtyard in tears. Doha hadn't seen Gunwoo since the day at the pond, which felt like ages ago.

"Gunwoo! What's the matter?" Doha asked.

His friend was sobbing so hard they couldn't understand him.

"Gunwoo, calm down. We don't know what you're saying."

Yuni offered him some corn, but Gunwoo, who normally ate any food in sight, shook his head and continued to cry.

The boy took shuddering breaths as he tried to stop crying.

"What's the matter, Gunwoo?" Doha asked again. He

rubbed his friend's back, trying to comfort him.

"Have you seen my parents?" Gunwoo asked.

"No, what happened?"

"Last night, my mom made me hide in the bushes behind the house. She told me not to come out no matter what happened. And then I heard the soldiers come. I could hear a lot of yelling and screaming, and they were breaking everything in the house. And then they took them both away!" Gunwoo began crying again. "I hoped they'd come back, but they never did, and I don't know where they are."

Yuni and Doha looked at each other in horror.

When the North Korean KPA had rolled into town five days before with a fleet of trucks and hundreds of men, they'd immediately taken over the town administration. Then they began arresting everyone affiliated with the local government. They'd imprisoned Police Chief Song and all his officers on the very first day. Then they went after the village leader, Mr. Choi, and a few of the elders. When Doha's father tried to speak on their behalf, he was told to focus on the care of the KPA wounded, or he would be arrested also. Now the town was occupied by an enemy force, and everyone was uneasy. Doha had not been allowed to leave his neighborhood or see any of his friends.

"They said it was because my older brother joined the military police," Gunwoo choked out. "They said he'd escaped, but our parents didn't, and would have to pay for his crimes. Doha, you have to help me, please! I have to find them."

Doha looked at his sister, who clutched at the neckline of her shirt, her eyes worried.

"We should talk with Abeoji first," Yuni said. Their parents were at the clinic, as usual, and their grandmother had gone to visit a friend.

Gunwoo let out a keening sound of such anguish it stabbed at Doha's heart. "I need to find them now! I'm gonna go myself, then." He turned away, his usually proud form wilting from the weight of his fear.

"Wait, Gunwoo. Let me get ready and I'll go with you," Doha said. He quickly rushed through his morning routine and joined his friend.

"Doha, I don't think this is a good idea," Yuni said. "Let me go run next door and talk to Abeoji first."

"Noona, you go talk to him and I'll go ahead with Gunwoo."

"Be careful, Doha," she shouted after him.

The boys ran into town together, stopping first at the market square, but everything was closed. There was hardly anyone out on the streets. Only North Korean soldiers on patrol everywhere, their tan uniforms looking drab and dusty.

With the town so deserted, Doha was sharply aware of how much they were sticking out. He suddenly thought of Sunjin. His sister had told him that the KPA were paying Sunjin's mother to cook and clean for them.

"Gunwoo, we can't just wander around. Let's go ask

Sunjin; he might know."

"I'm not asking that red traitor anything," Gunwoo responded fiercely.

"Gunwoo, don't be like that. He is still our friend."

"He's no friend of mine . . ."

"He'll help us. I know he will. I'll go ask him."

Anger gave way to desperation and Gunwoo gave a short nod. He stayed several lengths behind as Doha ran to Sunjin's house. Sunjin's house was busy, North Korean soldiers coming in and out, Sunjin's mom serving them, but with a strained expression on her face. Sunjin was filling cups with water and cleaning up after the men.

"Sunjin," Doha whispered several times. Sunjin looked around and casually backed away from the house before dashing out.

"Doha, what's up?" Sunjin said, then caught sight of Gunwoo lurking several houses back.

"What are you doing here with him? You've got to be careful. His family's been branded traitors."

"Sunjin, we need your help," Doha said. "We've got to find Gunwoo's parents. Do you have any idea where they are?"

Sunjin shook his head. "And even if I did, I couldn't help him. We'd get in trouble too."

"Sunjin, it's Gunwoo's family. He's our friend. Just please find out where they might have taken them."

Sunjin hesitated, sliding a look at Gunwoo. The big boy looked frightened and suddenly small. His face now no different than when they'd first met five years before.

"Wait here," Sunjin said, and slipped back inside. It took what felt like an eternity, but was at most fifteen minutes, before he returned. Gunwoo darted forward quickly.

"Where are they?"

Sunjin hushed him and pulled Gunwoo and Doha to the side of the house.

"They took Chief Song and his men to Dangjin Prison to stand trial for war crimes or something like that. But the government officials they took to the farthest valley of Palbongsan, on the west side. I don't know why or what's there, but that's all I know. Be careful."

At his words, Gunwoo took off down the road.

"Gunwoo, wait!" Before Doha could follow, Sunjin grabbed him by the arm.

"Doha, I don't think Gunwoo should go there alone," he said. "I think something bad happened to them."

With a sad look, he said sorry and went back into his house.

Doha raced after Gunwoo, catching up with the bigger boy fairly quickly. Doha had always been a faster runner.

"Gunwoo, wait! I think we should go get my father," Doha said.

"Why, Doha? So that he can be arrested also?" Gunwoo asked bitterly. "Don't worry, I'll go alone. You can go home now."

Unsure of what to do, Doha kept pace with his friend. He

desperately wanted to go home and get his father. But what if what Gunwoo said was true? What if he went to get his dad and caused him to be arrested by the KPA? His father was already being watched. No, it was better for Doha to go instead. They wouldn't possibly arrest two twelve-year-olds, he hoped. He was definitely afraid. Sunjin's warning not to let Gunwoo go alone had reminded him about what had happened to the ROKA soldiers. The North Koreans had shown no mercy, even to wounded men who could do no harm.

Doha stayed with Gunwoo on the ten-kilometer trek to Palbongsan. It took them over two hours to walk. They could see it long before they reached it. Several times they hid as trucks and North Korean soldiers marched by them.

Palbongsan meant "eight peaks mountain," with its highest peak standing over three hundred sixty meters high. The peaks lined up all in a row and made for a beautiful landscape. It was a favorite place for people to go hiking and appreciate nature's glory. The boys had to walk around the mountain to get to the west side valley. They knew they were close when the beauty of their surroundings was jarred by the loud weeping and wailing of distraught family members. Doha began to slow down, but Gunwoo raced ahead. The scene they came upon was gruesome. Women wailed around bodies lying thick on the grass.

Doha couldn't help but stare at their feet. Most of the shoes were straw. Doha knew what that meant. He'd seen them in his father's waiting room. Those who were too poor to own a pair of even rubber shoes. They were peasants. Mostly farmers or poor villagers. He'd heard that the Communists were targeting mostly police and government officials. So why were there so many poor people here? What had they done to deserve to die?

Suddenly, he heard Gunwoo scream and then begin to sob. "Appa! Appa!" He was kneeling next to a body.

Doha immediately noticed the shiny western shoes on its feet. Black patent leather, like the foreigners. Gunwoo's father had been so proud of the shoes he'd gotten from his eldest son, a police officer in Daejeon. He polished them until they gleamed. Townsfolk commented that they could see Gunwoo's father from miles away just from the shine of his shoes. He wore them every day to work at the administrative offices where he was in charge of meticulous recordkeeping. Gunwoo had been proud of the fact that his father had been a headmaster of a high school in North Korea. A stern-looking man, Gunwoo's dad was actually very kind and generous—he would always give out toffee candy to any child who greeted him. But now, Doha almost didn't recognize him. His face had been badly beaten and his body stabbed multiple times. But the worst were his eyes. They were missing. Doha's legs gave out and he sank down next to Gunwoo. What had this kind man done to warrant such a horrible death?

"Appa, Appa! Don't leave me!"

Gunwoo's head was pressed against his father's blood-covered hands. Doha sat silent, his own hands clenched in tight fists as his friend wept wildly. He felt helpless and heartbroken but also so terribly guilty. For his first thought had been to thank the heavens it was not his own father. And for that, he could not forgive himself.

"I hate them! I hate them all!" Gunwoo lurched to his feet, screaming at the sky. "Communist bastards! I'll kill them!"

Doha grabbed hold of his friend, desperately trying to calm him. It was a long and hard struggle, as Gunwoo raged in a terrible anger, lashing out violently against Doha until he fell against his friend, exhausted. Doha could do nothing but hold him tight.

"Eomoni! Where's my Eomma? I want my Eomma!" Gunwoo sobbed.

As Doha blinked back his own tears, he realized they had not found Gunwoo's mother. But where were they to look?

"Gunwoo, Doha." A woman approached. Doha recognized her as someone who also worked in the administrative offices. She too had been beaten, her face bleeding and bruised. She was limping badly and there was lots of dried blood on the bare legs that showed beneath her skirt. In her hands, she held a small pad of paper and pencil.

"Gunwoo," she repeated. "They took your mom to Doha's father's medical clinic. Go find her there. She was badly injured, but she's alive."

At her words, Gunwoo sat up in a rush.

"Eomoni is alive?" Hope and relief showed on his ravaged face. He went to stand up, but then stared down at his father.

His grief contorted his face once again.

"But Appa," he whispered. "I can't leave him."

"You have to," she said. "They're coming back to bury them. You can't be here when they do. You have to leave him."

Doha got up and was pulling Gunwoo to his feet.

"Ahjumma, you have to come too," Doha said. "You need a doctor also."

She nodded. "I will. I just need to finish writing down the names of who is here," she whispered. "So we have a record of who they murdered."

"Hurry, and come with us now," Doha said. He was feeling nervous about the idea of leaving her. She was hesitating when they heard the approach of a truck and watched as the other women who were crying over the dead began to scatter.

Doha grabbed Gunwoo by the arm and pushed the woman away from the approaching truck.

"Appa," Gunwoo cried out, but he didn't fight Doha as they scrambled away.

By the time they reached the clinic, dusk had fallen. Due to the woman's injuries, it would have taken more than five hours to return from Palbongsan but for the kind farmer who had given them a ride in his cart and dropped them off near town. Doha and Gunwoo walked the rest of the way, supporting the woman between them. When they finally arrived at the clinic, they collapsed in the crowded waiting room. Gunwoo rushed away, calling out for his mother, while the nurses half carried the injured woman to a chair and began to examine her.

Exhausted, Doha stumbled to the even more crowded exam room. His father gave Doha a worried look before turning his attention to his patient. On the other side of the room, Gunwoo had found his mother and was sobbing hysterically in her arms. Every cot was occupied with injured women and children, many on straw mats on the floor.

Dr. Han took a break and gently pushed Doha into his office.

"Yuni told me what happened, and I'm proud of you for helping your friend. But I was so worried about you." Doha's father hugged him tightly. "These are dangerous times, Doha. Please promise me you'll be extra careful."

"Abeoji, we found Gunwoo's father," Doha said, finally releasing the tears he'd been holding in as he sobbed at the horror of the death. His father held him and patted his back gently until he was all cried out.

"I was so afraid to go, but I didn't want Gunwoo to be alone," he said. "I'm sorry I didn't ask you first."

Dr. Han gently wiped away his son's tears and smiled. "Doha-ya, you were right to go with your friend, even though you worried us. There are moments in life when a person must decide between what's right and what's safe. It is one of the most difficult decisions in life, and I would never be angry at you for choosing to do what's safe. But I will always be proud of you for doing what's right."

Relieved by his father's words, Doha sat down in exhaustion. "Will Gunwoo's mother be okay?"

Dr. Han nodded. "It will take her a long time to heal, but she will survive. Now, I know you are tired, but I have another job for you."

"Yes, Abeoji?"

"We don't have enough room to take care of all the injured," Doha's dad said. "Doha, can you run over to Dr. Ma's and ask for help?"

Doha swallowed back his tired complaint. Dr. Ma's clinic was on the other side of town.

"But where are all these patients from?" he asked.

His father's lips tightened grimly, and his eyes were serious. "These soldiers were trained to shoot first, ask questions later," was all he said. "Stop home first and eat. Your mother and sister are there getting dinner. And then tell them to hurry back."

With a gentle push, Dr. Han urged him out of the clinic. Doha ran straight home.

"Eomma, Noona, please hurry back to the clinic!" he yelled.

"Doha-ya!" His mother, sister, and grandmother all descended on him, pulling him into a crowd of arms and kisses and yelling.

"We were so worried about you!"

"You have to be more careful!"

"My little puppy is home safe, and that's all that matters,"

Halmoni said with a big hug.

As they sat him down at the table to eat dinner, Doha yanked at his mother's skirt.

"Eomma, I have to go to Dr. Ma's clinic to ask for help, but can you please take extra care of Gunwoo for me? His father is dead. We saw him."

Doha swiped at his tears with the back of his hand.

His mother hugged him tight. "That's no sight for such young boys," she said in sorrow. "Will you be all right?"

Doha nodded. "I have to go after I eat, but please take care of Gunwoo for me."

Avoiding his mother's sympathetic eyes, Doha finished eating quickly and raced out of their courtyard and ran for the main road. The middle of town was still empty of villagers but full of North Korean soldiers patrolling the area. Doha slowed down and tried to avoid their attention. He cringed when he saw them pull a local shopkeeper out of his house and beat him. It made him run faster, with anger, misery, and guilt tearing at him. It took him thirty minutes to reach the other clinic. The building was a lot bigger than his father's. He quickly relayed his father's message and watched as the doctor and staff began to bustle about. A nurse brought Doha a cup of hot corn tea that he blew on and drank as quickly as possible. Pretty soon, a male staff member motioned him to come out. In front of the clinic, Dr. Ma had pulled around his old truck. It made a lot of noise, but it would get them back in ten minutes tops. Inside the cab of the truck, the engine was too loud for conversation. This suited Doha just fine.

On the way through town, a group of North Korean soldiers stopped them and ordered them out of the truck.

Doha trembled with fear as Dr. Ma explained where they were going. After a few minutes, the soldiers waved them on. Doha wondered if they might have been the ones who'd killed Gunwoo's father and all the rest of the people in the mountain valley.

Doha clasped his shaking hands tightly, still badly frightened and angered by the encounter. The soldiers were no more than violent, cruel bullies.

"Dirty Communists," Dr. Ma muttered as he started the truck.

Doha couldn't help but agree with Dr. Ma.

Junie

I have to grab a box of tissues to wipe my tears and blow my nose. I can't even imagine seeing something so terrible.

"Grandpa, that must have been so horrible for you," I say. "Is that part of your trauma?"

He nods bleakly. "Sometimes I still see Gunwoo's father in my dreams."

Chapter 12

ALMOST TWO MONTHS HAD PASSED since the North Koreans had taken over Seosan. It was a difficult time. Food was scarce because the soldiers had commandeered the supply house and were now rationing food out to all the villagers. The hardest hit were the families of those killed by the Communists.

Gunwoo and his mother had been unable to leave Seosan due to her long recovery from severe leg injuries. To help them, Doha's father hired Gunwoo's mom to clean and take care of the clinic. Meanwhile, Gunwoo would go out to the farms to help make money.

Life in Seosan had changed drastically. Minki's family moved south after Mija's death. And Kitae's family left for Busan as soon as the KPA took over. With enemy soldiers patrolling the streets, Doha's mother kept him close to home.

No more catching frogs with his friends. No more wandering around town at all times of the day and night. This new life was one of constant fear. Instead, he spent all his days helping out at the clinic with the rest of his family. Even his grandmother would come for a few hours every day.

For Doha, his greatest worry was for his father. With the loss of the town leadership, most of the villagers brought their troubles to Dr. Han. And there were more patients than ever in his clinic. The KPA were living up to their reputation as a brutal occupation force. Every day, new patients would come in after being savagely beaten by North Korean soldiers. The KPA took what they wanted, when they wanted, without regard for who they were taking from. The only happy people were the Communist sympathizers who'd been released from the prisons when the KPA arrived. They were the ones who wore red armbands proudly and would lead weekly Communist propaganda events, which they called educational. To entice people to come to them, they offered up bags of rice if you signed up. Once, Doha's mom mentioned that she wanted to go get a bag of rice to give to Gunwoo's mom, but his dad sharply declined.

"No, it's not safe. Remember, nothing in life is free," Doha's dad said. "There is always a price. And when you don't know what it is up front, then you must be prepared for it to be too heavy a burden when they come for you."

Dr. Han was very wise. But for someone who did not believe in taking anything from anyone else, he was generous to a fault. He helped all who needed his help or asked for his time. It was why he was always tired.

"Yeobo, you must stop them from coming every night!" Doha heard his mother yelling at his father one night. Doha had stayed up very late watching the line of people waiting to talk to his father. He found it fascinating and disturbing to eavesdrop and hear their stories.

"You're busy enough with all your patients—they can't expect you to solve all their problems too! And I'm scared they will bring more attention to us!"

Doha couldn't hear his father's soft response, but he knew what he would say. When Doha had asked a similar question, his father had turned very serious. "My son, war is horrific and dehumanizing. It numbs us to suffering, pain, and death. Therefore, it requires average citizens to take extraordinary measures. For if we don't do what we can to minimize the suffering of others, we will lose our humanity."

His father's words had affected Doha deeply and he realized this was something his entire family believed in and was a motto they lived by. Even before the war, his father's kindness was well known throughout the county. Poor farmers who gave sacks of potatoes or corn for treatment or medicine. Widows who would wash the clinic's bedding and linens in lieu of payment.

His grandmother would pack small packages of food for Doha and Yuni to deliver to the elderly. When Yuni was not helping at the clinic, she was helping to care for the children of the women who had to work. And his mother made sure to share all their food with the clinic staff and anyone who was in need. She constantly reminded the family how lucky they were because Dr. Han was so well-respected in the community. They were one of the few families that still had daily white rice, but just like everyone else, Doha's mother mixed it with barley, millet, and beans to make it last longer. Doha missed eating plain white rice, but he knew of so many who had so much less. He had learned to be grateful for what they had.

The thing he missed the most was his friends. School had not opened after summer vacation. He couldn't see Sunjin because he was not allowed to go to town, and Gunwoo was always busy.

But then one day, every single one of the North Korean soldiers were gone. They had all disappeared in the middle of the night. One day they were everywhere, policing everyone, indoctrinating the villagers on Communism. And the next day they were all gone.

It became obvious what had happened when, a few days later, the Republic of Korea Army arrived back in town. They came with dozens of badly wounded soldiers, and once again the medical clinic was over capacity. There were so many injured that they had to send half of them over to Dr. Ma's clinic. But the worst cases stayed under Dr. Han's care, too injured to be moved any farther. There were fifty soldiers, taking up every inch of space on both floors of the clinic.

The whole family was forced to help out with all the patients. Doha was tasked with running errands and bringing water and food to the patients on the second floor. Normally, the second floor housed twenty patients that needed long-term care on straw mats covered with blankets. Now the room was crowded with soldiers, and the smell of infection was made worse by the continuing heat wave.

After a long morning at the clinic, Doha was relieved by a nurse who came in for the afternoon shift. Doha immediately ran outside and took a deep breath. It was such a relief to breathe the fresh air without the smells of alcohol, peroxide, and sickness.

"Doha, why don't you go play with your friends?" his mother said. "You've been working hard. Go take the afternoon off."

"Thank you, Eomma!" With a happy wave, Doha took off before anyone else could stop him. It had been so busy in the clinic that Doha had no idea what was happening in town.

His first thought was to go to Sunjin's house. Now that the ROKA was in town, what would happen to the North Korean collaborators? A vision of Gunwoo's father dead among so many bodies flashed through Doha's mind. He shook his head. *No, the ROKA wouldn't do that. Only North Koreans are that evil.*

But the thought was troubling, and Doha began to worry. The ten-minute run felt incredibly long with his anxiety.

When he reached town, he was shocked to see Gunwoo crossing the main road with a group of ROKA soldiers.

Doha called out his name, but Gunwoo was too far away to hear him. A horrible feeling struck Doha deep in his gut. It couldn't be what he was thinking. Gunwoo wouldn't do that. But why was he walking toward Sunjin's house? Why was he leading a group of soldiers there?

"No, Gunwoo, don't do it! Gunwoo!"

Doha was breathing hard, trying desperately to reach the group that was now stopped in front of Sunjin's house. Angry shouts filled the air, and then he saw a frightened Sunjin and his mother step out into the street. The ROKA soldiers were pointing their rifles at them. As Doha arrived, he could hear Sunjin's mom apologizing and asking for mercy.

"Gunwoo! What are you doing?" Doha shouted as he grabbed his friend hard by the arm.

Gunwoo flung Doha away and turned back to continue glaring at Sunjin and his mother. "I'm exposing the Red traitors."

Doha looked at the ROKA soldiers' faces. They were cold and hard. One of them moved forward to tie rope around Sunjin's mother's hands. Doha could now see the terror on his friend's face.

"But Sunjin's our friend!" Doha shouted.

"He's no friend of mine! He's the reason my father's dead and my mother is disabled for life! He chose to be a Communist traitor. He's no friend."

"Sunjin didn't do that! The Reds did it!"

"He helped them! They both did!" Gunwoo yelled. "They killed my father."

"Gunwoo, you know we didn't have a choice," Sunjin said quietly. "They took my brother and forced us to support them. We did what they told us to do in order to survive. We're not traitors."

"Shut up! Shut up! Don't listen to him! They entertained the Reds in their house. They're traitors!"

Sunjin's mom began crying, pleading for them to at least save her son.

"Doha, please help us!" Sunjin begged.

The soldiers tied Sunjin's hands. Doha rushed forward and pushed his hands up, asking them to stop.

"Leave them alone! They're not Communist sympathizers! They were forced to do it!"

A soldier slammed a rifle butt into Doha's abdomen. He fell to the ground, his breath completely knocked away. The soldier stood over him in a threatening manner.

"Are you one of them?"

Gunwoo stepped between the soldier and Doha. "No, he's not! He's Dr. Han's son. The doctor who's taking care of all the wounded soldiers."

The soldier stepped back, but his face was stern. "He needs to stay out of official business."

The soldiers led Sunjin and his mother away, pulling roughly on the ropes that tied them together.

Sunjin looked back in tears, calling Doha's name.

"Doha, please help us! Please ask your father to help us! Please, Doha! Tell them we had no choice! Tell them we're not collaborators! Doha!"

The soldier leading them turned back and backhanded Sunjin across the face. Sunjin fell against his mother, who tried to hold him up with her bound hands.

"You had a choice!" the soldier yelled. "You should have died rather than help those filthy Communist pigs!"

Tears rolled down Sunjin's cheeks as he followed the soldier quietly. The only sound now was the weeping of Sunjin's mother as they were led away.

Anguished, Doha tried to follow, but Gunwoo held him back.

"Are you crazy? Didn't you hear the soldier? They'll arrest you too!"

This time Doha shoved Gunwoo away.

"I don't understand you, Gunwoo!" Doha yelled. "Sunjin's our friend! You've eaten at his house many times. We've played together for years! How could you do this?"

"He's not my friend! You're my friend. But if you keep defending him, you won't be anymore!"

Doha stared in disbelief. What had happened to Gunwoo? He shook his head sadly. "Gunwoo, I don't know you anymore."

Gunwoo stepped right up to Doha's face. "Maybe that's what happens when your father is murdered for rejecting

Communism. And your mother is stabbed almost to death just because her son became a military policeman. Maybe the Gunwoo you knew is dead because the Reds destroyed his family. I would have rather died than do anything for the Red scum. Sunjin should have known better."

His intensity was too much for Doha. "I understand how you feel . . ."

"Then stand by my side, not Sunjin's!" Gunwoo cut in.

"Gunwoo," Doha said carefully. "This isn't right."

"Then you're no longer a friend of mine." Gunwoo stepped back, his eyes still burning with the intensity of his emotions. He turned and followed the soldiers, walking away without a single glance back.

Doha shivered as a chill went through him. What had happened to his friend?

Junie

"No! How could he do that? I don't understand!" I explode in anger. "He put Sunjin and his mother in terrible danger! That's just wrong!"

Grandpa is silent as I rant and rave. When I'm finally done, he says, "Maybe this is a good time to take a break."

"No, no, I'm fine, Grandpa," I say, as mildly as I can. "I can keep going if you can. . . ."

∽Chapter∽
13

IN ORDER TO HELP SUNJIN and his mother, Doha knew he had to talk to his father. He was the only one Doha could think of who could save his friend.

Doha raced back to the clinic, shouting desperately for his father.

"Doha, what is it? What is wrong?" His mother came out first.

"I need Abeoji! Sunjin is in terrible trouble! The soldiers took him and his mother to prison. They said they were Communist collaborators!"

"Omo! Yeobo! Yeobo!" Doha's mother hurried inside, calling for her husband. Doha entered the waiting room and collapsed onto a stool, exhausted by everything that had happened.

Dr. Han came out quickly, wiping his hands on a towel. "Tell me everything."

The words came tumbling out of Doha as he tried to explain the situation. His father listened carefully, asking only a few questions. When Doha finished his telling, he could see the serious expression of concern on his father's face. Dr. Han squatted in front of Doha and wiped his tears away with a clean handkerchief.

"Doha, I want you to listen carefully," his father said. "Stay here. Don't go anywhere. I know the commanding officer. I'm going to go and talk to him. But you must stay here, okay?"

Doha nodded. He watched as his father gave instructions to his nurses and then walked out of the clinic, still wearing his white doctor's coat. An enormous sense of relief washed over him. Sunjin would be all right. Doha's father would save him.

Not long after, Doha's mother took him by the hand and walked him home. Halmoni had made chicken soup. Although Doha wasn't hungry, his grandmother gently coerced him to eat every bite, stroking his back the whole time. His mother and sister ate quickly and returned to the clinic while Doha waited anxiously for his father.

"Rest, my little puppy," Halmoni said, "so you can grow strong and healthy."

Doha went to his room, crawled into his blankets, and closed his eyes.

He woke up to the sound of his grandmother greeting his father. Several hours must have passed as it was now completely dark. In the living room, he could hear the hushed voices of the grown-ups. Creeping to the outer door, Doha listened.

"The ROKA soldiers are just as bad as the North Koreans," his father said bitterly. "They refuse to listen to reason. Everything is black and white. Good or bad."

"What does that mean for Sunjin? Where are they?"

Dr. Han heaved a deep sigh. "They are being held in jail at the police station. They've got so many people crowded in there. Most of them are poor peasants who only signed up with the Reds' People's Committees so they could get free rice! Their only crime is hunger!"

Doha's mother let out a shocked cry. "I almost signed up for that. I could have destroyed our family!"

"Aigo, aigo, what is happening to our country?" Halmoni asked. "What will happen to them?"

"I tried to talk to the leadership, but they refused to see me on this matter. They say there will be trials held for all the prisoners. I'll have to make sure to go to Sunjin's and speak for them. That's the best I can do right now," Dr. Han said.

"My son." Halmoni's voice seemed quite urgent. "Maybe you should stop. What if they arrest you also? What would we do?"

"How can I not speak up when something so wrong is happening? If we are silent now, then they will still come for us later. It will not stop."

There was a long silence.

"What will you tell Doha?"

"I'll tell him the truth," his father replied. "But not now. Let him sleep. I have to go back to the clinic and check on my patients."

"Eat first, my son," Halmoni said. "You need all your strength."

Doha crept back into his room and went back to bed. His father's words had reawakened the awful fear from earlier in the day. His friend was in jail waiting to be put on trial for the crime of helping the Reds. His other friend was the one who'd put him there. What kind of tragedy was this? And if his father spoke up, it could put him in danger also. Doha felt utterly helpless.

Early in the morning, Doha's father came to wake him up.

"Doha, I know you are really worried about Sunjin and his mother, but try not to be too anxious," his father said. "The ROKA are not like the Communists. There will be a trial. And I will do all I can to talk to whoever will help them."

Doha wiped the tears from his eyes and nodded. "Thank you, Abeoji."

His father patted his cheek with a smile. "I know it will be hard for you to see your friend in prison. It isn't fair. Even though we know Sunjin and his mother are innocent, and that they were forced into helping the Communists, there have been a lot of bad feelings and people are not reacting rationally. I can only hope the trials at least will be fair."

As his father got up to leave, Doha couldn't hold back his feelings. "I hate Gunwoo!" he cried. "He told the ROKA that Sunjin and his mother were collaborators. He turned them in."

The tears began to fall faster as Doha couldn't hold back his emotions.

"Why, Appa? Why would he do that? I don't understand."

His father sat down and gathered Doha into his embrace, letting him cry as he patted his back. "Gunwoo is angry with the world," his father said. "And in his pain, he doesn't know that he is hurting others. That he is doing wrong."

"I don't care! I'm so mad at Gunwoo and scared for Sunjin."

His father pulled away to look into Doha's face. "My son. You are a good friend in a difficult situation. But do not hate Gunwoo. Pity him. For he may end up hating himself far more in the future."

Doha wasn't sure about that. But he didn't know what to think anymore. "Will it be okay if I go visit Sunjin? Maybe I can bring him food?"

His father hesitated but finally nodded. "Yes, but you must go with your noona."

With one last affectionate ruffle of Doha's hair, his father rose to his feet and left the room.

Later in the morning, Doha's mother packed a small wooden container full of food, including fruit, and tied it with a brightly colored wrapping cloth for easy carrying.

"Doha, I don't know if the prison guards will let you bring this to Sunjin and his mother," she said with a worried frown.

She turned to Doha's sister and handed her the package.

"Yuni, you explain to the guards for Doha," she said.

"Yes, Eomma," Yuni replied. "Let's go, Doha."

Full of nervous energy, Doha hurried to slip on his shoes and wait for his sister at the front gate. He chafed at the slow pace his sister kept. He wanted to hurry her but knew she'd get mad. Yuni was a kind and gentle person, but she had only one pace. Slow and steady like an ox. Although Doha could have run to the prison and back in the time it took Yuni to walk to the police station, he swallowed back his impatience and stayed by her side.

"Doha, weren't you afraid when you saw the soldiers take Sunjin away? They could've taken you too!"

Shrugging, Doha kicked a stone hard, watching it raise clouds of dust where it hit the road. "Gunwoo told them to leave me alone," he said bitterly. "But honestly, I still can't accept what he did."

Yuni nodded. "But we all know Gunwoo. He's been hurting bad. We have to understand and forgive him."

"But what about Sunjin and his mom? Gunwoo sent them to prison! No matter how badly he suffered, I can't forgive him for ratting them out! What if something terrible happens to them? How can he live with himself?" Doha choked a little on his words as he could feel the frightened tears he was so desperately suppressing.

"Sunjin and his mother are good people who have already suffered too much in life," Yuni said. "I'm sure they will be released. Abeoji will help them."

His sister's warm hand slid into his and held it tightly. He rubbed his eyes and focused on the road before them. His father was the smartest person in the world. He would trust in his father to save his friend.

Junie

"Grandpa, you can't stop there! I need to know what happens!"

"Junie, I just need a glass of water."

"Oh, okay," I say sheepishly and dash off to the kitchen.

I rush back with ice water, then anxiously watch him drink it. Grandpa takes his time, leaving me squirming in my chair.

~Chapter~
14

IN THE TOWN SQUARE, THE marketplace was busy with people again. But it was not the normal buzz of usual business. There seemed to be a watchfulness. An air of distrust and apprehension. As they passed the stalls of seafood vendors, a fight broke out between a merchant and a customer. The two women were shouting at each other.

"Oh, it's the squid ahjumma!" Yuni said. "She talks in such a mean voice, but actually she's really nice. Whenever I go buy seafood from her, she always gives me a sweet treat. I wonder why she's fighting with that woman?"

Doha looked over at the woman. She wasn't familiar to him. The fighting intensified, and both Doha and Yuni were shocked when the customer called the squid vendor a very bad word. He was not as surprised then when the customer got slapped. His grandmother told him that if he ever used words like that he would be beaten.

The woman became so angry, she began screaming at the top of her lungs. She accused the squid merchant of being a Communist sympathizer. An immediate chill went down Doha's spine. This was even worse than the curse words she'd used before.

"Oh no, what is she doing?" Yuni asked in shock. "The squid ahjumma might be mean, but she's never been a Red."

Doha was close enough to see the horror on the merchant lady's face. She was trying to appease the other woman, who kept screaming until the soldiers who were stationed at the marketplace came to her aid. Doha and Yuni watched as the soldiers started to tie the merchant's hands together. When her husband came out to stop them, they tied him up also and dragged them both away.

Doha could not believe what he was seeing. He glanced at the customer and saw a mix of smugness and guilt on her face. Was she happy about what she'd just done? Was she perfectly fine sending innocent people to jail? What was wrong with her?

But it was his sister who really surprised him. Yuni, who was slow to anger, was visibly upset. She rushed toward the woman before she could leave.

"Ahjumma," Yuni said loudly. "The squid merchant is not a Communist sympathizer. Why did you say that?"

The customer glared at Yumi. "How dare you speak so disrespectfully to your elder! Who are your parents?"

Yuni bowed deeply. "Forgive me. My father is Dr. Han, and I don't mean any disrespect. But I must please ask you to take back your accusation."

A crowd was now forming around them. Other merchants were yelling angrily at the customer for falsely accusing the squid merchant.

"You've never liked her and always accused her of ripping you off!" the vendor from the nearby fruit stand shouted. "That's a horrible thing you did!"

The customer waved her hands angrily in the air. "You don't know anything! I saw her talking to the Reds and smiling at them. Giving them free seafood."

"That doesn't make her a collaborator!"

"We all had to smile at them in order to survive!"

The customer tried to leave, but Yuni stepped in front of her. "I'm very sorry, Ahjumma! But please take back your accusation!"

The woman slapped Yuni hard and pushed her out of the way. "If you don't stop bothering me, I'm going to report all of you as Communists!"

Her words quieted everyone, and the woman walked away. But for the first time, Doha felt a terrible rage overcome him. The sheer injustice of everything he had witnessed was too much. Gunwoo's father brutally murdered, Sunjin and his mother dragged to prison, his whole world thrown upside down by political ideology. Unable to control his temper, Doha grabbed a tangerine from the fruit stand and threw it at the woman's back, screaming "Don't you hit my sister!"

When the woman turned around in fury, Doha whipped another one at her chest.

"Ah, you nasty brat!" Before she could attack him, an egg came flying through the air and hit her on the side of her head.

When he turned around, Doha's mouth gaped open to see his sister holding another egg in her raised hand.

"You are a horrible, evil woman," Yuni said fiercely. The woman's eyes went wide, and she beat a hasty retreat.

His sister put down the egg but continued to glare at the retreating woman. Behind her, the merchants who had gathered to support her were all holding some kind of food item at the ready.

Yuni turned to the merchants in alarm. "We have to stop her! She made a false report!"

The fruit vendor put her arm around Yuni and squeezed her for comfort.

"That woman will never take it back," the woman said grimly. "She is a terrible person. The only hope we have is to try to talk to the authorities. But we will do that. You go home now."

"But the squid ahjumma—they took her to prison!"

"There's nothing you can do," the fruit vendor said. She urged them to leave.

Yuni took Doha by the hand and slowly walked out of the marketplace.

"Noona, are you all right?" Doha asked anxiously.

She shook her head. "It's supposed to be better now," she whispered. "The Communists are gone. But why is life still so scary?"

The soldiers hadn't even tried to listen to the squid merchant or her husband. They just heard "Communist sympathizer" and took them away. It was frightening.

"Maybe they knew the ahjumma, and that's why they believed her?" Doha asked.

"That's not right! They are bad people! They are garbage dog excrement . . ."

"Noona!" Doha cut her off in surprise. He'd never heard his sister use bad words before.

Yuni's lips tightened and she began to walk faster, dragging Doha along.

"They took her to the prison," she barked. "Let's go help them and Sunjin."

Running to keep up with Yuni's long, quick strides, Doha marveled at the change in his usually mild-mannered sister. The normally placid, slow-moving ox was now on a rampage.

At the prison, the soldiers were stern and intimidating. Yuni respectfully approached the desk guard and asked if they could bring food to Sunjin and his mother. They motioned for her to leave the food on the desk as they wrote down Sunjin's name. The desk guard gestured for them to leave, but Yuni stayed put.

"Sir, I wanted to report that we just came from the

marketplace and a woman falsely accused a merchant and her husband of being Communist sympathizers," she said. Her voice trembled but she showed no fear.

The desk guard slowly put down the papers he was shuffling through and gazed at Yuni with cold eyes. He was a middle-aged man with a severe hair part that was slicked back with pomade so thick that it made his hair look waxed.

"And how would you know that it is false?" he asked. Doha shuddered, and he pulled at his sister's arm in warning. The desk guard's voice dripped with disdain.

Disregarding Doha, Yuni continued. "Because I know them—"

"You know the Communist sympathizers?" His eyebrows raised in mock surprise. "Tell me again who you are bringing this food to. Are they also fake Communist sympathizers?" He tapped at the package sitting on his desk.

"Fake? They aren't Communist sympathizers at all! They were forced to because—"

Before she could continue, several soldiers surrounded Yuni and Doha as the desk guard walked around his desk to stand deliberately close to them.

"Who are you, and what is your association to the prisoners?"

"Sunjin is only eleven, and he has been friends with my little brother since they were babies," Yuni answered. "We are the children of Dr. Han, who is taking care of many of

146

your soldiers at our medical clinic."

"Just because your father is a doctor doesn't mean he's not a Communist sympathizer also!"

"No, he isn't! We aren't!"

"How do we know? We have confirmed testimony that the prisoners you are bringing food to are Red supporters, yet you claim they are falsely imprisoned. How do we know you aren't here to smuggle contraband to them?"

"It's just food . . ."

"Since we cannot confirm that this is merely food, we will confiscate this package."

The desk guard prepared to throw the package into the trash.

"No!" Yuni cried out. "Please don't do that!" She tried to stop the desk guard but was dragged back by the soldier behind her.

"Oh, you want me to check it first?" the guard asked with a nasty smile. He untied the package and then dumped everything onto the floor. Rolled eggs, rice balls with meat and vegetables, were ground into the dirty floor. So much precious food wasted.

"Why did you do that?" Yuni shouted. "People are starving! How could you treat food like this?"

The desk guard stepped around the desk and shoved Yuni, causing her to fall on top of the mess of food. He kicked the rice balls at her as she flinched in dismay.

"How dare you question our authority?" he shouted as he

grabbed her by the hair and yanked her up to her knees.

"Noona!" Doha ran to help his sister and was pushed away by the guard.

"Don't touch him!" Yuni shouted, and then gasped in pain when he pulled her hair harder.

"Leave her alone!" Doha charged at the man, head-butting him in the stomach. As he glared at their tormentor, Doha suddenly became aware of how quiet the room had gotten. All the soldiers were watching the desk guard to see what he would do. The man smirked and took off his belt. He nodded to the soldiers next to him, who grabbed Doha by the arms.

"No, please stop!" Yuni pleaded.

"I will teach you to respect your elders," the desk guard said.

The first bite of the belt on Doha's back turned his legs into jelly. Doha cried out in agony. In all his life, he had never been hit for any reason. The pain was excruciating. He could see his sister try to stop the whipping and being shoved aside. By the third lash, Doha couldn't hear his sister's screams over his own hysterics. It was the seventh hit that caused him to faint from the pain. Only later did he find out that the guard continued to whip him three more times before dropping him on top of the crushed food.

Junie

"Grandpa!" I'm so upset I'm finding it hard to even speak.

"But they were the South Korean soldiers! Why would they treat you like that? And that woman! How could they just believe her like that? That's not fair!"

"That is war," Grandpa says.

Chapter 15

DOHA DRIFTED IN AND OUT of consciousness. He felt both cold and feverish. Sometimes he would open his eyes and see his father's pale face anxiously watching him. Then the next time he would wake to the sound of his mother's tears. But he could never stay awake long enough to reassure her.

When he finally woke up, he was on his stomach, and someone was placing soothing cloths on his injuries. He could tell it was his grandmother by the way she hummed an old song as she worked.

"Halmoni, what happened?"

"Doha!" Yuni cried. She'd been sitting on his other side. She crawled over to face him and held his hand tightly. "I'm so sorry! It was all my fault! I should've protected you!"

"No, Yuni, there's nothing you could have done," Doha's mother said as she entered his room holding a bowl of rice gruel. She knelt beside him and waited for Yuni and Hal-moni to help him sit up. Doha moaned in pain. His mother slid a padded floor chair behind Doha, but he could only lean on it sideways.

From the corner of his eye he caught sight of the huge bruise and the long red laceration on his sister's arm.

"Noona, your arm."

Yuni covered her arm with her hand. "I'm okay, Doha. I only got hit once. You got hit ten times!"

If one lash looked that bad, he must look far worse.

"I'm sorry, Noona," he replied.

"Don't apologize, Doha. That evil man should never have hit you!" Yuni's eyes flashed in anger again.

Even through his pain, Doha had to smile. "Noona, you were kind of amazing. I've never seen you so angry."

Yuni grabbed his hand tightly. "And you are so brave!"

"Aigo, both my children almost gave me a heart attack that day," Doha's mom said. "Doha, your noona carried you all the way home on her back, both of you looking like bloody messes. Your halmoni almost fainted when she saw your back."

Doha blinked in awe. "Wah! Noona carried me by her-self? I always said you were slow as an ox, but I didn't know you were as strong as one too!"

"Ya!" Yuni yelled, but with a smile.

As his mother fed him, Yuni told Doha that he'd been unconscious and sick with fever for four days and their father had gone to the ROKA leadership to lodge an official complaint.

"I was so scared for Appa," Yuni said. "What if they decided to arrest him falsely like they did the squid ahjumma?"

"We were all afraid," Doha's mother said. "Especially your halmoni. She said not to complain, don't bring more attention to us. But he wouldn't listen. He was so upset! I've never seen your father that angry before!"

"Halmoni stood outside the whole time," Yuni added. "She wouldn't come in to eat until Appa came home."

"How could I eat while my son was in danger?" Halmoni sighed. "Look what they did to my little grandson. What kind of monster does this to a helpless child?"

"Abeoji is okay?" Doha asked anxiously.

His mother smiled. "Yes, he's fine."

Doha looked at all their faces. "Then why do you still look so worried?"

"Abeoji went back to military headquarters today to speak for Sunjin and his mother, and to complain about what has been happening in Seosan," his mother replied. "People are turning on each other, accusing innocents of being Communist sympathizers. It's a dangerous position for your father to be in."

People like Gunwoo and the woman who accused the squid lady. He shuddered at the thought that his father could be arrested also. Fear and pain made him close his eyes as he was overwhelmed by his tears. The women of his family gathered into a tight hug, surrounding him with love.

"It'll be all right, Doha," his mother soothed. "Your father will be fine. We've been praying for his safety."

"Halmoni went to the temple early this morning to pray to Amita Buddha," Yuni said.

"I sent praise one hundred times to Amita the divine Buddha of Infinite Light," Halmoni said. "He will take care of your father."

Doha was tired, and his mother tucked him back into bed. Doha stayed on his side with Halmoni next to him.

"Doha, your sister and I have to go back to the hospital, but Halmoni will look after you. All you have to do is sleep, all right?"

Already drowsy, Doha nodded as his eyes closed. He hoped that when he awakened his father would be safe at home.

"Appa? Appa!" Doha shrieked. He sat up painfully, as he'd had another bad dream. They were becoming a nightly occurrence.

His door slid open and his father entered the room. "Appa is here, son."

Doha had to swallow back his fear. "In my dream, I heard crying and I was so worried . . ."

His father hugged him. "I'm fine."

But Doha could hear something was wrong in his father's voice.

"What is it, Abeoji? Please tell me," Doha asked. "Is it Sunjin?"

At the mention of Sunjin's name, Dr. Han closed his eyes and nodded somberly. "I'm so sorry, Doha," he said. "I tried everything, but they wouldn't listen to me. There wasn't even a real trial. Just a rushed affair with no chance to defend themselves. I can't understand how this is our government now."

"What happened to them?" Doha asked.

His father slowly shared the entire ordeal of what had happened. There were so many people accused of being Reds or Communist sympathizers that the prisons had become overcrowded and they were holding people in the administrative offices. Their claim of fair trials for the accused were nothing but lies. They weren't interested in justice; they were only interested in wiping out all Communists. The army unit based in Seosan was moving south. The top-ranking officer had received orders from headquarters to kill all prisoners before leaving Seosan. Dr. Han pleaded with them to at least release Sunjin, since he was so young. But by the time he got approval, it was too late. All the prisoners had been transported to a larger prison facility in Daejeon.

"Will they get a fair trial there, Abeoji?"

"We can only hope," his father said. But the way he said it gave Doha no comfort.

"Will I ever see Sunjin again?" Doha asked.

His father leaned forward to smile into Doha's eyes. "I

don't know. But what I do know, my son, is that one day this war will be over. And it will be up to you and the other youth to rebuild this country and make it a better one. One that will allow all of us to live a life free of fear. One day."

Only much later did Doha understand what his father meant.

BOOK III

Junie

Chapter 16

I'VE NEVER SEEN MY GRANDFATHER cry. His tears now devastate me even more than listening to his entire story. I feel as if my heart has been pierced by a thousand needles.

"Don't feel sorry for me. I know I am the lucky one," Grandpa says as if reading my thoughts. "Because my father was a doctor, we almost never went hungry. The worst that ever happened to me was that beating. I had it easy."

"Did you ever find out what happened to Sunjin and his mother?"

Grandpa reaches for a tissue, wipes his damp eyes behind his glasses, and blows his nose.

"It took many years before South Korea finally had a real democratic government. After President Rhee, there were thirty years of brutal military dictatorships. They had absolute power. In fact, they were no different than the North

Korean government. They would not allow anyone to speak out against the government, including surviving families of those killed by the South Korean Army. For forty-plus years they were not allowed to speak, for fear of being called a Communist and being jailed or worse. That is how bad leaders stay in power: by using fear to silence people from speaking and stop journalists from reporting. But that all changed when the Truth and Reconciliation Commission was created and began investigating the massacres. At last, people could speak about what had happened to them."

"So what did they find?" I ask.

Grandpa takes a moment to compose himself. "They found bones, skulls of children with bullet holes in them. They found that up to seven thousand civilians—men, women, and children—were killed in Daejeon. Killed by their own government for possibly being Communist sympathizers."

I look up at him in shock. Daejeon, where Sunjin and his mother were taken.

"Then does that mean Sunjin was killed?"

Grandpa stares off into space for a moment. "For a long time, I believed that Sunjin and his mother had survived the war and were living somewhere safe and happy. But when I heard the news, I knew in my heart that Sunjin was dead. He died a long time ago, when he was only eleven years old."

I'm silent. I sit and wait for Grandpa to continue. I know it was almost seventy years ago, but the pain on Grandpa's face is now. He must have carried it with him all these years.

"Sometimes I wish I could have kept pretending that he was alive," Grandpa says. "But that's so selfish of me. I need to know that he died. I need to remember how he suffered. Junie, always remember that silence is a weapon. When people don't speak up, and let evil continue unchecked, they too have become corrupt."

"What about Gunwoo? Was he ever punished?" Even knowing how much he suffered, I can't help but be angry at the betrayal that happened so long ago.

"A year after Sunjin was sent to Daejeon, Gunwoo and his mother left town," Grandpa says. "I heard they went to be with his police-officer brother in Busan. I never saw Gunwoo again."

"He was a bad guy."

Grandpa gives me a chiding look. "He was only twelve years old, just like me. And he had suffered terribly. Try to put yourself in his shoes."

"I am sympathetic," I say indignantly. "But having something terrible happen to you doesn't make it right to stab your friend in the back!"

"Or turn away from your friend?"

I blink and stare at Grandpa. "What do you mean?" I ask.

"When a friend asks for support, you should help them to the best of your abilities, even if you feel it isn't worth it," he says gently. "Because a true friend is hard to find."

I feel the sharp sting of his words. He's right. I turned

away from my friends because I didn't want to deal with what they were doing. I didn't believe in it. My dad once told me about dreamers and cynics. Dreamers are idealists who still believe the world is good. Cynics are realists who view the world with skepticism. Then he told me that most cynics were once dreamers who became disillusioned. I guess this is true. When I was in first grade, my mom did the whole "is the glass half-empty or half-full" question with me. I remember saying the glass was half full. Whenever my parents would fill up my cup with juice, or milk, or water, they would always stop halfway. I don't think they ever gave me a full cup of anything. Probably because they worried I would spill it. At the time, half-full was still quite a lot. I don't remember when I started noticing that it was actually half-empty.

I think back to my conversation with Patrice. Was I ever supportive of her plan? Did I do nothing but put it down?

I guess I really am a cynic. And if my friends are idealists, then my realism would feel negative to them.

I'm a jerk.

"You're not a jerk," Grandpa says.

Huh? Did I say that out loud?

"I can see on your face that you are feeling guilty, Junie," he says with a knowing look.

"Was I a bad friend, Grandpa?"

He reaches over to grab my hand tightly between his.

"No, you are my kind, sweet, lovely granddaughter," he says. "You're not a bad friend. You were suffering also. But now you can go back and be the friend they need."

Looking up at my grandpa, I realize that he tried everything to help his friends, even risking death and taking a brutal beating. What am I risking? Nothing. Just some time, maybe a little pride. But nothing worth losing my friends for.

I'm suddenly filled with a rush of love and gratitude.

"Thank you for being my grandpa."

He hugs me. "I love you, Junie."

At home I find myself thinking about Grandpa's story. I am still wrecked by it, and I understand why Grandpa said it was his trauma. I am reminded of Mrs. Medina's words about how the silent and boomer generations are old now and it is important to record their stories before it's too late. And I realize what a terrible loss it would be to our family if his story was never recorded. I take out a composition notebook and try to jot down everything he told me. This is my oral history project. The story of my grandfather. I'm excited to record it all so that I will not forget what he has been through.

Next time I will bring the video camera, so his stories will be memorialized forever.

Chapter 17

BACK AT HOME IN MY room, I try to figure out how I'm going to make up with Patrice. Should I call her or wait to see her in school? I hate talking on the phone. But if I wait, I'll have to get through the weekend, and I don't know if I can do that. I want to get it over with, but I'm also afraid. I look over at the clock and see it's 4 p.m. I wonder if I should call Amy first. Feel her out. She might know how I can approach Patrice.

Just as I convince myself to call her, the doorbell rings. I don't think anything of it until I hear my mom calling me.

"Yeah, Mom?"

"Junie, come down. It's Patrice and Amy," my mom says.

I freeze. I wasn't ready to see them in person. Right now.

"Junie, you want me to send them up?"

"No, I'm coming down."

I take a deep breath and I head downstairs. I see them standing awkwardly in the living room as my mom hovers nearby.

"Hey," I say.

"Junie, we've been so worried. Are you okay?" Amy asks.

Patrice doesn't say anything, but she is looking at me with a worried expression on her face.

"I'm all right now," I respond without elaborating. I'm still not sure what to say.

My mom claps her hands and says, "Junie, the girls have brought you all the assignments you missed! Isn't that wonderful of them?"

I nod. *Not really*, I think to myself.

"Why don't you all sit down, and I'll go get some refreshments?" Mom heads to the kitchen, and I know she'll show up with a ton of food.

I sit down on the love seat, and Patrice and Amy both sit together on the larger sofa.

"Thanks for bringing me my assignments," I say. "Although I guess I have to do them now, so maybe no thanks?" I smile awkwardly.

Amy beams back at me before looking concerned again. "Junie, what happened? Why'd you miss school?"

The truth is I don't want to talk about it, but they're my friends, and I should tell them what's happening to me. But I'm tired of talking about it. Is it because of the depression that I don't want to talk about it, or do I not want to talk about the fact that I have depression? I have no idea. But I'm just so tired all the time.

"I have depression, but don't worry! I'm going to start seeing a therapist," I explain as they both gasp in surprise. "It's to help me manage my emotions and keep me from hurting myself."

Amy's eyes well up with tears. "Did you try to hurt yourself?"

I immediately regret my words. "No, don't worry, I didn't."

"But you thought about it, right?" Patrice says.

Surprised, I just stare at her. She gazes back solemnly. "My cousin Ashley got hospitalized for suicidal thoughts."

I bite my lower lip and nod.

"Oh, Junie, I'm so sorry." Amy comes over to sit next to me and give me a hug.

I glance at Patrice, who is also glancing at me, and then we both look away. It feels so awkward. I decide I'm just going to apologize at the count of five. I breathe loudly and count to five, and then I say, "Patrice, I'm so sorry!" At the same time Patrice says, "Junie, I'm so sorry I was mean to you!"

We both stop short in surprise, and then we start to laugh. It feels so good I almost want to cry. When Patrice comes over to hug me, I end up bursting into tears.

"Junie, please don't cry. I'm sorry!"

"No, I'm sorry, Patrice! I was such a jerk!"

"No, I was!"

Amy throws her arms around both of us.

166

"I love you two jerks!"

Which makes us both laugh. It is the best feeling in the world to know that your best friends still love you, no matter what.

"Junie, I'm so sorry that I was only thinking about what I was feeling and how angry I was, and I didn't even see that you were hurting. I was such a bad friend."

"No, you're not," I protest. "I should have been a better friend also. But I was only thinking about myself."

"Junie, we're your friends," Patrice says in a serious voice. "If you are hurting or having problems, you have to tell us. That's what friends do."

Amy nods emphatically. "We're here for you. Don't shut us out."

Had I done that? Shut them out? I hadn't told them anything about my suffering. Not all last year. Not how I felt about being the only one without a cell phone. Not anything about how sad I was that they texted without me.

All the things I'd been dealing with. They were bubbling inside me. But I didn't share any of my feelings. I did what I always do. Chama. I suffered by myself. I made it my problem alone. Sometimes to Chama is a good thing. It is about inner strength and resilience. To endure. But if I always endure everything on my own, how can anyone know what I'm going through? My friends aren't mind readers, but I expected them to know how I felt. I shut them out and then was disappointed by their actions.

"I'm the worst," I proclaim.

They squeeze me tighter. "No, you're not. You're just not much of a sharer," Amy says.

Patrice nods and releases me but keeps a tight grip on my hand.

"Junie, you've never been one to complain or talk about your problems. We've always had to force it out of you," she says. "We should've known something was up and pushed you to tell us. So that's why we're here. We want to know everything. Talk."

Tears threaten to spill out again, but I blink them away and nod. It's time to be honest from now on.

The front door slams shut and Justin walks into the living room shouting for food. He stops short when he sees us, giving us the strangest look.

"What are you three weirdos doing?"

"Shut up, Justin," I say, a little embarrassed, as I push out of my friends' embrace.

Patrice and Amy sit up and giggle hello.

Justin gives them a small wave and heads to the bathroom.

"Junie, your brother seriously glowed up!" Patrice says in admiration.

"Wow, he got so hot," Amy agrees.

I give both my friends a look of horror. "Ew, gross. Do you want me to vomit?"

Patrice and Amy start laughing, and I can't help joining them. It feels good to laugh with them again.

Chapter 18

MY MOM DROPS ME OFF at school on Monday. She and dad are going to take turns for drop-off and pickup. They don't plan on making me take the bus. I'm so relieved, but guilt eats at me. My mom sees my face and pulls me into a big hug.

"I know what you're thinking. You think you are imposing on us and you feel guilty." She gives me a knowing look. "But you don't have to feel guilty at all. You are our top priority. And if work interferes, we will ask Grandma to pick you up. So don't worry. It's all going to work out, okay?"

I nod. I still feel guilty, but I'm going to let my relief override it. At first I thought Justin had ratted me out. But when I confront him, he is offended.

"Yo, that's not my style," he says. And I know it's true.

"Besides, if Mom knew about Tobias bullying you, the

whole school would know about it too. Like, it would be all over the internet."

This is true also. And why I never told her. Mom would raise a massive stink, and I would never be able to show my face in public again.

"But Junie, if he ever touches you again, you'd better tell Mom or I will, understand?"

I nod. My brother is fairly laid-back until he's not. And then he's absolutely scary.

Fortunately, he's on my side. And I don't feel guilty about the rides anymore when I discover that Justin has managed to worm his way into the morning car schedule. Which means I have to get up extra early, since his school starts thirty minutes before mine. When I complain about it, he tells me to shut it.

"I need that twenty minutes of extra sleep."

Ugh. Meanwhile, I have to wake up thirty minutes earlier. But I decide not to complain, because anything is better than riding the bus.

Mom drops me off early and I head to the gym to wait for my friends. We spent all Sunday planning. And now that I've accepted the phone my parents got me, I'm on the group text chat, which I'm still not used to.

I walk into the gym and sit in our regular spot. I'm the first one again, but I don't mind. I can see where they painted over the walls and equipment. A part of me wishes I had seen the graffiti. Sometimes seeing something makes it more real than just hearing about it. But why do I need to see what I've actually experienced?

Patrice and Amy arrive together, soon followed by the others. We immediately discuss our plan. To produce videos about the lives of students of color and to explain what racism feels like. We're also going to create a club, specifically to create a safe space for Black students and other students of color to share experiences. Patrice already approached our English teacher, Ms. Simon, who enthusiastically supported the idea.

"Is it okay if I shoot and edit the videos?" I ask. "My dad let me borrow his laptop and I love the video editing program on it."

"Cool!" Patrice says. "Amy and I will write out the scripts, and Hena, Lila, and Marisol will help get all the other students for the interviews."

As we walk through everyone's duties, I can feel my anxiety sneaking up on me again. Why am I doing this? What if I mess it up? What if all this work ends up being for nothing?

I pinch my leg hard enough to make my eyes water. *This is all worth doing*, I tell myself internally. *No matter what happens, I'm in this together with my friends*. Even though I can feel my rapid heartbeat at the base of my throat, I ignore it and focus my attention on the conversation.

After school, we all head over to Patrice's house, where we are holding a planning session. Her mom, Mrs. Thompson, is a vice principal at a nearby high school, but not the one we will go to. Patrice is deeply grateful for that. She says going to high school where her mom works would cramp her love life. Hena's always like, *What love life?* Which is pretty funny because while lots of boys like Patrice, she's the queen of no.

While we are talking, Mrs. Thompson arrives home with two boxes of Krispy Kreme donuts and milk for us, and we sit around the kitchen table as Patrice tells us her new idea.

"So, I've been thinking," Patrice announces, and we all bust out in giggles at once.

"Yeah, okay, so I have a lot of thoughts," she says with a rueful smile. "So, the whole safe-space idea is great, but to be honest I think it's more important to educate everyone else."

Everyone is nodding, including me. "But how would we do that?" Amy asks.

"What if we have a school-wide discussion on diversity? We could show our videos and discuss issues like racism, sexism, and homophobia related to current events, like the Black Lives Matter movement or celebrating Pride."

"Will the school let us do something like that?"

"If we can convince Ms. Simon, she can convince the administration."

"But it's going to depend on how good our videos are," Patrice says.

I bite my lip. I need to say what I want, carefully. "I think it's great to have the video be like the discussion point for the program," I say slowly. "And I'm sure we can make it great! What we need is really good, powerful messaging. To me, a message I would like to see is not to be a bystander. To speak up! Speak up and say something when someone is being racist or sexist or some other kind of terrible -ist, if you know what I mean."

Everyone agrees, and for the next hour we talk and debate the wording of the script. We end up with a lot of good talking points, which Patrice and Amy plan to write up, and Hena will edit.

"So when's our deadline?" Lila asks.

"Yeah, when do we need to get everyone for the interviews?"

Please not too soon, I think to myself.

"Let's make a timeline and put it in a calendar," Hena says. She whips out a clean piece of paper and starts setting out tasks.

"We have to write the script, invite people to be on the video, interview and film them, edit the videos, and prepare for the school event. Hmmm, how about the beginning of November?"

I'm relieved, but Patrice looks unhappy. "I was hoping for earlier."

"I think it's better for us to do a good job rather than rush this," Hena says. "We want to open people's eyes and maybe even change their thinking."

Patrice reluctantly agrees.

By the time my mom comes to pick me up, Hena has given all of us deadlines and specific assignments and I'm so impressed by my friends that I forget to worry about how I'll do.

In the car my mom asks, "How was your day, Junie?"

"Great!" I say, and I mean it. Between the project with my friends, the oral history assignment, and my regular work, I'm going to be extremely busy for the next few months. I'm looking forward to seeing Rachel and telling her about the positive changes I'm making in my life.

Chapter 19

AFTER SCHOOL ON THURSDAYS, I go to see Rachel at her office. I spend all my time enthusiastically telling her about my dual projects. She asks me how I feel during the discussions with my friends. I tell her honestly that when I start to feel negative, anxious, or overwhelmed, I focus on how much I like just being with my friends. She tells me she is proud of me and that I'm already using good mindfulness skills. We go through my journal and discuss my emotional highs and lows each day. Not every day is a success. I still have bad moments. I still struggle. I still hear the voice that tells me I'm worthless, that nobody likes me. But not as often. Not as loud. And she tells me that's okay. I will not get better all of a sudden. But I'm on the right path.

I let my mom know what we said after every session, and I can see that she is happier. But the worry is still there in her eyes. I know it will take some time for her too.

On Fridays, Grandma comes to pick me up, and Grandpa is usually in the car with her. The first thing they ask me is if I'm hungry.

It's funny because I'm usually not until they ask me, and then I'm ravenous.

At their house, Grandma starts cooking right away, but as soon as she sets the table, she gets a call from a client and has to leave.

I look at Grandpa with a pitying look, but he only smiles at me.

"Lucky for me you're here to keep me company and help me eat all this good food," he says.

Grandma has set another feast. Grilled mackerel, purple rice, spicy bean-sprout soup, and lots and lots of delicious side dishes. I don't know how she does it. Grandma works a very busy job and still cooks amazing meals. Meanwhile, my mom thinks putting an egg in instant ramen is gourmet cooking.

"Wow, Grandma is the best cook," I say, devouring a huge scoop of rice and soup. "But Grandpa, what happened to Mom? How come she can't cook?"

Grandpa is shaking his head. "Your mom can't even make rice," he says flatly. "I don't know what went wrong. We both taught her over and over again, but she always messes up rice. If you can't make rice, you can't cook."

That's true. Korean food has to have perfect rice: not too

dry, not too wet. If I didn't know better, I would assume my mom messes up the rice so she can get out of cooking.

While we are eating, I ask Grandpa if he will be my interview subject for a school project.

"What would I talk about?"

I tell him what the project is about, and he is silent for a very long moment. I know not to interrupt him when he's thinking.

"I don't think I can talk about Gunwoo and Sunjin again," he says. "But what if I tell you about meeting your grandma and moving to the US?"

I perk up. I've never heard their story before.

"Grandma always says you guys were an arranged marriage," I say. "I've always wondered about that. It doesn't sound very romantic."

"That's what you think, but it's quite a romantic story." His eyes twinkle at me. I've always read about eyes twinkling and I remember my friends laughing and saying eyes can't really twinkle. But I swear my grandpa's eyes do! His entire face crinkles when he smiles, and his dark brown eyes are little star-filled night skies.

"Wow! Really? Can we start now?" I jump to my feet to go grab my phone out of my bag. I've been playing with the camera app and it's pretty good.

"Let's finish eating first. I'm still hungry."

I sit again and wolf down my food. I'm excited to start my project.

As soon as Grandpa finishes his last bite, I quickly clear the dishes, wash the plates, and run to set up my phone with the little tripod my dad bought for me. Grandpa is relaxed in his armchair. I center him in my video.

"Grandpa, you look so cute!"

"Cute?" he growls at me. "I'm not cute, I'm handsome."

"Yes, very handsome and cute." I chuckle. "Let me know when you're ready."

"I'm always ready!" he grouses good-naturedly.

I hit record.

"Okay, Grandpa, will you please introduce yourself and tell us your year of birth, and where you were born? Then tell us an important event from your life."

"My name is Han Doha. That is the proper way to say my name in Korea, which is where I'm from. We say the last name first. I was born in Seosan, South Korea, in the year 1938."

He pauses. "What's the question I'm supposed to answer?"

Stifling my giggle, I say, "Tell us about an important event from your life."

"Ah!" He nods and then clears his throat. "Did I ever tell you how I met your grandma?"

"No, you didn't. Grandma told me that it was an arranged marriage. Wasn't it strange marrying someone you didn't know?"

Grandpa grins mischievously. "She wasn't a stranger to me," he says. "We'd met once before; she just never remembers."

I can tell this will be a great story. "Where did you meet her?"

"I was studying at Korea University in Seoul when my friend suggested we go down to Ewha, to see the pretty girls."

"Ew, Grandpa! I can't believe you were checking out girls!"

He laughs. "What, I was young once!"

"What's Ewha?"

"It is an all-women's college, and one of the best in Korea. I remember the first time I saw her. I thought she was so pretty, especially when she turned her nose up at my friend."

"She did?"

"Yeah, turned her nose in the air and pretended like he wasn't even there. He was quite insulted, but I was enchanted."

"Did she talk to you instead?"

Grandpa shakes his head. "I didn't even try. We'd just been introduced to her by one of her friends, but I could tell she had no interest in talking to any of us. If she were here, she'd tell you she had no time for silly boys!"

"She still says that!" We both laugh. Grandma is always telling me never to worry about boys and to spend my time worrying about myself instead. She always tells me, *Let the boys worry about you; you don't have to worry about them!* But if my mom is around, she always corrects Grandma and says that they will be happy with whomever I end up dating. Which is a cool way of telling me that my family would be supportive no matter who I might love later in life. And Grandma will just nod and smile. My uncle Paul is gay, and they've always been accepting of him and his partner, Simon. Except that Grandma still holds a grudge against Simon for making Uncle Paul move all the way to Seattle.

"Your grandma liked studying more than dating," he says proudly.

"So how did you get her attention?"

"I never did. I saw her a few more times. There was always some boy trying to impress her and failing miserably. So when I decided she was the one for me, I told my parents to hire a matchmaker and approach your grandma's parents with a marriage offer."

"Oh, how romantic," I say sarcastically.

Grandpa laughs. "Well, it worked, didn't it?"

"So, what happened next?"

"Well, the matchmaker told us that your grandma had rejected many offers already, to her parents' deep frustration," Grandpa continues. "And she didn't have very high hopes for me. I was a country boy and my father a doctor with a small, rural medical clinic. How could I compete with the son of some wealthy banking family?"

"Then how'd she pick you?" I'm so invested in his story that I forget about the recording and almost knock my phone over.

Grandpa tilts his head as he thinks. "You know, she never told me why she agreed to meet with me."

"So you went on some dates?"

"We had a couple of meetings, the first with the family and then once alone," he says. "I'll never forget our first time alone. I took her to see the cherry blossoms, and as we sat on a bench, the petals rained down on our heads. She would catch them in her hand and laugh with such happiness. I thought my heart would explode with how full it felt."

Aw, my grandpa is a romantic. I could imagine the scene all in my head. I've seen photos of my grandpa when he was younger. He wasn't a handsome model type, but he was really cute, with a smile that made him more attractive than any movie star. Okay, so I might be biased. However, my grandma is straight-up beautiful, now and then. They must have made such a cute couple.

"It was there that she asked me whether I would be willing to move to America. I was surprised. I'd never thought of it, but I wasn't opposed. I asked her why, and she told me that she had made a promise to herself during the war that she would one day live in America. She would not marry anyone who wouldn't agree to move there. So of course I said yes. And that's why we moved here right after our wedding."

This is all news to me. I don't know why I've never thought to ask my grandparents about their lives before. I'm learning so much about them.

"Can you talk about what it was like moving from South Korea to America?"

Grandpa shifts deeper into his chair as if to get comfortable.

"Well, we came as graduate students. I applied to Emory University business school and Grandma applied to Georgia Tech for a master's degree in mechanical engineering."

My mouth falls open in shock. "Mechanical engineering? Grandma? But she's a real estate agent!"

"That wasn't her dream job," Grandpa explains. "In college, your grandmother was a physics major who dreamed of one day working on spaceships."

"Whoa, Grandma! That's so awesome!"

I wish Grandma was here. I would give her the biggest hug.

"Why didn't she tell me?"

Grandpa spreads his hands. "You have to understand, Grandma is a very proud woman. A very smart woman. She had a really hard time working at Ford when she graduated."

"She worked at Ford?" I've surpassed shock now; my mind is officially blown. I just can't believe this news.

"Your grandma was the only woman in her section and also the only Asian in her entire department," Grandpa said. "They didn't want her there, and they showed it every day. They made her life hell on earth, and every day Grandma came home and cried. Finally, I couldn't stand it, and I told her to quit. At the time, I was still working at part-time jobs while trying to complete my PhD in business management. The racism was hard, but there were a lot of nice people I saw every day who made life bearable. But your grandma had nobody. Not one person at the Ford plant would even smile at her. It was a terrible place for her. It's why we moved to New York."

"Poor Grandma." My heart hurts to think of my pretty grandma suffering. "I really need to record her side of the story too," I think out loud.

"You absolutely should!" Grandpa agrees. "And you should also ask her about her war story. It is very different from mine."

"How?"

"That's her story to tell. You must ask her, so you can record it. Promise me."

"Yes, Grandpa. I definitely will!" I had made up my mind that recording both of my grandparents' stories was an important project not just for school, but for me and my family.

Chapter 20

"So, Grandpa, how did you end up in New York and then Maryland?"

Clearing his throat, Grandpa asks me for a cup of barley tea. "Junie, please pour me some boricha if you want me to keep talking."

Grandma brews a large pot of barley tea every day and leaves it on the stovetop. It is still hot, so I pour it into two mugs. I put a few ice cubes in mine, because I don't like to burn my mouth. It smells earthy but in a good way, with a hint of sweet nuttiness. I bring over the mugs and watch as Grandpa sips his hot tea and says, "Ah, delicious. Now, where was I?"

"New York?"

"Right! Our friends told us that it would be better for us to move to New York to be around more Asians. Back then, there weren't many in Atlanta. So, we packed everything up and drove to New York. We decided it was a great time to sightsee. This is such a beautiful country. But even that was hard. It was 1971, and your uncle was four years old. We would drive around and see beautiful landscapes, and then at night we would struggle to find a motel that would take us."

"What do you mean, take you?"

"We were foreigners who spoke English with an accent," Grandpa said. "Many nights we would drive up to a motel with a vacancy sign, only to be told at the front desk that there were no vacancies. Some nights we had to sleep in the car at a visitor's center parking lot off the highway. At least we'd have a bathroom to use and water to drink. Several times we walked into little diners or restaurants that would not seat us. Or if they did, the waitresses would ignore us and finally we would be forced to leave hungry."

My blood is boiling. I can't even imagine how difficult it must have been for them.

"We had a hard time." Grandpa smiles ruefully. "We were on the road for five days, and only one night could we get a motel room."

"That's horrible!"

"Yes, racism was really bad back then. But we finally arrived in New York City and we were able to stay with friends until we found a small apartment in Queens. We opened up a small jewelry store with the money we had saved from our jobs. We both learned to make jewelry, and we imported some Korean products, like vases and jewelry boxes."

Korean vases are beautiful and very different looking. My mom has a few that my grandparents gave her, and she cherishes them. And I have a jewelry box that Grandma bought me a few years ago. It's black with a mother-of-pearl design of flowers and butterflies. The only thing I keep in it is the gold baby ring that most Korean kids get at their one-year birthday. It is my greatest treasure.

"I didn't know you owned a store!" I say. "Are mom's vases from back then?"

"No," he says as he takes a sip of his hot boricha. "We'd only had it for a year when there was a robbery and we lost everything. Grandma was pregnant with your mom and we had no insurance. It was a really difficult time. Our landlord was a terrible person who kicked us out immediately without giving us a chance to recover. I think he took advantage of us because we spoke broken English."

I'm so mad I explode. "But you both speak English really well! And you and Grandma are bilingual!"

"Grandma's trilingual," Grandpa says with a grin. "She speaks Japanese also."

"Yeah, trilingual!" I sputter. "All they can speak is one stupid language." I stop and cross my arms. I'm aware of the fact that I only speak one language too. "I'm sorry, Grandpa, please go on."

"I understand how you feel, Junie," Grandpa says. "It must be hard to hear this."

I nod and chew on my nails. I know it must have been harder to live through it.

"We had to borrow money from friends in order to feed our children. At the time I had to work three different jobs, and your grandmother started working a few weeks after having the baby. Trying to find a job was a struggle for both of us. Many times, they told us they didn't hire Chinese or Japanese. They didn't even know what Korean was. They didn't care what kind of Asian we were; they just hated all of us."

The sad thing is that what my grandpa is telling me doesn't surprise me at all. It makes me angry and upset, but I know all these stories are true. Not just because it's my grandpa and I believe him. I'm not surprised because this is America.

"What kind of jobs did you work?" I ask.

"I could only get part-time employment like delivery service or janitor. Manual labor jobs that didn't care that I spoke broken English. And the only place that would hire Grandma was a Japanese restaurant and bar. Your uncle was six and had to stay at our friend's house until late at night. And Grandma took your mom with her to the bar and left her sleeping in the basement. Sometimes she'd go check on her during a break, and your mom would have been crying for a long time. They would never allow this to happen nowadays, but we did what we had to do to survive. Your grandma cried a lot during that time."

I wanted to cry just listening to my grandfather.

"Did you and Grandma think you'd made a mistake coming to America?"

Grandpa made that hand gesture again. Opening them palm-side up as if to say not sure.

"It's hard to say. There were definitely moments where I wondered if we shouldn't have come. But as difficult as it was for us in America, there were friends and family who were suffering in Korea also. At that time, South Korea had another brutal dictator as president who claimed rule under martial law."

"Martial law? What's that?"

"It means that normal laws don't apply, because the government has called in the military to enforce their law over all its citizens. It's a terrible power. So many South Koreans died protesting. We don't know what would have happened if we'd stayed there."

"But you wouldn't have dealt with racism, at least." I feel a little bitter at this, as if it is their fault for coming here and making me suffer from racism also.

"Then you wouldn't have been born," Grandpa says. "Or you would have been born, but to another father."

I am struck by this statement. He's right. Everything would have been different. My mom wouldn't have met my dad. I can't imagine, and wouldn't want, anyone else as my father. But still. I would never have had to deal with Tobias either.

"How did you deal with all of it?"

"All of what?"

"The racism." I wipe the tears away from my eyes. "How come it didn't get to you? Weren't you depressed? Didn't it make you want to just run away and never have to deal with it?"

Grandpa gets up and comes over to hug me. The video is still running on his empty chair, but I can't be bothered to turn it off. I let myself cry in my grandfather's arms as he gently pats my back. When I'm finally cried out, he gets up to give me a box of tissues and waits as I blow my nose.

"I'm sorry, Grandpa."

"No, Junie, never apologize for showing your feelings. That is not something my generation of Koreans is good at doing, but it is a beautiful thing to see how Americans can be so open and honest about how they feel."

"Are you talking about that Chama thing?"

Grandpa smiles and nods. "We Koreans have learned to hold in so much suffering. But we also have the ability to love deeply. This country has been so difficult and yet I love it very much. I still believe in the American dream. Your grandmother and I came with very little money, and now we are comfortable in our old age. This country has been very hard on us, and yet it has been very good to us also. For every terrible racist we have had to deal with, there have been many more wonderful people who have helped us and cared for us. That is why I never regret moving here. I don't know if we would have been better off in Korea, but I do not doubt that I gave my children a chance at a better life during a very turbulent time in our own country, and I am grateful for that opportunity."

"Sometimes it doesn't feel like they want us here." I heave a shuddering breath. "It makes me want to run away. I'm so tired of it."

It's quiet in the room, and then Grandpa sits back in his armchair with a sigh.

"I understand, Junie. It is easier to run away and pretend that racism doesn't exist. But some people can never do that," he says. "In this country, Black people must face racism every single moment of their lives."

"Racism is hard for me, too, Grandpa!"

"I know it is," he says. "And yet you know it is not the same. For them, racism kills."

I feel ashamed of myself. Of course it's not the same. It's why Black Lives Matter has become such an important movement. Because there are Black people being killed just for being Black. I hang my head.

"When we were in Atlanta," Grandpa continues, "we had to put your uncle Paul in a preschool while we worked and went to school. Even though segregation was supposed to have ended, the preschools were all white or all Black. The only one that would accept him was a Black preschool. I'll never forget how warm and kind they were to us. How they accepted Paul and he made so many good friends."

"Uncle Paul went to an all-Black preschool?"

"Yes, and he loved it. Even though the other Koreans

didn't approve. They even formed their own Korean-only preschool and urged us to bring Paul there, but he didn't want to go. He loved his school and he loved his friends."

"They formed a preschool just so Uncle Paul wouldn't go to a Black one? That's terrible!"

"Ah no, it's more complicated than that! They formed one so that immigrant Koreans could work together and form their own community where it didn't matter that their English was bad," he explained. "It was for very good reasons, and if it had been open when we were first looking for a preschool, we would have sent Paul there. And I'm sure it would have been great. What they didn't understand was why we let Paul stay in the Black preschool. Paul stayed there because he was happy, and he was learning. That's all that mattered to us."

"Asians can be racist also," I say.

"Yes," he agrees. "They see how the people in power treat them, and they don't want to be treated like that."

This is a lecture, and usually I hate being lectured, but this is also part of Grandpa's story.

Grandpa reaches over and pats my hand. "Junie, my point is, no matter how difficult racism is for you, it is much worse for the Black community. When you get tired, think of how tired they must be. When you are angry, think of how angry they must be also."

I'm nodding. This is why Patrice is fighting so hard for change.

"It feels impossible to fight back," I say in a discouraged

voice. I can feel my depression affecting my mood, telling me I can't do anything. I can't help anyone else when I can't even help myself.

"That's because the hateful voices are the loudest ones. They are afraid of how the world is changing. You must remember that we have the ability to change people's hearts. Running away or doing nothing never changes anything. Staying and fighting racism by educating people is not easy. Many times they don't listen. Many times they won't change. But we continue to talk to them, to teach them, and one day their hearts might open."

Something clicks in my mind and I see that Patrice is very similar to my grandfather. She wants to start conversations, make people think and learn. Grandpa is the same. I need to be more like the both of them. But how can I? I'm not brave or strong.

"Junie, there are many different ways to fight. And it is up to you to find out your way. For example, your mama is the type of fighter who likes to go to protests and make speeches and argue with people. She is very solution-oriented and has no problem challenging authority. It's why she's such a good lawyer. On the other hand, your father does not like confrontation. His activism is more about writing letters to politicians and helping fundraise for specific programs he cares about. One way is not better than the other; we need all types of people if we are going to fight for a better world. The only wrong thing is to not do anything at all."

I understand now. I need to find my way, whatever that might be. I need to be brave and a good friend.

"Grandpa, I'm going to try to be more like you. I'll try to be brave."

"You are already brave, my child," Grandpa says to me. "I believe in you. Will you believe in yourself?"

I nod.

He smiles at me. "Good girl."

He gives me a second to compose myself and then he asks, "Are we done with the video thing?"

"Nope, Grandpa, I'm going to record all your stories! So what do you want to talk about next?"

He rubs his hands together and raises his eyebrows at me. "Did I ever tell you about when I ate my first slice of apple pie and ice cream?"

I continue to record my grandfather as I listen to all his stories, and I am suddenly so grateful that Mrs. Medina assigned this project. Hearing my grandfather's stories directly from him makes me feel so much closer to him than ever before.

Chapter 21

AT SCHOOL, THE DIVERSITY PROJECT is moving along. Patrice, Amy, and Hena finalized scripts, and we've been interviewing students every day at lunch. Ms. Simon allows us to use her classroom to record. I've been filming them all and then at night I've been uploading them on my father's big-screen computer. It's been a lot of fun playing with the editing equipment and music. I'm starting to think that this is something I might want to do for a career.

We've also formed a club with Ms. Simon as our teacher sponsor. Which is great because we can meet once a week during lunch in her classroom. Lila is the best graphic artist in our group, so she created a cool graphic with the words *Diverse Voices*, which is our official club name. Patrice and Amy made photocopies and plastered them all over the school. Even though it is a club for students of color to meet and talk about prejudices they deal with, we are open to everyone who wants to come and learn. Our first meeting is Wednesday at lunch, and we even got a stipend so we can have snacks. Patrice is especially excited.

For the meeting, I drew a poster for Diverse Voices with little chibi cartoon versions of all six of us. When I showed it to my friends, they all loved them, especially Amy, who is an uber fan of all things manga. I'm posting it up on the bulletin board near the front entrance when I see Esther Song staring at me.

"Hey," I call out to her. "Want to come to our first meeting?"

"Ew, no," she replies with a sneer.

I don't let her response get to me, and instead I just say, "We're going to have lots of different snacks! I'm going to bring some chocolate Peppero sticks and Yakult drinks."

For a second I swear I can see some interest, but then she turns away.

Friday, I get picked up by Grandma and Grandpa as usual, and I record Grandpa's stories. I ask Grandma if she'll let me film her, and she shakes her head.

"Your grandfather is best for your project," she says. "He likes to talk too much. So he is perfect. Me, I don't like talking."

"But Grandma, I want to hear your war story also!"

"Ah, that story?" She nods. "One day I'll tell you. But not now. I am too tired."

And then she goes and cooks. Which some people might think is weird, but I understand. Sometimes I find talking much more exhausting than actual work.

I look at my grandpa with a *what do I do* gesture, and he whispers in my ear. "Don't give up," he says. "Keep trying, and one day she'll tell you."

I'm disappointed, but I set up my phone to keep recording my grandfather. I now have twenty of his stories recorded, and I've enjoyed every single one of them. I plan to put them into a movie to give to my entire family. I think they will love it.

"So what are we talking about today, Junie?"

"You said you would tell me about why you moved to Maryland."

"That was all because of your grandma."

The great thing about Grandpa's stories is that they don't really end. One story will lead to another one through some connection, and then he weaves them all together. Sometimes he repeats stories, but I don't mind. I still enjoy hearing them. A few times, Grandma has been home during his recordings. And those are my favorite times because Grandma will always add something to the story. Like today.

"What do you mean, because of me?" she demands from the kitchen. She comes out and gives us a plate full of cut-up fruit. "I could have stayed in New York for the rest of my life. You're the one who said you wanted to move down here and finally be able to garden. I had to give up my New York real estate practice and take another broker's license test for this big suburban area, just so I could work here."

"Well, the truth is it was your mother's fault," Grandpa says to me. "If your mother hadn't moved to Washington, DC, for work, we'd probably still be in New York."

On the coffee table is a bowl of honey-roasted peanuts. Grandpa reaches for them, but Grandma is faster and snatches them away.

"No more of these for you! Eat fruit instead," she says, as she puts a fork with a piece of cantaloupe in his hand. "And don't blame Sasha! You couldn't stand the idea of being too far from your only grandchildren!"

"That's true." He reaches over and pinches my cheeks. "Who can blame me when my grandchildren are so smart and beautiful? Who do you think you take after, Junie? Your mom or dad?"

I smile. "I take after Grandma, of course."

Grandpa busts out laughing. "Good answer!"

Chapter 22

AT SCHOOL THE FOLLOWING WEEK, Lila and Marisol come to Ms. Simon's classroom at lunch with some of our flyers.

"We saw these in the eighth-grade hallway," Marisol says as she hands them over. Lila looks like she's going to cry. When we see the flyers, we know why. Someone has written all over them with racist hate words. We are all quiet. Ms. Simon reaches over and takes the flyers. We can tell how furious she is by how her lips have disappeared into a tight line.

"I'm going to show this to the principal right now," she states. "Wait here for me."

She marches off, her heels making loud, angry clacking noises on the wood floors.

Marisol moves closer to us and whispers. "So, it must be an eighth grader, huh?"

Lila is nodding vigorously and says a bad word in Spanish, which normally would make me snicker admiringly.

"It could be anyone," Patrice says, "but for sure it is definitely a student."

I agree with Patrice. I keep looking at the handwriting, and it looks so familiar to me. I've seen it before. That weird scrawl of small and large letters that slant to the left instead of to the right.

I think it might be Tobias. But do I say anything? What if I'm wrong? Would I be accusing someone just because I'm biased? I'm not sure what to do.

"Listen, my mom told me that the police think the gym graffiti and the boys' bathroom graffiti are two separate people," Patrice continues. "The gym was spray paint, but the bathroom was a black Sharpie."

"Like this flyer." Lila points to the black markings.

"My mom says they think the gym graffiti was actual vandals who don't go to the school."

"Well, why won't they tell us this?" Hena fumes. "This is kind of important!"

Patrice nods. "Probably because the police are still investigating. But this is our problem." She stares down at the flyer. "This is someone we go to school with, and we need to find them and expose them."

"How do we do that?" Amy asks.

"I don't know, but we'll think of something."

I'm taking in everything they are saying, and suddenly I

have a thought. "You know whoever did this had to have done it during the school day," I say slowly. "It isn't like the vandals who broke into the school at night. This was done during school hours."

They all look at me. "Meaning someone might have seen them." Patrice smiles.

I nod. "What we have to do is encourage people to do the right thing and speak up."

Before we continue, Ms. Simon comes back. "I've talked to the principal, and we are not taking this lightly. Principal Sumner is taking it to the police, but he also wants to have a professional diversity trainer come and talk to the entire school."

Patrice's eyes light up. "Ms. Simon, what if we show our videos and present our message along with the professional trainer?"

Ms. Simon looks unsure. "Is this something you all want to do?"

Patrice and the others all look at each other and agree. I'm not sure, so I just stay quiet. When they look at me, I nod firmly. "We should do this."

I can see my words make them happy. This is me being the supportive friend Grandpa told me to be. I can't wait to tell him about all this.

"Well, I'll ask the principal. I just want to make sure that it's safe for all of you to do this."

"Why not?" Patrice asks. "Everyone knows who we are

and what we're doing. Bringing it to the whole student body's attention is why we formed this club and are making these videos. We should be allowed to share them."

Ms. Simon nods. "And to do it with a professional trainer may be the best way. It will be their job to help understand and teach tangible action plans. Okay, I'll speak to Mr. Sumner. I'm sure I can convince him, but I need all of your parents' approval to do this."

I'm nervous about it, but I'm trying to be brave. I will be brave. But then that little voice of negativity starts to chatter in my head.

What can you really do, Junie? All this is useless. You're useless. You should give up. They're all waiting for you to disappoint them again.

Breathe, I tell myself. *Just breathe.*

The videos for school are taking a lot of my time, and instead of going to my grandparents' place on Friday as usual, I go to Patrice's to show my friends what I've got so far. We've decided to focus on showing how racism affects Black students and other students of color, and why silence about racism is just as bad.

Ms. Simon shows a video clip of the diversity trainer the school has hired. His name is Michael Giles, and he is great. He starts by talking about his experience growing up Black in Mississippi and moves on to talk about systemic racism and how we don't even realize how embedded it is in our world. I am struck by all he has to say and how much I didn't know.

"He's amazing!" Patrice's eyes are glowing with admiration.

"What all of you have been doing here is the same thing," Ms. Simon says. "You are helping to educate your fellow students who've never experienced being anything other than part of the majority. I think you all are just as amazing."

Her words are like an energy shot to all of us. We are determined that the diversity assembly will be the best we can make it. The date is set for the first Thursday in November. It gives us more than a month.

"Junie, it's up to you to really make these videos great," Patrice says. "We're counting on you."

"No pressure or anything," Hena jokes as she pokes me in my side.

I smile weakly. I really hope I do a good job. The voice of depression is speaking to me again, getting louder. Telling me I'm no good. But I stomp on it by chanting my words of affirmation out loud. "I can do this. I am good enough. I can do this. I am good enough."

In therapy, I talk to Rachel about my fear.

"Tell me what you're afraid of, Junie."

It's hard to put into words, but I try. "What if everything we're doing makes it worse?"

"Makes what worse?"

"The racism. What if it makes them angrier and they lash out at us?" I think of the flyers and the graffiti. "What if next time someone gets hurt?"

"This is a very valid concern," Rachel says. "And I don't have an answer for you. This is a difficult position to be in. The question for you is whether or not the fear is greater than your desire to help your friends. And there is no judgment here. Whatever you do is fine. You have to decide what your position is and what the consequences of that decision will be. Because there will always be consequences to any action or inaction."

I know she's right, and I also know what the consequences would be. Disappointing my friends. But also disappointing myself.

The group wants to meet on Friday again, and so I call Grandpa and tell him I won't be over, but promise to come next week.

"Don't you worry about me, Junie!" Grandpa says. "You focus on your school projects and come see me anytime."

I feel guilty, but I want to put all my extra time into being with my friends and getting ready for the event.

The next Friday, I finally go to see my grandpa, but he's not feeling too well.

"Grandpa, what's wrong?"

"I'm just tired," he says. "I think I caught a cold. Probably from your grandmother because she's always running around."

Grandma is insulted. "I'm not running around; I'm a working woman!"

"Why don't you retire already?" he complains.

"I like my work, and I'll keep doing it until I can't." She turns to me and caresses my cheek. "Junie, make sure your grandfather drinks lots of tea and let him rest, okay?"

"Yes, Grandma." I wave as she heads out the door.

Instead of recording, I just tell him all about what's happening in school and how everything is going. He smiles and tells me I'm a good girl. As I show him the diversity video, I see he's fallen asleep in his armchair. He looks pale. I'm worried. Since Grandma is still out, I call my mom. When she comes to pick me up, she talks to Grandpa and asks to take him to the doctor.

"I'm perfectly fine! Just tired. Don't worry." He is grumpy and waves off our concern.

I can't shake my weird feeling, and I give Grandpa a tight hug. "Don't be sick, Grandpa," I tell him. "We need to finish our recordings!"

He gives me a tired smile and hugs me back. "I love you, Junie."

"I love you, too, Grandpa."

Chapter 23

LATE SUNDAY NIGHT, I WAKE up because I hear my mom's anxious voice talking on the phone. I come out of my room and see my parents getting dressed.

"What's going on?" I ask.

"Grandpa got rushed to the hospital," my father says. "We're going to meet your grandma there right now."

"Is he all right? What happened? I want to see him!"

"No, honey, you stay here," he says. "We'll call you as soon as we hear some news."

I spend the next hour wide awake in bed, anxiously waiting for my parents to contact me.

Finally, my dad calls.

"How's Grandpa?" I ask desperately.

"He's in the intensive care unit. He had a pretty serious stroke, but they are hopeful they caught it in time," my dad answers.

I let out a shuddering breath, and tears of relief stream down my face. "When can I see him?"

"I don't know yet, honey. But as soon as you can, we'll bring you here."

I fall in and out of sleep but am wide-awake when my dad comes home in the early morning hours. I jump out of bed and yell out to him.

Justin pops his head out in confusion. "What's going on?"

I ignore him and run down to my father in the kitchen, where he's making himself coffee.

"Did you see Grandpa? What did the doctor say? Where's Mom?"

Justin pads into the kitchen behind me. "What happened to Grandpa?"

"They are calling it a massive stroke. We're lucky he didn't die. But he's still not conscious yet, so we don't know how it has affected him."

"What's a massive stroke mean?" Justin asks, his eyes now wide open in shock.

"He had a series of blood clots in his brain," Dad says gently. "It cut off oxygen to his brain. That's what a stroke does."

"Was he in pain?" I ask.

"No, honey." My dad gives me a big hug and then pulls Justin into his embrace too. We are all quiet for a long moment as we think of Grandpa.

"I assume you guys don't want to go to school today."

We both shake our heads a hard no.

He smiles. "I don't blame you. Let's all wait for Mom to tell us when we can go in to see Grandpa. Until then, try to go back to sleep. You'll need your rest."

I don't think I'll be able to sleep, I'm so worried about my grandfather. But as I lie in bed, I'm overcome by tiredness.

My dad's voice wakes me up immediately. He's telling us to get ready to go to the hospital. I beat my brother to the bathroom and brush my teeth and wash my face as fast as possible. I throw on any clean clothing I get my hands on, then grab my phone and zoom down to the kitchen, where I'm surprised to see Dad's made us pancakes. I don't want to eat, but I can see from his face that he won't take no for an answer.

"Junie, you have to eat to keep your strength up," he says. He puts a few mini pancakes on my plate with fresh strawberries. Even though I don't feel hungry, I slowly eat all of them. My brother shows up and swallows ten of them without chewing, chugs a glass of milk, and then says, "Let's go!" He doesn't even notice that his shirt is on inside out.

Bethesda Hospital is made up of several buildings in a large complex all connected by glass corridors. It doesn't really look like a hospital, but I guess that's a good thing. The parking lot is crowded, and we end up parking far from the building that Grandpa is in. Once inside, we walk through a lobby that seems more like an office building than a hospital. We head to the seventh floor and find Mom waiting for us by the elevators. I can see she's been crying, but she smiles as soon as she sees us.

"He's awake and talking a little bit," she says. "But please don't be alarmed when you see him. Because of the stroke, he's having a hard time speaking."

The seventh floor looks like what I'd expect a hospital to look like, with wide white corridors and nurses stations. It has that weird rubbing-alcohol smell that makes you scrunch your nose.

At Grandpa's room, I see Grandma holding his hand. I rush to his side.

"Grandpa! I was so worried!"

He tries to smile at me, but only the right side of his mouth goes up. The other corner droops down. His cheek seems to sag on his left side. But his eyes are the same. They still twinkle as he smiles.

"Juuunie, aga." He hasn't called me aga in a long time. Since I was eight and told him I wasn't a baby anymore. He's talking again. But only in Korean. I don't understand him. I am trying not to cry because my parents told me not to in front of Grandpa.

"He says don't worry," Grandma translates for me. "He says he'll be okay."

He is talking again and looking at me and then Justin. His voice still sounds like Grandpa but slower and weaker, with a slight slur.

"He says, 'I'm so lucky to have my beautiful grand-children here. I'm so proud of them both.'"

I can hear Justin sniffle, and he turns away. I sit on the bed and hold Grandpa's right hand. I can feel him squeeze it slightly. Mom told us to keep things as normal as possible.

"Grandpa, you have to get better soon so we can continue recording our family history."

He does the lopsided smile again and agrees in Korean, which even I understand. Justin then takes his turn talking to Grandpa about school and soccer until we notice Grandpa's eyes starting to close.

"Okay, kids, it's time to let Grandpa rest," Mom says. "You can come back tomorrow after school to visit him."

We give him and Grandma hugs, and we reluctantly leave. Out in the hallway, Mom explains why Grandpa is speaking in Korean.

"Sometimes after a stroke, people lose their ability to speak," she explains. "But in your grandpa's case, because he is bilingual, he has lost his ability to speak English and has reverted to his mother tongue, as it is probably easiest."

"Will he get it back?" Justin asks.

She nods. "The doctor says he should, but we don't know when."

I can feel the tears threatening to come out. Mom hugs me. "It's okay. You can cry now. I just didn't want you to do it in front of Grandma and Grandpa."

I nod and let my tears fall silently into my mom's jacket. I'm so relieved Grandpa is alive that it doesn't matter to me if he never speaks English again. I'll just have to learn Korean. When I'm done, she hands me a tissue and turns me toward the elevator.

"You guys go home. I'll stay here until your uncle Paul

comes. He should arrive some time tonight."

She walks us all the way out of the hospital. I wave good-bye to her until I can't see her anymore.

In the car, Dad asks if we want to go back to school as it's only eleven thirty in the morning. Neither of us is up for it, so instead he takes us to our favorite diner for milkshakes, burgers, and fries.

"Dad," I say. "Will Grandpa really be all right? Is he safe from more strokes?"

"I don't know the answer to that," he says. "Medicine has advanced a lot, and people can definitely recover from strokes, but there's no guarantee that they won't have another one. We have to make sure Grandpa takes better care of himself."

Justin sees how worried I am, and he pats me on the head, which I hate. "He's going to be okay. Just wait and see, Junie."

He sounds so confident. I wish I could be, but the depression voice is thinking terrible things. I blink hard and shake my head. I won't let it overwhelm me. I repeat positive words and tell myself he is going to be fine. Over and over to drown out the negative voice.

I think back to all the times I've heard Grandma nag at him about his blood pressure and not eating too much salt. I always thought she was being mean for limiting his favorite salted nuts, but she was trying to keep him healthy. I vow to myself to help her from now on.

The next day at school, I'm not really focused. My friends and teachers all know what's happened to Grandpa, and everyone is very kind. I just want to get through the day and go see him. That's really all I can think about.

After school, my dad picks me up and takes me straight to the hospital. Justin has a game, so he's supposed to come later, after dinner. In Grandpa's room, I see my uncle Paul. He's tall and lanky and looks like a male version of my mom.

"Junie, sweetheart!" He gives me a big hug. "How's my favorite only niece in the whole wide world doing?"

"I'm fine, Uncle Paul. Just worried about Grandpa."

Uncle Paul strokes my hair gently and smiles down at me. "I know how close you are to him," he whispers. "He couldn't have a better granddaughter than you."

After Mom hugs me hello, Grandma shoos my parents out. "Go take your wife out for dinner! She needs a break!"

My mom seems reluctant to go and looks at me uncertainly. "It's okay, Mom. I'll be here with Grandpa."

Grandpa waves a weak hand at them to go.

"We'll come back with Justin after dinner, then," Mom says. She kisses me on the forehead and leaves with my dad.

I sit by Grandpa's side, and Uncle Paul sits on the other side of the bed next to Grandma and has his arms around her.

"Hi, Grandpa!"

"Juuuuunie-ah!" He smiles his lopsided smile. He asks me a question in Korean, and I understand it.

Before anyone can translate it for me, I say, "School was fine! I did all my homework in class, so I don't have anything to do but spend time with you."

"Oh, Junie, you understand some Korean! So impressive," Uncle Paul says as he gives me a fist bump across Grandpa's bed. "That's better than me, I admit it!"

Grandpa speaks again. It's slightly garbled but Grandma understands him clearly.

"Dad says it's not too late to learn, Paul."

Uncle Paul rolls his eyes, but I lean forward eagerly. "I want to learn! Can you teach me, Grandma?"

She looks surprised and then happy. "I'm happy to, but you should also take lessons. There's a Korean-language school that is based in our church. We can sign you up to take Korean class with kids your age."

"Juuuunie-ahhhh!" Grandpa says excitedly.

"He's so happy that you want to learn Korean," Grandma says.

There's a tugging on my jacket sleeve. Grandpa puts out a shaky hand, his pinky pointing out at me. "Yaksok?"

I nod and make a pinky promise with him. "Yes, Grandpa, I promise."

Uncle Paul smiles at me. "I always hated Korean school, but I bet you'll do really well, Junie!"

"I'll do it for Grandpa," I say. "So I'll understand him always."

His grip on my hand is tighter than it was yesterday. The twinkle in my grandpa's eyes now glimmers with the extra sheen of tears.

Chapter 24

AT SCHOOL, THE DIVERSE VOICES club is gathering more members. It's nice to see that there are some students signing up who just want to show their support. Every week we've had at least fifty members show up, and it has been great. Ms. Simon starts off each meeting reminding everyone that it is a safe and supportive place for people to be honest and open, but that anyone who is not respectful will immediately be asked to leave. We've had no issues. I've really enjoyed our meetings, and it has given me a chance to interview more students for our video.

We are three weeks away from the presentation. The plan is that Patrice and Hena will introduce the club and the rest of us, and then I will introduce the video. But I don't want to. I just don't know how to tell them that.

I'm almost finished with the video. It's twelve minutes

long, and I want to edit it down to ten minutes, but I think it's pretty good. I'm anxious to share it with the others, and if they like it, I want to show my grandfather. He's still not feeling well. My mom thinks it's because he's in a hospital, and she thinks he'd be safer at home. Which I think is kind of weird. It's a hospital—you go there to get better, not sicker.

I need Grandpa to get better so he can come home and help me finish my oral history project. Even though it's not due until the end of the semester, I decide that I'll finish off a first draft, so my grandparents can see how good the video is. And just maybe Grandma will agree to record her story for me also.

Mom picks me up after school, and I ask her if I can go home first and go see Grandpa after dinner.

"That works out," she says. "I wanted to make some soup and rice for Grandpa anyway."

"Homemade?" I ask dubiously.

Mom gives me an exasperated look. "It's that kit I got from the Korean market. The ones you guys raved about."

"Oh, the restaurant one? Awesome!" When we were in New York, we found that our favorite restaurant had a soup-starter base that would replicate its famous soup at home. Even my mom couldn't mess it up.

As she prepares dinner, I try to finalize the edits to my oral history project, but Mom finishes cooking before I'm done. I decide I'll work on it tomorrow.

Mom packs up a lot of food to take to the hospital. "Your grandma and Uncle Paul must be so tired of hospital food." She packs the containers into a large insulated bag. "I know I am."

"Can I eat my dinner now?" I ask. I hate eating at the hospital. The smell kills my appetite.

I quickly mix a bowl of rice into the spicy tofu soup my mom made and gulp it down. I'm so hungry I'm barely chewing my food. As soon as I'm done, my mom and I head to the car so we can leave for the hospital.

When I see Grandpa, I'm alarmed. He doesn't look good.

"Mom, did he eat his dinner?" my mom asks Grandma.

"He ate very little," she replies. "He keeps shaking his head and tightening his lips. I think it's because the hospital food tastes so bad, but he's not allowed to eat anything else."

Grandma looks tired. She stands up and takes the bag of food my mom brought.

"Why don't we have a change of scenery and go eat in the lounge," she says. "Junie, since you ate already, will you keep your grandfather company?"

"Yes, Grandma."

Uncle Paul looks at me with uncertainty. "You sure you'll be all right alone, hon? I can stay with you if you want."

I look at his tired face. He's been sleeping on the short little armchair at the hospital, even though Mom told him to come stay at our house. I shake my head. "I'll be fine! You should definitely get some fresh air, Uncle Paul."

He ruffles my hair. "Call me if you need anything."

As soon as he leaves, I scooch closer to Grandpa. His eyes are closed. I don't talk, just let him sleep. Several minutes later, he opens his eyes. When he spots me, he smiles.

"Junie-ah, waseo?"

It takes me a moment to remember that *waseo* means "you came."

"Grandpa, how are you feeling today?"

"Gwaenchana," he says.

"You don't look okay," I say, eyeing him worriedly.

"Gwaenchana, gwaenchana," he repeats. As if saying *okay* twice really makes everything fine.

"Junie-ah," Grandpa starts. Then he says something in Korean, and I have no idea what he said.

My face must show my confusion because Grandpa strains himself to say something more.

"Please . . . promise . . ."

It's pretty garbled, and his lips are trembling with effort, but I can understand what he is saying.

"Grandpa, you're speaking English!"

I'm so excited that his English returned. That has to mean he's doing better!

"Grandpa! What is it? You want me to promise something?"

He nods with effort and stumbles over his words. "L-l-look."

"Look?" I repeat.

217

"Af-af-after Gr-gr—" His face is so contorted by his effort to speak.

"Look after?" I'm trying to help him.

"Gra-gran-grand . . ."

"Grandma?"

"Mm."

"You want me to look after Grandma?"

He nods slightly.

"P-p-p-prom-ise . . . take care . . . Grandma . . ." Drops of sweat are beading on his forehead.

"Yes, Grandpa. I'll always take care of Grandma." I take his pinky in mine and shake it gently. "Yaksok."

His face relaxes and his lopsided smile flashes. "Good . . . girl."

I try to relax also. He spoke English again. That's supposed to mean he's getting better, but then why am I so anxious? Grandpa's face is so pale now. I wish Mom were back so I could ask her to ask the doctor. I want to talk to him, but his eyes are closed, and he seems to be sleeping. I'm so anxious I stare at his face and check constantly to make sure he's breathing.

When the others come back, I tell them how strange he seemed but that he spoke English. Grandma tries to wake him, but he seems deep asleep.

"Maybe we should call the doctor," I say.

"Don't worry, Junie. The doctor will stop by later tonight. I'll ask him then," Grandma says. "Sasha, go and take Junie home. It's getting late."

I'm reluctant to leave. Something makes me want to stay longer. Mom gently steers me out as Uncle Paul and Grandma wave at us. "I'll be back soon," Mom tells them, and we head home. I can't shake this weird crampy feeling deep in my gut. It kind of hurts, and makes me think I have to go to the bathroom. But it also scares me.

"Don't worry, Junie," Mom says. "I'll drop you off and go back to find the doctor. We'll take care of him."

Even though her words reassure me, the weirdness is still there. When I get home, I work on Grandpa's video until very late at night, but I find myself thinking of more questions I have for him. I want to know more about his life. I think of all the times I didn't go to my grandfather's in order to work on the diversity project instead, and I regret them all.

There's a knock on my door, and I look up to see my dad walk in.

"Go to sleep, Junie," he says as he strokes my hair. "Tomorrow is still a school day."

I wake up several times during the night from a nightmare where I'm trapped in a glass room. I can see everyone outside my window, but they can't see or hear me, even though I'm banging my whole body against the wall.

The alarm finally rings, and I get ready.

I go down to breakfast and see Dad packing lunches. Justin is shoveling cereal in his mouth like he's plowing snow. He's not even swallowing his first bite; he's just filling his mouth so he looks like a bloated chipmunk. Once the last bite is gone, he grins at me, snatches up his schoolbag, and takes off. I sit down and reach for the cereal and pour out nothing but sugar dust. Justin has eaten the last of the Chocolate Frosted Flakes.

I growl, which makes my dad laugh. He opens the door under the sink and pulls out a new box of cereal from behind the bag that stores all the other plastic bags. Don't ask me why they do that. I know it's weird.

With a happy sigh I open the box and pour a new bowl of cereal. My dad's the best.

"Yes, I know," he says, as if he can read my thoughts. "I hide stuff from Justin all the time; otherwise he will eat everything."

Holding a finger to his lips, he moves the bag of plastic bags and shows me his hidden stash of Doritos (Justin's favorite), gingerbread cookies (my favorite), caramel popcorn (Mom's favorite), and a big bag of mini chocolates (my dad's kryptonite).

"You have my permission to help yourself to whatever you want, as long as you promise not to tell Justin or your mom," he says with a grin.

I can't help but laugh, and for the time being the weird feeling that's been bothering me is gone.

At school, I'm distracted. All I can think about is going to the hospital and showing Grandpa my school-project video. During lunch, when my friends are discussing all the aspects of the coming assembly, I can barely focus. That sick sensation is back in my stomach. I don't know what's wrong with me.

Someone is calling my name. I look up and see Ms. Simon's serious, sad expression.

"Junie, please grab your things and come to the office with me," she says in a soft voice that frightens me. "Your father is waiting for you."

I slowly pack up my lunch bag and wave goodbye to my friends, who are all looking at me with similar expressions of concern. The walk to the office feels endless and yet suddenly I'm there and I can see my dad's face and I finally know what the sick feeling has meant.

"Grandpa?" I whisper.

He nods and folds me into his embrace. "He passed this morning."

The words crush my heart. I should've finished my project sooner. I should've have spent more time with Grandpa.

I don't even remember walking to the car. My brother is crying in the front seat. We don't say a word to each other the entire ride. Dad tries to say something, but I can't hear him. I feel like I'm trapped inside my own head. The world is muted except for this loud buzzing in my ears. I am muted. I can't hear anything, and they can't hear me screaming.

Mom's not home. I go straight to my room and turn on my dad's laptop. I want to see Grandpa's face. Some extra footage of Grandpa that I didn't use is left open on the screen. I click on the first one.

"Aren't you tired of hearing me talk, Junie?" Grandpa asks.

"Never!" my voice responds.

He's here. I see his smiling face, hear his deep voice. He's fine. Everything's fine. He's not gone. Not my grandfather. He can't be. I haven't finished recording my project with him. There's still too much to do. He can't leave me.

"Junie-ah, let's take a break and raid the kitchen for some sweets!"

"Okay, Grandpa!"

I'm staring at the screen, frozen on Grandpa's face. I don't believe he is gone. I can't. I just saw him yesterday. He was supposed to get better and come home. He's not supposed to die yet.

My chest hurts so much I can't breathe. But I don't cry. I can't cry. It feels like something is broken inside me. I feel like I'm broken.

Chapter 25

"JUNIE-AH!"

"Grandpa!"

I open my eyes and I am all alone. But I swear I've heard my grandfather's voice, as clear as a bell. At those moments, I think there must be something wrong with me. Because this new life without Grandpa doesn't feel real.

In my home, everything seems normal except for the mood. My whole family is hurting, but I can't focus on anyone's pain. Mine is too much to bear. I feel both overwhelmed with emotion and completely empty.

At the funeral home, I am sure that this is all just a bad dream. That I will wake up and hear Grandpa calling me to him.

"Junie-ah!"

It's not my grandpa; it's my great-aunt who came from Korea. My grandpa's older sister Yuni, who looks at me with Grandpa's eyes.

"Junie-ah, I haven't seen you since you were a baby," she says in Korean.

I bow and let her hug me, but I don't speak.

I keep getting looks from people at the funeral and then at the burial site. Everyone's crying but me. I'm like a robot. I show no emotions. I nod. I shake my head. I point. I can communicate simple things. But I'm incapable of answering anything more than a yes or no. I am numb.

Pain makes everything hard. It's hard to wake up, it's hard to move, it's hard to eat, it's hard to exist in my space that feels like it's shrinking more and more until it's choking me and I wake up gasping for air and realize I'm still in my nightmare.

The depression voice has taken over my head. It tells me how stupid I am. How utterly useless for not letting anyone know how worried I was. How much time I wasted on school and friends instead of being with my grandfather. How disappointed I am in myself. How angry I am at Grandpa for dying. My brain is swirling nonstop with thoughts and feelings that I can't control. The voice in my head won't shut up. So I just stop talking.

"Junie, your parents have told me that you've not spoken a word since your grandfather passed," my therapist says. "It's been four days. I'm here for you whenever you feel like sharing with me."

I shake my head. I don't want to talk about it. I don't want to talk about anything. I feel bad for my mom. She's lost her dad, and she also has to worry about her daughter's depression again. I feel bad, but I can't help her. I can't help myself.

"Have you been taking your meds, Junie?"

I nod. My dad gives them to me every morning.

"I know it probably doesn't feel like it's helping, but I'm sure it is. It's keeping you from being far more depressed under the circumstances."

That makes sense. I can still get out of bed. Still eat a meal, even if it's tasteless. Still do things, even if I don't want to. I just don't want to feel anything anymore.

"It's okay, Junie," Rachel says to me. "You don't have to talk to me. You can just sit here and play with toys or draw a picture."

In front of me is a drawing pad. Without thinking, I decide to draw. At the end of the session, Rachel looks at my picture and smiles.

"You are incredibly talented," she says. "Is this your grandfather?"

I nod. I've drawn him sitting in his armchair, smiling. A pose I'm so familiar with. The sharpness of missing him stabs me in my heart like shards of broken glass.

Rachel tears the picture out of the book and hands it to me. "I think you should give this to your mom. She would love it."

Taking the picture, I stand up to leave.

"Junie." Rachel rises and grasps one of my hands. "Everyone grieves differently. It's okay if you don't feel like talking or crying or laughing or doing anything. Life's never going to be the same, because you lost someone you love. But it will get better, I promise."

Her words give me some hope. With a quick nod, I walk out to the waiting room where my dad is waiting.

"How did it go?" he asks.

I shrug and then give him the picture of Grandpa.

He whistles softly under his breath. "Junie, this is incredible. It looks exactly like him."

Before we can leave, Rachel asks my father to come see her in private for a moment. There is a mother with her teenage daughter sitting on the left side of the room. I go to sit in a chair on the opposite side and face the wall. After a few moments, my dad comes back out and we leave the office. In the car, he gently asks me how I'm feeling. I just stare down at my picture of Grandpa.

That night, I can't sleep. During the day my head is foggy, and I don't really think clearly. But at night, my brain races with so many thoughts. The doctor said Grandpa had another stroke and that is why he died. When he was not himself, I should have insisted they get the doctor right away. I knew something was wrong. If the doctor had come then, could they have saved him? If only I were an adult, I could have made myself be listened to. But I'm just a kid. I have no power.

I can't stop all these thoughts. And I blame myself for not seeing him more often. I'm so angry and I'm so sad.

I jump out of bed. Maybe I need to drink some milk or some hot honey-and-lemon water. I wish I was at Grandma's and could have some of her barley tea. That would be perfect.

As I head downstairs, I hear my parents speaking in the kitchen. I tiptoe down the stairs and sneak closer. I can hear my mother weeping softly and talking.

"I'm so worried about Mom. She's devastated. I'm glad Paul is with her, but he can't stay forever. He has to go back to work."

"We'll convince her to move in with us," my dad responds. "It's not healthy for her to be alone in that house with all those memories."

"I know. I've already mentioned it so many times, and she keeps refusing. You know how stubborn she is. She said it's her house and she's perfectly capable of staying by herself. But you know the widowhood effect. Look at your parents!"

My own heart almost stops at her words. I was too young when my other grandparents died, but I'd heard so much about how my father's father couldn't bear to live without his wife. And he literally wasted away. The thought of losing my grandma also makes me want to scream. I cover my mouth to keep from making any sounds.

"Your mother is one of the strongest people I know. She eats healthy and she exercises regularly. What other almost-eighty-year-old do you know who does the breast-cancer-awareness 5K race every year?"

"Your father was healthy too. It's not physical health; it's mental health."

"I know. And we have to make sure we watch her carefully. Help her get back to work and keep busy."

I can hear Mom start to cry again. "I can't lose my mom too."

No longer thirsty, I slowly walk up to my room. I'm remembering Grandpa's last words to me. "Look after Grandma." He made me promise to take care of her. Had Grandpa known he was going to die? Is that why he asked me? Because he was worried about her?

In my room, I close the door and feel my legs give out as I slump onto the floor. The tears I've been holding back all this time come hard and fast.

"Oh, Grandpa. Even at the end, you were worrying about Grandma."

All the emotions I've been suppressing erupt, and I'm sobbing so loudly my parents come and find me. I sob out everything I've been holding in. Mom listens and cries with me, rocking me in her arms. Dad just sits and holds my hand.

Finally, I find my voice again.

"Mom, Dad, can I stay at Grandma's for a while?" I ask. "I don't want her to be alone."

"Will you be all right?" Mom asks.

I think of my promise to Grandpa, and I wipe away my

tears and nod. "I need to do this for Grandpa. I promised him."

These words fill me with a purpose that clears out the fog I've been under. It drowns out the voice of depression. I will not let Grandpa down. I will take care of my grandma.

Good girl, Junie-ah. Good girl.

Chapter 26

My PARENTS DROP ME OFF at Grandma's, and I leave my bag in the guest room she's made up for me. Uncle Paul left in the morning to go back to work. Before leaving, he gave me a big hug and said, "Thanks for staying with Grandma, Junie."

"I'll take good care of her, Uncle Paul."

He smiled, and for a moment he looked just like Grandpa. "I know you will! See you next month."

Now alone in the house, I look for Grandma and find her sitting on the sofa, a blank expression on her face. I sit down next to her and wait for her to notice me.

"I don't know why you want to stay with me, Junie," she says after several minutes. "I'm not good company. Not even sure I can cook any food for you."

Grandma is definitely more low-energy now than I've ever seen her.

"It's okay, Grandma! I know how to make ramen with an egg. And I can make us grilled cheese sandwiches. But best of all, I can order food on my phone!" I show her the food-delivery app that my mom told me to download. She said to order as much as I want and make sure Grandma eats.

She just nods vaguely and turns on the television. It's a Korean channel that she gets through her cable network. It's some kind of variety show, but I can tell that she is not really watching it, just staring off into space.

"Grandma, did you eat any lunch?" I ask.

"Hmmm? Oh yes, I ate something," she answers without looking away from the TV. I look in the kitchen. It doesn't look like she's made anything in a while. She hasn't even brewed her daily pot of barley tea. It's so odd not to smell the fresh, earthy, nutty smell that I've grown to associate with my grandparents.

That's one thing I know I can do. I text my mom and ask her how to brew it and then follow her instructions carefully. Thirty minutes later, I bring over a mug of the hot tea.

Grandma gives me a small smile.

"I didn't know you can make boricha," she says.

"Mom just texted me the instructions. Did I do a good job?"

She takes a sip and nods. "Perfect! Grandpa would really like it!"

Then her smile fades, and she puts the mug down and returns to staring at the TV. I change the channel to a nature program, which I'm hoping is more calming. But when a killer whale catches and eats a baby seal, I immediately change it back to the Korean variety show. My grandma doesn't react at all. I don't think she even noticed what I did. I think of Grandpa and wonder what he would do. He was the best at getting Grandma out of her bad moods.

I have to do something drastic. My dad let me bring his laptop with me. I go to my room to finish the special video project I started just for Grandma. Only through the editing process did I find that I had recorded lots of wonderful footage of Grandpa talking about Grandma. It made me think of what Grandpa would have wanted me to do with all of it, and then it hit me. Grandpa told me that he'd never done anything romantic for Grandma, not even a love letter. Here was my chance to make one for her. I've been working on it the last two nights. I'm almost done. I just need to add music and smooth out all the rough transitions.

It's almost dinnertime when I finally emerge from my room. My eyes hurt and my back feels achy from being hunched over the laptop for hours. But I'm done.

In the living room, I see that Grandma's fallen asleep on the sofa. I turn off the TV and decide the first thing I'll do is order food for us. My rumbling stomach reminds me that I barely ate lunch. Looking at all the restaurant options, it dawns on me that Grandma doesn't really like to eat out. She doesn't even like pizza, which is kind of bizarre to me because who in the world doesn't like pizza? I love it so much

I sometimes wonder if I am really related to her. Grandma's a great cook. She's always cooking all kinds of foods, not just Korean food but Spanish, Chinese, Italian, Vietnamese, and even Russian. A long time ago, she knew a Russian chef who taught her how to make the most delicious beef stew. My mouth waters at the very thought of it. Because she's such a good cook, we rarely eat out with Grandma. I'm not sure what to do.

All of a sudden, Grandpa's voice pops in my head.

"Your grandma is always trying to make me eat healthy foods."

Of course! Grandma always had salads or green vegetables at every dinner, no matter what she was serving. I remember now that my mom bought these gourmet salads for my grandparents from a new salad-only place. Grandpa complained the whole time, but Grandma ate her entire salad.

I text my mom and ask her what she ordered. And she immediately texts me back that she'll handle it and get it delivered. Within thirty minutes Mom shows up with a big bag of food. Grandma wakes up when the doorbell rings, and she goes to greet Mom.

"Sasha, you didn't have to go through all this trouble," she says in surprise. "I was going to ask Junie to order us a pizza."

"Grandma, you don't eat pizza!" I say, as I take the bag and carry it into the kitchen.

"Yes, but you love it! You and Grandpa would always eat an entire large pepperoni pizza by yourselves!"

That sad smile again. It hurts my heart.

"I remembered Mom bought you a fancy salad that you really liked. So I asked her to get it again!"

"But you don't like salad," Grandma says. "You're just like your grandpa."

Mom is unpacking everything on the kitchen table. "Which is why I got her karaage instead!"

My mom is the best. She also went to my favorite little Japanese café and got me a bento box of Japanese fried chicken with rice, miso soup, and potato salad. The potato salad is kind of an odd combo, but it really works. Mom joins us for dinner with a salad of her own.

"Grandma, since Mom is here, can I show you a video I made?" I ask around a big bite of my fried chicken and rice.

She frowns. "I'm not sure I'm in the mood to watch any school videos for you, Junie."

"Oh, it's not for school," I say. "It's a video that Grandpa would have wanted me to show you."

Mom's face lights up while Grandma looks surprised. "Junie, that sounds wonderful! How did it come about?" Mom asks.

"It started with my oral history project," I explain. As I tell them both all about how I first began recording Grandpa, I notice that Grandma is absentmindedly eating. This makes me so happy that I talk as much as I can, forgetting to eat my own food. When I finally run out of things to say, I eat my cold chicken as fast as possible. Lucky for me, it is still delicious. Grandma has eaten half of her salad. Mom looks at me and gives me an approving wink.

"So, are we ready to watch the video?" I ask.

When they agree, I lead them to the living room, where I've connected the laptop to the big-screen TV with the cable my dad gave me. Mom and Grandma sit on the sofa as I start the video.

Immediately Grandpa shows up on the screen. He's sitting in his armchair wearing his favorite red sweater, and his short white hair sticks up on the top of his head. He smiles at the camera.

"Are you ready, Junie?" he says.

"It's all you now, Grandpa," my video self replies offscreen.

"So, this is for Grandma only?"

"Yep."

He stares at the camera and scratches his head bashfully. "I don't know where to start."

My video self laughs. "Why don't you start with when you first saw her?"

"The first time I saw your Grandma, I fell in love." He then proceeds to tell the story of how they first met when they were both in college. I sneak a peek at my grandmother and can see her eyes shining with tears, her hand holding my mom's tightly, but I can see that she is smiling.

"Grandpa, did you ever tell Grandma you loved her?"

He shakes his head sadly. "Because it isn't what I was raised to do. It was not the Korean way. But I will say it now. I love you, my beautiful wife. Ever since the first time I met you when you were at Ewha. It may have been an arranged marriage for you, but for me it was always a love match. Yeobo, saranghae!"

Grandma is now crying. "Nado, saranghae yeobo! I'm sorry I never told you also." She sobs so hard I pause the video, because I don't want her to miss any part of it.

The Korean words for "honey, I love you" sound especially bittersweet to me. Especially knowing that they are words they never shared with each other.

"Grandma, keep watching," I tell her. I wait for her to wipe her eyes and compose herself before pressing play.

My voice on-screen is speaking.

"Did Grandma ever say 'I love you' to you?"

Grandpa smiles and says, "She tells me she loves me every day. When she makes my favorite dishes. When she makes me drink healthy smoothies that taste terrible. When she nags me about taking my high-blood-pressure medicine. When she forces me to take her out somewhere, to make a memory together, even though I'd rather stay at home and watch TV. All these little gestures tell me she loves me."

The video then transitions to a montage of scenes with Grandma coming over to feed Grandpa, taking away his salty nuts or candy, bringing him his medicine and vitamins, laughing at him, nagging him.

I sneak a peek at my grandma and my mom, and I can see both of them smiling and crying.

The last scene of the montage is when Grandma snatches his favorite salty nuts and replaces it with a bowl of blueberries.

"They're sour!" he complains.

"Eat them anyway," Grandma says as she walks away. "They're good for you!"

Grandpa smiles into the camera and gestures to Grandma's departing form. "See what I mean? She loves me."

The scene transitions back to Grandpa in his red sweater.

"So Grandpa, how do you show Grandma how much you love her?"

He scratches his head sheepishly. "I don't really know."

The scene transitions to another montage. When Grandma leans over to place a fruit plate on the table, Grandpa is staring at her with so much love in his eyes. When Grandma is nagging at him and Grandpa simply answers, "Yes, Yeobo!" When Grandma asks if we like her new dress that she just bought, and he tells her how beautiful she looks. That she is the most beautiful woman in the world. And the last scene, when Grandma leaves a dark green smoothie in a tall glass for Grandpa to drink.

"Do you want to taste it?"

On-screen me shows up and sniffs at it and then makes a revolted face.

"Grandpa, it smells like farts."

"You'd better drink it all, Yeobo!" Grandma yells out from the kitchen.

Grandpa makes a stinky face at me, and then he raises the glass and drinks every drop. I am gazing up at him with awe and disgust.

He belches and grimaces. "Tastes like farts also."

"How can you drink that?"

"Because your grandma told me to," he answers simply.

Grandma comes back out with a plate of clementines. She takes the empty glass and pats Grandpa on the head, saying, "Good job!" The look Grandpa gives her is shining with his love.

"Did Dad drink that every day?" my mom asks. I pause the video to hear my Grandma's response.

"Every day," she replies. "It is so healthy. It has kale, broccoli, and spinach, but I add apple cider to make it sweet."

"Mom, I know what it tastes like," my mother responds. "You made me drink it once, and I almost threw up. Only Dad would willingly drink that for you."

Grandma laughs and wipes her eyes. I turn the video back on.

On-screen we see Grandpa with the red sweater again.

"Grandpa, anything else you want to tell Grandma?"

He leans forward and clasps his hands. "Yeobo, thank you for making me the happiest man in the world by being my wife for fifty-seven years! You are the best wife, and I am so lucky to have you. Saranghae!"

The video fades to black.

We are all quiet. I can feel Grandpa's presence in the room. I want to talk to him, tell him how much I love him. How much I miss him. I sit where I am on the floor next to my laptop, trying not to cry. Suddenly, I feel arms wrap around me from behind. My grandma sits behind me, holding me tight. I can hear my mom sniffling in the background.

"Junie-ah, thank you so much! This is the most wonderful present anyone could have ever given me."

I turn around and hug my grandma. Wherever Grandpa is, I'm sure he is smiling too.

Chapter 27

"So, Grandma, what made you pick Grandpa?" I ask. "Grandpa said he didn't know why you agreed to even meet with him."

It's been several days since I showed Grandpa's love video to Grandma and she has watched it ten times so far. She laughs and cries every time.

We are sitting in the kitchen, plucking the tails off the bean sprouts Grandma is making for dinner. It's a long and tedious process, but I don't mind it because I can see Grandma needs this kind of mindless work right now.

Grandma's eyes grow soft. "I recognized him as one of the polite boys who came to meet me at school. But he never tried to talk to me. He was very respectful that way. I thought he didn't like me, so I was surprised when I saw his picture on the marriage proposal. He was the only one who smiled in his matchmaking photo. He had such a sweet smile. It made me think he was a good man. And I was right."

Grandpa was the best. The sharp pain of missing him is still there, but it helps to be with Grandma. Especially knowing that it's what he would want me to do.

I am suddenly reminded of another promise I made him. To make sure I recorded Grandma's war story. I'd tried before, but she hadn't wanted to talk about it. Would she be willing now?

"So, you know how I did the videos with Grandpa?" I ask.

"I'm so glad you did, Junie," Grandma answers. "It is such a wonderful record of your grandfather."

"Well, I promised Grandpa I would record your stories also."

"Ahhhhh." Grandma gives me a look that says *I know what you're up to.*

"No, really! He made me promise to record your war story. He said it was very important in explaining why you wanted to come to America."

Once again, a faraway look creeps into Grandma's eyes.

"I guess that's true," she says. "All right, then."

"Great! When can we do it?" I'm antsy to get started, afraid she might change her mind.

"After we clean all these kongnamul," she says.

Determined to finish quickly, I rip off the tails of the bean sprouts as fast as I can.

It takes almost two hours before we sit in the living room and I set up my little recording area. Grandma insisted on finishing the soup and side dishes she was going to make with the bean sprouts, and then changed her clothes and did her hair and makeup. It was a lot different from Grandpa, who didn't even brush his hair before I'd record him.

I check the screen, and she looks beautiful as always. She's the most nongrandmotherly-looking grandma I know. Her straight black hair reaches her shoulders and is graying only at her temples.

"Whenever you're ready, Grandma."

She plays with her fingers and takes a deep breath.

"I'm ready."

I press record. "Grandma, please introduce yourself and tell us your year of birth, and where you were born. Then tell us an important event from your life. Specifically, your time during the war."

Grandma looks at the camera with a serious expression. "My American name is Jinjoo Han. Han is my married name. But my Korean name will always be Lee Jinjoo. Because Korean women keep their maiden names."

"Oh, is that why my mom kept hers? I thought it was because of her work."

Grandma nods. "Yes, your dad wanted her to change it like the Americans do, but I told her to keep her traditions."

I like that and I decide that if I ever get married, I too will keep my name. Junie Kim is who I am.

"Can you tell us when and where you were born?"

"I was born in Incheon, the year of 1940," she says. "When I was ten years old, the Korean War began, and my entire life changed."

Chapter 28

"Dried squid!"

"Fresh eggs!"

"Pickled octopus!"

"Blood sausage!"

"Rice cakes!"

The litany of food items available for sale in the Sinpo Market was always fascinating to Jinjoo. Dozens of little stalls packed tightly together with row upon row of food and clothing and other merchandise. The smells were both delicious and revolting, and oh so familiar. Fried mung-bean pancake with spicy sauce, wafting in the air with the bricks of pungent soybean paste hawked by a nearby merchant, so strong you could taste it. Sweet rice cakes with gooey walnut paste next to stalls of fish cake and raw seafood. This was home.

Jinjoo forgot that she was in the middle of an intense game of hide-and-seek, and instead watched the hotteok lady making fried gooey sweet pancakes. First, she pulled off a lump of the rice dough and molded it into a small pocket filled with sugar and nuts and sesame seeds. Then she threw it on the griddle with barely any oil and pressed it down with a circle spatula, crisping it into a white-and-brown pancake that she added to the pile on the side of her grill. It was still early in the morning, but Jinjoo had raced out of the house without eating breakfast. Now her stomach grumbled loudly.

"Jinjoo-ya," the hotteok lady said. "Your eyeballs are going to fall out onto my grill if you keep staring like that."

Jinjoo dug her hands into her pants pockets and pulled out a fistful of lint, a red ribbon, and a shiny silver coin. Wiping it against her shirt, she held it out to the hotteok lady with a beaming smile.

The woman looked at the coin with a raised eyebrow.

"Five chon? Wah, Jinjoo, you are rich today! Are you buying for your friends?"

As if she'd spoken the words to a magic spell, all three of Jinjoo's friends suddenly appeared at her side.

"Jinjoo, where'd you get so much money?"

"Jinjoo, can I have a hotteok too?"

Jinjoo looked back into the surprise and awe of her friends' faces and felt her chest puff out in importance.

"Father had me deliver a watch to an important client on

the other side of town yesterday. You know, where the Japanese tile houses are," she said. "The lady gave me five chon for bringing it so quick."

"Wow!" The friends edged even closer, staring at the coin as intensely as Jinjoo had stared at the hot hotteoks. Jinjoo had to bite her tongue from bragging that five chon was nothing compared to how much her father used to give her. But that had been over a year ago, when there were more wealthy foreigners around with fancy watches they needed fixed. Nowadays her father hardly gave her any change because of her mother's disapproval. Her mother didn't like the way Jinjoo was being spoiled by her father.

Don't just give it to her! Make her work for it, her mother always said.

Which was why Jinjoo had been so keen to deliver the watch.

Feeling incredibly generous, Jinjoo ordered two hotteok, and wrapped the second one in paper and carefully placed it into her deep pants pocket. The heat of the hotteok burned comfortingly against her leg.

"Why aren't you eating that one, Jinjoo?" the hotteok lady asked.

"I want to take it home to my eonni and brothers," she replied.

"You're a good kid, Jinjoo." With a smile, the hotteok lady gave her one more of the piping hot cakes and shooed the kids away.

Taking the delicious-smelling hotteoks, the group of friends dashed through the crowded road and sat on the curb of the sidewalk. They waited patiently as Jinjoo carefully split the two cakes into four even pieces and shared it with her friends. The first two to Taeyoung and Taemin, fraternal twins, who looked exactly alike except that Taeyoung wore her hair in long braids and Taemin kept his head shaved due to the heat. The third one to Yohan, Jinjoo's favorite friend, who lived the closest to her and sat behind her in class.

As they gobbled up the last of the sugary treat, they watched the busy streets filled with pedestrians, horse-drawn carriages, bicyclists, and every now and then a fancy automobile from the rich part of town.

"Who do you think that is?" Taeyoung asked.

"Maybe it's President Rhee," Taemin said.

"President Rhee?" Jinjoo snorted. "He'd have a whole street full of cars with him! My father said he doesn't go anywhere without a bunch of people to lick his feet clean."

"Not just his feet," Yohan said slyly.

They all snickered. Even though Incheon was close to Seoul, most people despised the tyrannical old guy with the foreign wife. They heard the grumblings of the grown-ups. It wasn't just the Communist supporters who hated Rhee.

"It's probably some rich bank president or hotel guy," Jinjoo said. "Or one of those Japanese rich guys . . ."

"Probably not Japanese," Yohan replied. "They all went back to Japan after they lost to the Americans."

A sudden cloud of dust enveloped them, and the kids leaped to their feet. A shopkeeper was vigorously sweeping the sidewalk in front of his store.

"Hey, ahjussi, you got us all dirty!"

"Get off the sidewalk! Filthy urchins," he muttered.

The children glared back. "Come on, let's get out of here."

"Let's go to the park."

They ran down the middle of the road, dodging pedestrians and bicyclists and rickshaw men. They ran down Bank Street, named for the series of fancy banks in gray concrete buildings that lined the street. Once Japanese banks, now Korean independent banks after World War II had ended. Incheon was an important city port where many westerners arrived in Korea. It was a mix of old and modern. Of ancient Korean houses and tall westernized buildings.

Finally, they climbed all the way to the top of the park and looked out over the view of Incheon port.

"Wah! Look at those American ships!" Taemin yelled out in glee.

"They're not American," Yohan corrected. "And those are freighters, not passenger ships. To carry cargo."

"How do you know?"

"Look at the flags, silly!"

One had a big red flag with a thick blue cross outlined by white. The other one was red with four small stars in a semicircle to the right of a big star. Jinjoo didn't recognize either flag.

"So where are they from?" Jinjoo asked.

Yohan scratched his head sheepishly. "I'm not sure, but I think one of them is the new flag of China."

Jinjoo narrowed her eyes suspiciously at her friend. "Which one?"

Yohan didn't respond, and Jinjoo crowed in delight. "Ha! You don't know! And if it is for cargo, what're those people doing on it?"

They all peered down to see people boarding the freighter.

Suddenly, Taeyoung shouted, "Look at all those buses and cars!"

A number of vehicles were pulling into the harbor lot and unloading even more people onto the pier. From their vantage point, the children could make out the khaki uniforms of American soldiers escorting women and children onto the ships.

"Huh. Those look like Americans heading to that ship," Jinjoo remarked. "Lots and lots of them."

Peering closely at the cars, Yohan pointed to one with small flags on its hood. "You're right. See the red and white stripes with a blue corner and lots of stars? That's the American flag."

"What's going on?" Taeyoung asked. Her eyes were round with worry. "Why are they all leaving?"

They all watched as buses and cars, even trucks, kept driving up as close as possible to the ship. Soon hundreds of people were gathering around the ships. Men, women, and children of all ages. Jinjoo and her friends watched for over an hour as they loaded more and more people on the ship with the blue cross. Even though it was full, they kept boarding.

"I don't get it. Why don't they get on the other ship? It's empty," Taemin asked.

"That's the Chinese freighter," Yohan said decisively.

"I thought you didn't know," Jinjoo said in suspicion. "What makes you sure now?"

"Because they're avoiding it," Yohan replied. "Westerners trust other western people but not Asians. That's what my father said."

Yohan's father worked at the city government office, so he would know.

Jinjoo turned her attention back to the ships. She could see the crew of the empty ship talking with some men who were trying to convince some of the people to board, but everyone refused. They kept boarding the blue-cross vessel. Taeyoung and Taemin got bored and moved away to play in the shade, but Jinjoo was fascinated by the activity going on in the harbor.

"How many people you think got on it?" Jinjoo asked.

"More than five hundred, maybe six," Yohan said. "Although it's a freighter, so it's used to carrying heavy cargo. But definitely way more people than should be on that ship. I guess they'd rather risk sinking than get on a Chinese boat."

"That's so wrong," Jinjoo said in disapproval.

Yohan agreed. "Americans are funny that way."

They could hear honking as a few more cars pulled up to the harbor.

"It looks like all the westerners are leaving Korea," Jinjoo said.

"Maybe the Reds are invading!" Taemin announced with a laugh.

"Bite your tongue, Taemin!" Yohan shouted. "That's not funny. We don't want North Korean Communist pigs here!"

The words sent a chill through Jinjoo's spine. It was a worry that her parents talked about constantly. Her mother had begun trying to persuade her father to move south, but business was still decent. Not as good as earlier years when the streets of Incheon were filled with foreigners, but enough to feed his family. Her father worried that if they left Incheon, he would not be able to make enough money to buy rice, like so many other poor Koreans. But her mother worried that they were too close to the thirty-eighth parallel that separated North and South Korea. Too close to the Reds, she would say. And with Incheon being a hotbed of Communist supporters, she didn't feel safe.

"Come on, let's get out of here," Jinjoo said, motioning her friends to leave. "I think we should go home now."

They could turn on the radio and listen to the news. Maybe then the sick feeling in Jinjoo's stomach would abate.

Junie

"So what country was the blue cross flag ship from?"

"Norway," Grandma responds. "I found out later that it was full of fertilizer and that it had to be emptied out completely for the evacuation. Over six hundred people, a lot of them women and children, boarded that freighter, which took three days to travel to Japan. Apparently, many people got sick from the smell of the fertilizer and overcrowding."

"Huh, they should've gotten on the Chinese ship," I say unsympathetically.

Chapter 29

"NORTH KOREA HAS INVADED! SEOUL has fallen!"

Out on the streets the local Communists were celebrating the news of the Red invasion with a makeshift parade. They wore red armbands and were setting off fireworks. Jinjoo could hear them from her house, which was on a side street several blocks from the main thoroughfare. Jinjoo hadn't left the house in days. Her mother had been too afraid to let them out ever since the North Korean Army had advanced into Incheon. Inside the house, they'd heard shooting and loud explosions. The soldiers had been going to houses and stealing food. They'd come to their house and ransacked everything. Jinjoo and her sister had kept their brothers inside the bedroom, too terrified to make a sound.

When they'd left, Jinjoo had walked out to see their kitchen and living quarters in huge disarray. Pots and pans thrown everywhere, their mother's pretty dishes smashed on the ground.

"Why did they do this?" Jinjoo asked.

Her mother and Shinae eonni, their live-in maid, were busy cleaning up. Jinjoo's mother was tight-lipped and angry. "Filthy animals! They took all our food and even your father's watchmaking tools."

"Is there no food for us?" Jinjoo's sister, Eunjoo, asked with worry. She was holding little Junha, who was crying, while Junsoo was running around picking up items on the ground and bringing them to his mother.

"Jinjoo, please take your brother inside before he gets hurt," their mother said, ignoring Eunjoo's question.

Jinjoo caught her brother, who struggled against her. His little four-year-old body was no match for Jinjoo's brute strength, and he, too, started to cry.

"I said take them inside and keep them quiet!"

The two girls rushed their little brothers back inside.

"Eomma is mad," Jinjoo whispered inside their living room.

Eunjoo frowned. She put Junha down, and then plopped some wooden puzzle toys in front of him and Junsoo. They both stopped crying as Eunjoo began playing with them.

"I think it's because the North Koreans took all our food," Eunjoo said in a worried tone. "What will happen to Junha? He's just a baby."

"He's not a baby! He's almost two! What about me?"

Jinjoo asked. "I'm bigger and hungrier!"

"But you can go without food for a little bit. Junha and Junsoo can't."

"Food, food, food!" Junsoo repeated as he galloped around the room.

"Let's wait for Abeoji," Eunjoo said. "I'm sure he will know what to do!"

After a while, Shinae eonni came in and brought them corn cobs broken into small pieces. Eunjoo helped Junha eat his corn, while Jinjoo and Junsoo devoured their pieces.

"Eonni, where's Eomeoni?" Jinjoo asked.

"She went out to your father's store to get some money," Shinae eonni replied. "Then she'll go to the market for food."

Junsoo reached for the other corn, but Jinjoo stopped him. "No, Junsoo, that's Eunjoo noona's corn."

"It's okay, Jinjoo. He can have it," her sister replied. "I'll just eat the rest of Junha's."

She handed it to Junsoo, whose lip stopped quivering. Jinjoo eyed them both angrily.

"This is why you're so weak, Eonni," Jinjoo said. "You don't eat enough food."

"Leave her alone, Jinjoo," Shinae eonni said. "Eunjoo, you are a very kind girl."

Eunjoo winced as Shinae patted her on the head a little too roughly. Jinjoo narrowed her eyes and glared at Shinae, noticing how the older girl had taken two of the largest pieces of corn for herself and eaten them all.

Jinjoo had never really liked Shinae eonni. She'd come two years ago from a small town far south of Incheon to work for their family after their first maid got married. Perhaps because Jinjoo didn't like her, she found her unattractive. She was lazy and sneaky in little things that she thought Jinjoo's mother and father probably didn't notice. Like always blaming broken things on little Junsoo, when most of the time it was her own carelessness. Or taking more food from Eunjoo, because she knew Eunjoo didn't eat a lot. They were small things that Jinjoo always noticed and despised, but that her mother would never listen to her complain about.

"Jinjoo-ya, Shinae has no family," their mom would say. "We're her family now."

What could she say to that? Nothing. So Jinjoo kept quiet and just watched her. She hated that she had to call her eonni out of respect, especially given that respect was the last thing Jinjoo felt for the older girl.

That night, Jinjoo's parents came home together. Her father carried his work bag close to his chest, as if it was very heavy. When he opened it, they saw why. It was filled with a sack of rice and not his usual work tools. He handed it to Eomma, telling her to hide it in their secret hiding place under the floor panels in the living room. It was where they kept their family valuables. Now rice would be kept in there also. Rice had become a precious commodity, to be kept safe from the North Korean soldiers.

At dinnertime, Jinjoo's mom gave everyone small servings

of rice mixed with barley and beans and told them to make it last.

"I hate the North Koreans!" Jinjoo said as they ate their dinner. She stared down at her empty rice bowl, still hungry for more. While they didn't have a feast at every meal, there had always been enough food to fill her stomach. But now, they had to ration everything they ate.

Looking across the table, she saw Shinae sneak a spoonful of rice out of Eunjoo's bowl and shove it in her own mouth while Eunjoo was feeding Junha.

Shinae moved to take another spoonful, but Jinjoo shouted.

"Shinae eonni!"

Startled, she looked at Jinjoo's angry glare and subsided.

"What is it, Jinjoo?" her father asked. "Why are you yelling at Eonni?"

Knowing that her parents would only yell at her for being disrespectful, Jinjoo said nothing but instead crossed her arms and glared at Shinae.

"Eat your food, Eonni," Jinjoo said to Eunjoo. "I'll take care of Junha." She took the little boy into her lap and began to feed him his rice. "Eonni, please eat all your food."

Even though Eunjoo was older than her by a year, Jinjoo was very protective of her older sister. Eunjoo had always been frail and would get sick easily, while Jinjoo was bigger and stronger with a healthy constitution. When they went out, Jinjoo was the one who usually carried little Junha on her back, while Eunjoo would hold four-year-old Junsoo's hand.

And because their mother was a bit absentminded, Jinjoo felt she had to help take care of her sister. The truth was that the person their mother cared for the most, and always came first, was their father. The children were more of an afterthought. And in their family, all the children knew that. Father, on the other hand, cared for all of them. Which was why Jinjoo squirmed her way next to her dad at dinner. Because she knew he would take care of her.

"Jinjoo," her father called. "Ah!"

She looked up to see her father holding a spoonful of rice and meat. Even as she could see the angry glare of her mother, she quickly opened her mouth and accepted the bite.

"Yeobo! You have to eat and keep your strength!" Jinjoo's mother said.

"I get plenty to eat! Don't worry about me," he said. "I worry about my little helper! Jinjoo needs to be strong so she can work with me at the shop, right, Jinjoo?"

"Yes, Abeoji!"

Junha gurgled as he tried to reach for his food and almost toppled out of Jinjoo's arms. Getting a firm grip of him, Jinjoo fed him the rest of his food as she avoided her mother's disapproving gaze.

In the middle of the night, Jinjoo woke to the urgent sound of someone frantically knocking on their door. Jinjoo sat up and stared out at the shadows of moving bodies across her bedroom door. Her sister was still fast asleep, her arms flung wide and her legs sprawled out over Jinjoo's. Jinjoo pushed her sister off and scurried over to the door. She slid it open and stared down the hallway to where the brightness of the lamps sent long flickering shadows dancing across the paneled wood before her eyes. She heard harsh whispers and weeping.

Jinjoo crawled out into the corridor and quietly made her way down to the living room. Peeking around the opening, she saw the room was full of adults who she didn't recognize. They were crowded around someone lying on the ground. Jinjoo craned her neck and was shocked to recognize her gomo, her father's big sister. Her mother sat next to her, stroking her back. Gomo was always so proud and dignified and wore Japanese pearls her son had bought for her when he'd become police captain. But now she was sprawled on the ground, her black hair a wild mess, as if she'd been ripping it out by the handful. Her blue hanbok skirt was twisted all around her, showing her white underskirts, and the bright blue of her hanbok jacket sleeve was stained. Her hands were dirty. Jinjoo squinted. Where her gomo's hands pressed into the floor mat, dark stains appeared. Suddenly, Jinjoo was very frightened. She didn't want to know what it was. She didn't want to know why her gomo lay as still as death, her eyes pressed tightly together even as tears coursed down her face.

The door opened, and Jinjoo saw her father appear with a young man she recognized as Mr. Pak from their watch store. This time Jinjoo knew what it was she saw on her father's hands. Blood.

She stood paralyzed in the hallway.

"Those dirty commie bastards." It was Mr. Pak speaking.

Everyone was quiet, just staring anxiously at the men. Jinjoo could barely breathe. Something terrible had happened, but what?

Gomo sat up and stared at Jinjoo's father. "Did you move them? Did you move my son? My poor son? Did you move him out of the cold street?"

Her father nodded, and she collapsed to the floor again. "They killed my son! They killed him! They dragged him out of bed with his pregnant wife and they killed them in front of me! They shot them down like animals! They aimed at her swollen belly! They killed that poor baby! They killed my grandchild!"

Jinjoo shoved her fist in her mouth to keep from crying out. Gomo's daughter-in-law was nine months pregnant with their first child. Gomo had been so sure that it would be a son.

"You're lucky they didn't kill you too!" another aunt was telling Gomo.

Gomo reared up and shoved her away. "They should have just killed me! I'm dead already! They took everything away from me!"

Jinjoo didn't even realize she'd made a sound until she saw her aunt's wild eyes light upon her.

"Jinjoo-ya! Jinjoo-ya!" Gomo started wailing. She opened her arms and Jinjoo felt compelled to run to her.

Gomo hugged her so tight Jinjoo could hardly breathe, but she didn't complain. She knew her aunt needed to hold her. To cry over her. To let out all her grief. Her aunt held her tight and began to beat her on the back with her fists. Hugging her and hitting her and screaming the entire time. Begging for her son to come back to her.

Jinjoo began to cry also. It wasn't that Gomo was hitting her too hard. The pain wasn't bad, but it was the overwhelming emotion that was all too much to handle. Her mother gently pulled her from her aunt's arms and led her out of the room. Standing in the hallway was her older sister, staring with wide eyes. Their mother pushed them into their room and tucked them back under the blankets.

"Eomma, was it the North Koreans? Are they going to kill us all?"

"No, Eunjoo," their mother responded. "They won't hurt children."

"But they killed the baby," Eunjoo replied. "They killed the baby in her stomach."

Her mother was quiet, her face shuttered and remote in a way Jinjoo had never seen before.

"Go to sleep," she said, and left.

Eunjoo scooted her body next to Jinjoo and huddled close.

"I was scared for you, Jinjoo. Gomo looked like a wild person. I thought she might really hurt you!" Eunjoo said. "Weren't you frightened?"

"Yes," Jinjoo whispered. "But not for myself. I was scared for Gomo."

"What do you mean?"

"Gomo wasn't herself," Jinjoo said. "She looked broken."

Eunjoo nodded. "What's going to happen to her?" she asked.

In the quiet of the night, after Eunjoo had fallen asleep, Jinjoo's mind was still racing from all that she'd witnessed. *What's going to happen to us?* she wondered.

Junie

"I don't understand, Grandma!" I'm in shock. "Why did they kill a pregnant woman?"

"To kill off the bloodline," Grandma replies. "So that there are no descendants to seek revenge."

"That's evil."

"War is evil, Junie, never forget that."

∘Chapter∘
30

DURING THE THREE DAYS OF family mourning, Jinjoo and her siblings weren't allowed to leave the house and hardly saw their parents. As the head of the family and chief mourner, Jinjoo's father stayed at the home of the deceased with Gomo for the entire mourning period. They saw their mother only when she would come home to feed them dinner, but as usual, she left their care to the maid and stayed by her husband's side.

Jinjoo was certain that Shinae was the worst maid in the world. Instead of taking care of them, she did almost nothing but sit around eating most of the food their mother had prepared. The fourth day was the funeral procession, and they didn't see their parents at all. It was all very sad and frightening.

In the daytime, it was hard to believe what had happened

to Gomo's son and wife. Even though it was so recent, it felt like it was a story about a long-ago event, and the danger didn't seem real except for a vague sense of unrest. Because she was stuck in her house, Jinjoo had no concept of what was happening in the outside world, where occupation by the Communists had become a reality. Out in their small court-yard, Jinjoo paced along the outside wall. She wondered what her friends were doing. Were they all right, or were they also stuck at home?

Sighing deeply, Jinjoo went back inside, where Eunjoo was playing peekaboo with Junha while Junsoo ran around trying to catch a fly with his hands.

"Noona, noona!" Junsoo called as he launched himself into Jinjoo's arms. "Let's play hide-and-seek!"

They played for an hour before Junsoo got tired and went to his room for a nap. Eunjoo had gone to bed with Junha, and both were now sleeping too. Bored, Jinjoo paced around the courtyard again. She was desperately wishing she could go out to the marketplace and look for her friends when there was a knocking on her front gate.

"Jinjoo!"

She opened the gate and saw her friends, twins Taeyoung and Taemin, waiting outside. They came in and sat on the narrow wooden porch that ran along the whole length of Jin-joo's house.

"Jinjoo, why haven't you come out lately?" Taeyoung asked.

"We're in mourning," she replied. "My gomo's son and his wife were killed by the Communists."

They both were shocked to hear the news.

"Wasn't he the policeman?" Taemin asked.

Jinjoo nodded.

Taemin whistled. "I heard my parents talking about that. I didn't know he was related to your family, Jinjoo."

"Is your father okay?" Taeyoung asked.

"Yes, why are you asking?"

The siblings looked at each other. "There's been a lot of rumors that all government workers and their families are being arrested."

Jinjoo's eyebrows furrowed in concern. "But my father is a watchmaker. He's not a government worker. Why would they arrest him?"

Taemin shook his head. "I don't know, Jinjoo. I'm just telling you what I heard. We haven't seen Yohan either. We thought you might know if he was all right."

Now the vague unease Jinjoo had been feeling roiled in the pit of her stomach, as if she'd eaten too many boiled eggs. "What else did you hear?"

After they left, Jinjoo wanted desperately to find her parents. She hadn't seen her father in four days because of the funeral rites. Was he really okay? And what had happened to Yohan? His father worked for the city government. Had he been arrested?

That night, Jinjoo stayed up late, waiting for her parents

to come home. But she couldn't stay awake long enough. Early in the morning, she snuck out of bed quietly to keep from waking her siblings. With their parents out so much, Junsoo slept next to Eunjoo, while Junha was in between his sisters.

Out in the kitchen, she saw her mother cooking rice and a seafood stew. Shinae was sitting in the corner peeling onions very slowly and yawning.

"Eomma, where's Abeoji?"

"He is escorting your gomo and her daughter to Suwon by train," she said. "Don't worry, he'll be back today."

It was not the answer Jinjoo had hoped to hear. She'd desperately wanted to see her father to know that he really was safe.

"Why is Gomo going to Suwon?"

Her mother's face was wrinkled with concern. "It's not safe for her to stay here because of what happened to her son."

"What about Abeoji? Is he safe?"

"What kind of question is that?" her mother snapped. "Of course he's safe. He's just escorting your gomo because she's too upset to go by herself. He'll be perfectly fine. Don't question that! You know better than to air such thoughts."

This was a superstition of her mother's. Never to say bad things out loud just in case evil spirits might hear and make them come true.

"I'm sorry. I just was worried because I haven't seen him for so long."

Her mother was silent, just focusing on cooking. Jinjoo shifted from one foot to the other as the silence extended.

"Eomma, do I still have to stay home, or can I go see my friends?"

Her mother hesitated. "Don't go far, and come home in an hour."

Relieved to be let out, Jinjoo agreed and raced out of their gate. She was heading to Yohan's house, which was only a ten-minute walk from hers. Yohan's family lived in a nice house with black lacquered double doors that Jinjoo had always admired. She arrived to find the doors broken and hanging off their hinges. Inside their large courtyard, the belongings had been thrown into a pile and destroyed.

"Oh, no," Jinjoo breathed. "Yohan, are you there? Yohan?"

She stood at the doorway, horrified by the mess. What had happened here? Where was Yohan? She was so afraid that they'd been hurt or worse.

"Hey, little girl, are you looking for the Pak family?"

Jinjoo whirled around to find an old grandma looking at her from the street.

"I'm looking for my friend who lives here," she said. "Do you know what happened?"

The old woman nodded. "They were lucky. They got out before the Reds came for them."

"They got away?" Jinjoo asked.

"As far as I know," the old woman said. "They snuck out

late at night, right before the Reds came into this neighbor-hood looking for them."

Jinjoo thanked the lady and slowly headed home. She was both relieved and sad. She hoped Yohan and his entire family had been able to escape. But she was sad not to have seen her friend before he left.

On the way home, she passed by Main Street and was shocked to see it filled with North Korean soldiers. Some drove by in jeeps and trucks while others patrolled the streets.

The world had changed so drastically in only a few days. This was why all the foreigners had been trying to get on the boats. They had known what was coming.

Junie

"Grandma, did you ever see Yohan or your other friends again?"

She nods. "Taeyoung and Taemin never left Incheon. I saw them both again when I went to college. And Yohan attended Seoul University medical school and became a very successful doctor."

I let out the breath I was holding, relieved to hear her friends had survived the war.

Chapter 31

IT HAD BEEN SIX DAYS since their father had gone to Suwon. Every day their mother would go out looking for him. Every night she'd come home and cry herself to sleep. Today her mother had just heard rumors that fifty people had been killed by the Communists at the police station. Their mother became frantic. She ordered Shinae to go with her to the police station, but the girl refused, saying she was terrified of dead bodies. Jinjoo's mother began to beat on her chest and wail in hysterics.

"Eomma, don't cry. I'll go with you," Jinjoo said. At the moment, she was more frightened by her mother's behavior than by dead people.

At her words, Jinjoo's mother calmed down. They walked through the Chinatown area where the police station was. The entire time, Jinjoo's mother didn't say a word. When they arrived near the vicinity of the police station, they heard the wailing first. On the wide dirt road in front of the station, there was a row of bodies covered by dirty straw mats. Several women were weeping over them.

Jinjoo's mom rushed over to the bodies and began pulling up the mats and checking the faces. Jinjoo was horrified. She'd never seen a dead body before, let alone so many. She shuddered and shut her eyes. But the images were seared into her memory. The bodies were covered in blood, some with faces bashed in. They ranged in age from old to young. Nobody she recognized, but it was still too much for her. She just wanted to go home.

She opened her eyes and saw her mother still looking at the dead bodies. The straw mat that was covering the dead body next to her had slipped, leaving the face exposed. Jinjoo wanted to cry. She wanted to run to her mother, but she was frozen in place.

"Eomma!" she cried out. "Eomma!"

"I'm sorry, Jinjoo. I shouldn't have brought you here," her mother said. Taking her hand, she led her away.

"Abeoji's not there, right?" Jinjoo sobbed.

"No, he's not. But I have to find out where he is."

They went into the police station, which was now full of North Korean soldiers. There was a crowd of people, mostly women and old men, standing in front of the desk officer. They were all asking about what had happened to someone they were looking for. Jinjoo's mother joined the queue but quickly shoved her way to the front. Pushed by the other people in the crowd, Jinjoo was forced to let go of her mother's hand and fell to the floor. Before she was trampled, a man helped her up and pulled her away to the far side of the room.

"What are you doing here, little kid? You could have gotten really hurt."

Jinjoo bowed deeply and thanked the man and then noticed that he was a North Korean soldier. He looked very young, not much older than Shinae eonni. But he had a kind face.

"Are you okay?"

Jinjoo nodded.

"Where are your parents?" he asked.

Looking at the crowd, she could see her mother at the front of the line pleading with the desk sergeant, who looked overwhelmed.

Jinjoo pointed. "She's over there."

"Mmm, I tell you what. I'll stay with you until your mom comes back, okay?"

Not knowing what to do, Jinjoo just nodded. He led her to a bench nearby and sat down with her. From his pocket, he pulled out a small bag of sesame candy and offered Jinjoo one. Unwilling to say no, Jinjoo took the small rectangular sweet and sat with it in her hand, eyeing him and then the candy a little suspiciously.

He smiled and popped the sesame-covered bar in his mouth. "They're fine. I promise I wouldn't give you something bad."

Jinjoo thought of all the dead bodies outside the police station. Blinking away the image, she couldn't help but notice the rifle leaning against his leg.

"You can eat it. I promise it's good. These are my little sister's favorites," he said a little sadly. "You remind me of her."

He didn't look like a bad man. His smile was gentle, and he seemed very nice. But he was a Communist. And she'd been taught that all Communists were bad. Jinjoo didn't know what to do. Should she not trust him, even though he'd saved her from being trampled? She looked down at the sesame treat in her hand. She was starting to unravel the wrapping paper when a hand slapped the candy away. Jinjoo stared up at her mother in shock.

"Don't you dare give my daughter candy!" her mother said fiercely.

The soldier's face grew serious and he stood up. "You should be more careful with your daughter. She was almost badly hurt by the crowds over there."

"Mind your own business!" Jinjoo's mother snapped. Grabbing Jinjoo's hand, she pulled her out of the police station.

Early in the morning, Jinjoo heard a lot of hurried movement and banging from the other room. She carefully snuck out of bed so she wouldn't wake her siblings, only to find her mother in a frenzy. In the center of the living room floor was a large white cloth with a pile of her mother's jewelry, her father's special watches, jade figurines, money, and other precious items. There were also four twenty-four-carat-gold baby rings, one for each of the children, that they'd received on their first birthdays. Jinjoo's mother would sometimes show the rings to Jinjoo and her sister, telling them they were theirs as soon as they got married. That had always bothered Jinjoo. Why did she have to be married to receive a ring that was hers?

But now all the rings were in a pile with the other family valuables, and their mother was tying it all up with a small parcel of clothing.

Eunjoo came out of the room holding Junha.

"Eunjoo, Jinjoo, Eomma has to go help your father! You have to be good girls. Take care of your brothers and listen to Shinae eonni."

"Eomma, where are you going?" Eunjoo asked in a frightened voice. "Please don't leave us!"

Their mother stopped packing to grab both Eunjoo and Jinjoo firmly by their arms and look at them intensely. "Listen to me. Your father is in a prison in Seoul. I need you both to be brave. We need your father, or we can't survive." Under her breath, she whispered, "I can't survive."

Jinjoo heard her and once again felt that mix of sadness and anger that her mother would always put her husband before her children. But she pushed the feeling away, because she also knew that they needed their father.

Her parents had had an arranged marriage, like all

other marriages in Korea. But the difference was that her mother had been madly in love with her husband from the first moment she saw him on their wedding day. Her father had grown fond of his wife, and it was a matter of pride for Jinjoo that her parents loved each other. But sometimes Jinjoo wished her mother's obsessive adoration of their father would not shut her children out. Not that their mother didn't love them. She did. But all her life, Jinjoo had instinctively known that her father cared for them more than their mother did. He had a special love and adoration for his children that their mother didn't seem to have. And sometimes, Jinjoo could sense their mother's jealousy when they received too much of his attention.

Jinjoo silently followed her mother as she rushed to Shinae's room.

"Shinae! Wake up!" her mother yelled.

The girl hurriedly rose to her feet and bowed.

"Here, take this money for food." Jinjoo's mother thrust a small wad of cash into the maid's hands. "But make this last. I have to go to Seoul. I should be back within a week. Take good care of the children."

Jinjoo saw Shinae's eyes light up at the sight of more money than she'd ever seen before. Now Jinjoo was worried.

"Eomma, do you have to go? Can't someone else help Abeoji?"

"There's no one who will help us, Jinjoo," her mom said. "These are dangerous times, and everyone is afraid. If I don't go, we may never see your father again. Do you want that?"

Jinjoo shook her head fiercely. "No, Eomma. Please be safe."

Her mother absently patted her on the head, put on her shoes, and hurried out the front gate. Jinjoo watched her mother's form disappear down their street before closing the door. She turned to see Shinae still staring at the money while both Eunjoo and Junha cried. Junsoo came running out of the bedroom asking for his mother.

A wave of helplessness nearly consumed Jinjoo. She feared they would never see their parents again.

Junie

"Oh, Grandma, I can't believe you had to see such terrible things when you were only ten."

Grandma pats my hand. "Should we take a break?"

"No, please don't stop."

Chapter 32

Two days later, Shinae eonni went out to the market for food and never came back.

Jinjoo was not surprised, but Eunjoo was devastated. There was no food in the house; Shinae had eaten or taken it all, along with the money their mother had left her.

"What do we do?" Jinjoo asked.

Eunjoo wiped her eyes and picked up their crying baby brother. "We have to go ask our neighbors for help."

"I'll hold him, Eonni," Jinjoo said. She put Junha on her back while Eunjoo took out the podaegi. She placed the podaegi's wide quilted blanket around Junha and took the long strap and wrapped it under his bottom, across his back, and then tied it in front of Jinjoo. Eunjoo took Junsoo by the hand, and the siblings went out of their house.

Several hours later they returned with the small amounts

of food their neighbors could spare. For the first time, Jinjoo became aware of how hard it was for everyone. Some neighbors had simply closed their doors, while others had given them as much as they could manage. It was clear that everyone was suffering.

Eunjoo took the rice they'd gotten and mixed it with the fish and soup to make a rice gruel for Junha. She then carefully split up the remaining food for Junsoo and Jinjoo, while giving herself the least. It was depressing to see how little food they were able to get.

The next day, the siblings went to an adjacent neighborhood to ask for food. This time, they were chased away with a broom from a few houses and called beggars. Jinjoo was angry and powerless. But the following morning, the children had no choice but to try a different neighborhood.

By the time they got home, they'd received even less food than the day before. For three more days the siblings went door to door asking for help. They went farther and farther from their own neighborhood and it took much longer to get home. Since they would walk so far, Eunjoo would use the podaegi with Junha while Jinjoo carried Junsoo on her back. Often, Eunjoo would be so tired she would collapse, leaving Jinjoo to feed their brothers. Their meager meals left everyone still hungry and cranky. The one thing Jinjoo was grateful for was that they'd avoided going into her friends' neighborhood. She couldn't bear the idea of showing the twins how bad their situation was.

On the morning of the sixth day since Shinae had deserted them, there was a loud knocking on their front gate. Jinjoo opened the door to see two policemen.

"Are your parents home?" the older man asked.

Jinjoo slowly shook her head.

"Do you know where they are?"

Again, she shook her head. The two policemen looked at each other, and one nodded.

"We received word that a group of children were begging for food. Would that be you kids?"

A sound behind her made Jinjoo turn around. Her sister was carrying Junha in the podaegi while Junsoo stood hiding behind her.

Gazing back at the policeman, Jinjoo didn't answer.

"We're going to have to take all of you to the police station," the older policeman said, reaching over to grab Jinjoo's arm.

Frightened, Jinjoo dodged and ran back to the house.

This time the younger policeman came forward. "Hey, don't be scared. We're just going to take you to the station so we can help you find your parents. There's also delicious food."

Eunjoo was already nodding and heading for the door, but Jinjoo held her back.

"And then you'll bring us home?" she asked.

The young policeman nodded with a smile. "Of course! We'll bring you right back home so you can wait for your parents. But you need help to find them. And I'm sure you're all very hungry."

Eunjoo pulled at Jinjoo's arm. "Let's go. Junha and Junsoo are hungry."

That was her sister's problem, Jinjoo thought. She was always thinking of others and not herself. Jinjoo didn't trust these policemen, and the last place she wanted to go was to the police station. She was still haunted by the memory of the dead bodies. The idea of going there terrified her, but all she could do was follow her sister.

Although the walk from their house to the police station was not very far, the policemen carried Junha and Junsoo, making it easier for the sisters. As they approached the police station, Jinjoo gripped Eunjoo's arm tightly and whimpered.

"What's the matter, Jinjoo?" her sister whispered.

Jinjoo shook her head and closed her eyes tightly.

"There's nothing scary here," Eunjoo said. "You can open your eyes."

She shook her head, refusing to open her eyes until they were inside the police station. Inside, the policemen led them to a side room with a large window looking out onto a side street. On the table, there was a pitcher of water and a few small wooden bowls.

"Wait here and I'll get you some food," the older man said.

The younger officer smiled and asked them to sit. Eunjoo sat with Junha on her lap, while Junsoo sat next to Jinjoo. The police officer then began to ask many questions, starting with their parents' names, their father's occupation, where the rest of their family was, when their parents had left, and so on. But when the questions began to turn to who they were friends with and where did they work, and why did their mother leave them behind, Jinjoo began to be alarmed. As the girls struggled to answer all the questions of the smiling police officer, Jinjoo knew why she didn't like him. His smile never reached his eyes. She kicked her sister under the table and answered first.

"We don't know," Jinjoo said. "We don't know where they went or why. We don't know anything! My sister's eleven years old and I'm only ten! How are we supposed to know anything?"

The policeman gave them another fake smile. "Let me go see where your food is."

After he left, Jinjoo admonished her sister about talking too much.

"But he's a police officer," Eunjoo replied in surprise. "We're supposed to listen to them."

"He's North Korean! He wants to find anyone who is antiCommunist!" Jinjoo explained.

Her sister's eyes grew round in shock. "I thought the police were still the police."

"No, we can't say anything about Gomo, and why Abeoji took her to Suwon," Jinjoo said. "You have to stop being so trusting, Eonni."

Another hour passed before the older policeman returned.

He brought them a large plate full of jumokbap, small fist-sized rice balls mixed with barley, seaweed, salt, sesame oil, and toasted sesame seeds, sitting on a white cloth to prevent sticking.

"Eat as much as you want. There's more if you're still hungry."

Jinjoo quickly counted twelve rice balls and handed out one each to her brothers and sister before hurriedly eating her own. Eunjoo and Junha ate one each while Jinjoo and Junsoo ate two. Jinjoo wrapped the remaining six carefully with the cloth and tied them up into a little sack. She then hid them in the podaegi that Eunjoo was still wearing.

"What are you doing?" her sister asked.

"I don't want them to take it away," Jinjoo explained. "We can take it home for dinner."

Another long hour passed and still no one came to talk to them.

Jinjoo walked out into the main office and waited to catch someone's attention. But everyone was busy and ignored her. She wandered around the building until she finally found a young officer working in a filing room.

"Excuse me, but can you tell me when we can go home?"

The officer looked confused. "Who are you? Where'd you come from?"

Jinjoo led the officer back to the room, and he looked more confused than ever. "Okay, stay here and I'll find out what is happening."

The officer was gone for a short time before he reappeared again.

"Okay, kids, I just heard that you are to sleep here for the night, and someone will drop you off at the orphanage in the morning."

Hearing the word *orphanage* sent shivers down Jinjoo's spine. So many times she had heard stories about how children who were taken to the orphanage never saw any of their family again. Her mother had once threatened her with being sent to the orphanage when she was naughty. Jinjoo had been more frightened of that threat than any beating she could have gotten.

When the officer left, she ran to hold hands with her sister.

"What do we do?" Eunjoo asked.

"We have to run away," Jinjoo said.

"But how?"

"I don't know." Jinjoo frowned in concern. "But we must."

"I have to go bathroom!" Junsoo whined.

Is this our chance? Jinjoo thought. "Okay let's go find it," she said.

Eunjoo stopped her and pointed to the corner, where there was a small pot. "I've been letting Junha go in there," she said.

"No, this time we need to go find the outhouse," Jinjoo insisted.

Holding Junha, Jinjoo led her sister and Junsoo out into the hallway.

"Where do you think you're going?" The older policeman stopped them.

"Bathroom, bathroom!" Junsoo whined as he held his hand to his crotch.

The policeman looked surprised and then quickly led them out the back exit and pointed to where the outhouses were.

"I'll wait here for you," he said as he crossed his arms.

"Drat," Jinjoo whispered as she ushered her brothers into the smelly outhouse.

After relieving themselves, they came out and washed their hands in the long sink behind the building. Jinjoo carefully looked all around her to get her bearings. This was the back of the police station in a large alleyway that opened to the main street after two other buildings. On the other side of the building, she could catch glimpses of the bay.

The policeman hurried them back inside. That night for dinner, they were given rice that was mostly barley and grains that made it crunchy. It was served with a broth made from dried fish and radish. It tasted so bad that they decided to eat the rest of the jumokbap instead. But Jinjoo picked out pieces of fish from the soup that she tucked in the middle of the little rice balls she made out of the barley and grain rice. After making eight of them, she tied them in her cloth again and kept it with the podaegi. During the night, they all went to the outhouse twice more, but always with a guard. Jinjoo checked the hallways several times, but there was always someone around. Frustrated and tired, they all tried to make themselves comfortable on the floor and fell asleep.

Early in the morning, they woke up to the sound of a series of intense blasts that shook the building. Alarmed, they sprang to their feet and looked out the window to see frightened people running in the streets. Jinjoo opened the door and stuck her head into the hallway. The police station was in full alarm, with officers and soldiers rushing in and out of the building. This was their chance.

Eunjoo was helping their brothers empty their bladders while Jinjoo pulled a chair over to open the window. There was so much activity in the streets, no one would notice them. Jinjoo jumped down and quickly tied Junha onto her back with the podaegi, then tied her sack of rice balls to the front strap. She climbed out the window and down, holding onto the ledge with her fingertips until she could safely fall to the ground. Eunjoo climbed onto the chair next with Junsoo, and he jumped into Jinjoo's arms, squashing their rice balls. Next, Eunjoo slowly climbed out.

"Hurry, Eonni!"

Eunjoo fell to the ground with a loud oomph. Jinjoo pulled her sister up, and the siblings joined the crowd of people running.

"Jinjoo, where are we going?"

"To find Appa!" Jinjoo said.

* * *

Junie

"What's the matter, Junie? Why are you looking at me like that?" Grandma asks.

"You were so brave." I stare at her in awe.

Grandma laughs. "I was stubborn and headstrong. Still am."

Chapter 33

ONCE THEY WERE FREE OF the police station, Jinjoo felt like she could breathe again. But the powerful blasts that filled their ears meant another danger was near.

On the street, as they were running, they found an old couple whose bag of belongings had spilled out onto the ground. Jinjoo untied Junha and passed him to her sister. She helped the old couple pick up all their valuables and retie their packages.

"Thank you, little one," the grandfather said. "Where are your parents? It's not safe! You must find them quickly!"

"They're not here," Jinjoo said. "We need to go find them in Seoul. Do you know the way?"

"Aigo, you poor children! How could your parents abandon you?" the grandmother cried.

A loud blast shook the ground beneath their feet.

"Children, you cannot go to Seoul now! It is too danger-ous," the grandfather said.

"But our parents . . ."

"For now, we must all leave Incheon. The Americans are bombing us!"

Not knowing what else to do, Jinjoo hurriedly retied Junha to her back, and the children followed the elderly cou-ple. The roads out of the city were filled with people walking with their hastily packed belongings. Several hours later, they were out of the city walking on dirt roads with thou-sands of other people. Eunjoo was now holding a sleeping Junha, while Jinjoo carried a tired Junsoo. But Jinjoo's arms and legs were sore, and she didn't know how much longer she could continue. As if recognizing their exhaustion, the grandfather announced that they would take a break. They pulled their little group over and found a grassy field by the side of the road. So tired was Eunjoo that she lay down side-ways and fell asleep, Junha still pressed to her back.

Jinjoo sat down and cradled Junsoo in her lap.

The old couple sat next to her; the grandfather fanned himself and his wife. He pulled a gourd of water out of his sack and offered it to his wife before drinking some. Smiling at Jinjoo, they offered her some water. Grateful, Jinjoo took a tiny sip. It made her even more thirsty, but she didn't want to drink any more of their limited supply.

"No, no, drink some more and give some to your brothers and sister," the kind grandfather said. "There's a well not too far from here that I know of. We can refill it on the way. But if you don't drink enough water you will all get sick in this heat."

Thanking them, Jinjoo shook her siblings awake and made them drink all the water. After a few more minutes, the grandfather announced that it was time to keep walking.

"Where are you going, Harabeoji?" Jinjoo asked.

The grandfather pulled Junsoo from Jinjoo's arms to carry him for her. "We are going to Suwon," he answered.

"Our gomo is in Suwon," she said. "Do you have family there?"

"Our son is there with his family. He's been waiting for us to join him so we can all go to Busan together, but we didn't want to leave our store."

"*You* didn't want to leave the store," the grandmother cut in. "I wanted to leave long ago! Before the North Koreans arrived!"

The grandfather nodded ruefully. "I was prideful. My garment store had been in my family for several generations. I didn't want to give it up."

"So what? It's just a building! You can always start another one. But family is irreplaceable," the grandmother said.

"Oh, my father had a watch store in the business district," Jinjoo said. "I don't know what's happened to it now."

"Watch store? Are you Lee Changwoo's children?"

Jinjoo nodded in surprise. "Do you know my father?"

"Of course," the grandfather said. "He is one of the most

honest business owners I know. Terrible thing about your gomo. I was so sorry to hear that. I understand he was taking her to Suwon, and that's the last thing I heard. What happened?"

Taking a deep breath, Jinjoo explained all that had occurred since her father had left town and what her mother had learned.

"So that's why you wanted to go to Seoul," the grandfather said. "But it is definitely too dangerous. I think we should take you to your gomo. Your father will most likely head there also. It is the safest place for all of you."

Jinjoo bit her lip as she looked at her sister. Seeing how tired her sister was, she took Junha to give Eunjoo a rest. She thought of what the grandmother had just said. That family was irreplaceable. A fierce rush of love and affection filled Jinjoo. She would protect her family, and she would find their parents, no matter how hard it was. She would find them.

Junie

"Why did the Americans bomb you?" Junie asks.

"The American ships bombed Incheon so they could land their troops."

"Oh, I see, because the North Koreans had taken over."

Grandma nods.

"How far is Suwon and Seoul from Incheon?"

"Let's see, why don't you pull up a map of Korea on your computer?"

Grandma points out where Incheon is on the west coast of South Korea. Seoul is to the east and slightly north of Incheon while Suwon is directly south of Seoul.

"Wow, Suwon was much farther," I say. "Why did you walk there when you needed to go to Seoul?"

"Because it was safer," she replies simply.

Chapter 34

It took three days to reach Suwon at the slow pace they walked. The elderly couple had shared their food and water supplies with the children, and Jinjoo had in turn given them some of their rice balls. But once in Suwon, the streets were chaotic, with people in a panic.

"I don't know what's going on here," the grandfather said in alarm. "Let's head to our son's house."

They followed along, trying to keep out of the way of the fleeing people. Until they finally reached a quiet, well-lit street. Jinjoo could see that it was a wealthy area of the city. The grandfather put Junsoo down and knocked on the door to a large house compound. The door opened immediately. A young woman appeared and cried out in relief.

"Abeonim! Eomeonim! Thank heavens you've arrived! There's no time to lose! We must leave immediately!"

"What's happening? Why must we leave?"

A man appeared and urged them inside.

"There's going to be another big battle here," he said. "We barely survived the last one. We need to leave for Busan immediately. It's the only safe place in Korea. I was fortunate to bribe a military driver to take us as far south as he can. But we have to leave now!"

The grandfather looked to Jinjoo and her family. "We need to help them find their family."

The son stopped and blinked in astonishment at the children. Jinjoo could see his surprise turn to fear and anger. Before he could complain, she stepped forward and politely thanked the old couple.

"Harabeoji, Halmoni, thank you so much for helping us," she said. "We can find our gomo from here. We know the way."

The grandfather did not look like he believed her, but his son urged him to come inside and prepare, and he guiltily accepted their words.

"Good luck, little ones," he said.

The grandmother pushed a sack of food into Jinjoo's hands before quickly rushing after her son. Jinjoo and Eunjoo bowed and quickly walked away.

"What do we do now?" Eunjoo asked. "We don't know where Gomo is."

Jinjoo went to the end of the empty block and sat down in a grassy spot, hidden from the house. "Now we wait."

Not long after, a large military vehicle drove up to the gate and rapped on the door. Jinjoo watched as the son stepped out and handed the driver a large wad of cash. The driver then loaded the back of the car with all their belongings, while the grandfather and grandmother got in the car with the son and his wife. When everything was loaded up, the car drove away.

"Wow, they must be really rich," Jinjoo said out loud. Taking her little brother's hand, she marched back to the now-empty house.

"Jinjoo, what are you doing?" Eunjoo asked.

"We need a safe place to stay tonight." Jinjoo unlatched the door that had been left unlocked and entered the house compound.

"Are you sure this is all right to do?" Eunjoo asked with wide, frightened eyes.

"They left already," Jinjoo said. "And they're not coming back." She locked the gate door after them and went inside the house.

Turning on the electric lights, Jinjoo immediately searched for food in the kitchen. She found seaweed and small dried anchovies and a basket of fruits and vegetables. Combined with the food the grandmother had given them, they had enough for a full meal. They ate ravenously, enjoying every bite until they were almost uncomfortably full. Jinjoo groaned with pleasure. It was the first time she'd ever seen her sister eat so much.

After they ate, they washed up in the sink outside the house in the warmth of the summer night. Eunjoo decided to wash all their clothing, so they raided the closets for large T-shirts that they wore while they washed everything. The little boys were happy to go naked during the wash. When they were done, they hung the wash on the clothesline and went inside.

Jinjoo found the main bedroom and opened the closet. She pulled out thick bed padding and blankets and spread it all out on the floor for their bed. She turned off the lights, and the children settled down to sleep. The little boys fell asleep right away, but Jinjoo and her sister stayed up late listening to the sounds of the night all around them.

"Jinjoo, what do we do tomorrow?" Eunjoo asked.

"We try to find Gomo."

"But what happens if we can't find her?"

"I don't know," Jinjoo whispered.

They were both quiet for a long moment. Jinjoo was starting to panic at the idea of not finding their gomo when Eunjoo spoke again.

"It's okay, Jinjoo," her sister replied in a sleepy voice. "We'll figure it out."

A few minutes later, her sister's soft snores made Jinjoo realize that Eunjoo was relaxed for the first time since they'd last seen their parents. Her sister, who worried about everything and had barely slept for days, was finally fast asleep.

In the morning, they set out to the main road to seek help.

But no matter who they asked, no one knew who their gomo was, or her daughter. After several hours, they returned to the house they were staying at.

Jinjoo was tired and frustrated. She lay down in the main bedroom to try to figure out what to do. After a while the smell of food roused her, and she hurried out into the courtyard. There she found her brothers chasing each other while her sister was standing in front of a large grill. On top of it sat a small pot of rice, another of soup, and a kettle of barley tea.

"How did you do this?" Jinjoo asked in amazement.

"Eomma taught me how to use the yeontan," she said as she pointed to the cylindrical coal briquettes piled up against the outside of the house. "Shinae never did a good job, so I learned how."

"But where did you find all this food?" Jinjoo asked. "I didn't see it."

"They have an icebox in the kitchen that you missed," Eunjoo said. "I also found kimchee!"

Soon, the meal was ready. Eunjoo didn't know how to make a lot of food, but she had learned to make rice and seaweed soup. Because there was no meat, she'd used a tin of tuna. While the soup wasn't as good as their mother's, and the rice was scorched on the bottom and a little too dry, it was all incredibly delicious to the hungry children. And when eaten with kimchee, it was perfect.

After dinner, they made sure all the coals were burned out before they washed up and went to sleep.

In bed, they waited for their brothers to fall asleep. Then the sisters began to talk about what to do.

"Should we stay here for a while?" Eunjoo asked. "We have food and a place to sleep."

"No, we have to find Abeoji," Jinjoo said.

"And Eomma, too," Eunjoo replied.

"She will be wherever Abeoji is."

"How do we find them?" Eunjoo asked.

"We should go to Seoul." It was the one thing Jinjoo was certain about. "If we stay here, we may never see them again, but if we head to Seoul, we can still find them."

Her older sister sat chewing her lip, a clear sign she was worrying again. Jinjoo could almost hear her thoughts. Walking to Seoul could take days with two little boys. What would they eat? Where would they sleep? Shouldn't they stay here where it was safe?

"Eonni," Jinjoo said. "The owners of this house left because it was not safe for them. Then it is not safe for us. We need our parents."

Eunjoo agreed. "Are you sure we will be able to find them?"

"Yes, I'm sure," Jinjoo said confidently.

They were quiet as they listened to the snoring of their little brothers. Soon Jinjoo heard the soft breathing of her older sister too. As she listened to their sleep sounds, Jinjoo let her worries subside and let the cadence of their breathing lull her to sleep.

In the morning, Eunjoo heated the barley tea and poured it into bowls of yesterday's cold rice and served it with roasted seaweed, sautéed anchovies, and kimchee.

After they finished, they cleaned the house, emptied the coal ash, and washed everything they had used before leaving. Even if the original family didn't return, they wanted to leave it cleaner than when they'd arrived. This was their way of thanking them.

At the main road, the crowds that had been there in the previous days had died down. They asked a random passerby for the direction to Seoul and were pointed toward the main highway. Having asked the grandfather the distances between Suwon and Seoul and Incheon, Jinjoo knew that it would probably take them three to four days to reach Seoul. Not because it was so far—the distance was about the same, thirty-five kilometers—but because she knew the boys would slow them down.

The road to Seoul was not crowded with people or vehicles. They were able to walk on the side of the road unbothered by others. When they were tired, they let Junha and Junsoo run ahead for a little while. Junha in particular was pleased to be free and run around on his own two feet. They just needed to point him in the right direction. When the boys grew tired, the girls carried them on their backs until they could no longer take another step.

At midday, the children stopped when they caught sight of farmhouses a small distance from the main road. Too thirsty to continue, they went to the nearest farmhouse to ask for water. Inside, it was completely empty. It seemed to have been abandoned for a while. In front of the house, there was an iron water pump. Jinjoo looked in the house and found a bucket. She pumped vigorously until water started pouring out of the faucet. She rinsed out the bucket before filling it again. The water was cold and only slightly metallic. They drank the water and ate their packed lunches and rested for an hour. Using the water to clean off as well as cool down, they sat in a grassy area to relax. But Jinjoo couldn't rest and began searching through the entire house.

"Jinjoo, what are you doing?"

She ignored her sister and looked in every corner of the house until she finally found a wooden bottle. She ran to the pump and rinsed the bottle until it smelled clean and then filled it with water. Not having a stopper, she used part of a clean cloth to plug the bottle.

"Now we're ready!" Jinjoo said.

Junie

Grandma pauses and clears her throat. I race to the kitchen to get more boricha. Grandma thanks me, then continues her story.

Chapter
35

IT WAS HARD FOR JINJOO to know just how far they'd come. The road seemed endless and the few people they saw would not stop to speak to them. And because the sisters were either carrying the boys or letting them walk, their pace was slow. When Junsoo wasn't trying to run the wrong way and eat anything that he could catch, Junha would throw a massive tantrum. It was impossible to pick Junha up when he was that upset. He would do the stiff-arm, back-arch trick that was guaranteed to make whoever was trying to pick him up fall over also. At that point, there was nothing to do but let him cry it out.

Jinjoo worried that if they didn't hurry, they would miss the opportunity to see their parents. It was a concern that she felt deep inside, a gnawing feeling that she couldn't explain but couldn't help but believe. All she could do was urge her siblings to walk faster.

By nightfall, the little family found themselves still on the open road. Seeing haystacks in a nearby field, Jinjoo suggested they sleep hidden behind them for the night. They ate the last of their packed food, and Eunjoo sang songs to their grumpy brothers.

Mountain bunny, bunny-ya
Where are you going?
Bouncing, bouncing as you're running.
Where are you going?

Jinjoo sang along, using her fingers to make bunny ears. Her brothers chortled in happy laughter.

"Noona," Junsoo said, pointing to Jinjoo. "You sound like an old frog when you sing!"

Junha screamed, "Frog," and bounced up and down.

Jinjoo pulled a sour face and punched the hay to make it comfortable. Everyone always made fun of her singing. Even her father had told Jinjoo that it was a good thing she had a pretty face and smart brain, because her singing would drive any potential husbands away. It had hurt her feelings, and she'd sulked for days. Though no one liked to hear her sing, she enjoyed it anyway.

She watched as Eunjoo played with their brothers and then got them ready to sleep, covering them both with the podaegi. Eunjoo kept singing and patting her brothers. They fell asleep instantly.

It struck Jinjoo that her sister was more like a mother than their mother. But right after she thought it, she felt guilty. Jinjoo stared up at the starlit sky, wondering where their parents might be.

In the quiet of the summer night, she could hear her sister praying. Although their mother was Buddhist, their father was Catholic, and they'd gone with him to a few services at Dapdong Catholic Cathedral. It was a beautiful building with its three-bell tower and western construction. It felt holy. It felt like a place you could pray to the heavens and be heard. Eunjoo loved the church and wanted to go every week, but their mother disapproved. To be honest, Jinjoo's interest in the church only grew in defiance of their mother. But at times like this she wished she could be at the church, sending her prayers to heaven in hopes that someone would hear her.

"Do you really think we will see our parents again?" Eunjoo asked.

Jinjoo swallowed back her fears and focused only on the belief in her heart. "Yes," Jinjoo replied.

"How do you know?" Eunjoo asked.

"I just know." Before her sister could ask any more questions, Jinjoo turned away onto her side and tried to sleep.

Jinjoo woke up to the laughter of her brothers. They were running around the haystack, chasing a white butterfly. As she watched them play, she heard the rumbling of approaching vehicles. Before she could stop them, her brothers raced to the side of the road to see what was making such a commotion. Jinjoo caught them just as the first American trucks rolled up. The large vehicles weren't driving very fast, and the children could see the faces of the American soldiers sitting in the backs of the trucks in their green uniforms and hard helmets, holding their rifles. Some of the soldiers waved and smiled as they stood gaping at the procession.

"Wow!" Junsoo shouted, and then waved his little hands as he smiled and jumped up and down. This made more of the soldiers smile, and many even laughed.

Jinjoo picked up her younger brother so he could see better. He put out his hand and leaned toward the trucks, as if he was trying to touch the Americans. Some of the soldiers leaned over to wave at Junha, making him laugh out loud. She couldn't understand the words the men were saying, but she appreciated their warmth toward her little brothers.

All of a sudden, a soldier in one of the last trucks waved at them and said something. As he came level with them, he tossed a big handful of small items that fell all around them. He said one more word as he waved goodbye. Jinjoo didn't know what he had thrown, but she bowed in thanks. Junha wriggled down to see what it was and began picking up the colorful objects with his brother.

Jinjoo looked at a yellow rectangular one and squealed in happiness. She knew what it was. Several years before, when there had been more foreigners in Incheon, an American man had given her one piece. He called it chewing gum and explained that it was for chewing until all the flavor was gone but not to swallow it as it was bad for your tummy. Jinjoo had enjoyed the sweet flavor but understood what the man had said about swallowing. Once she had chewed it for a while, all the flavor was gone and it tasted like nothing. But she'd enjoyed it tremendously. There was another small rectangle that was brown with gold ends. She didn't know what it was, but it smelled sweet.

"Junsoo, Junha, pick up every piece! It's candy!"

The little boys crowed in delight and filled their little pockets with everything they could find. Jinjoo searched the entire area to make sure they hadn't missed any. She gathered them all from her brothers and marveled at the big pile of sweets they now had. Only then did she notice that Eunjoo had never joined them.

"Eonni! Where are you?"

Her sister peeked out from behind the haystack.

"Are they gone?" she asked. "I was so scared. How come you weren't?"

As the little boys ran over to show Eunjoo their haul, Jinjoo wondered why it was she hadn't been scared by the Americans. Lots of Koreans hated them. They blamed them and the Soviets for dividing the country into North and South. They were the ones that had created the thirty-eighth parallel and separated families. But right now, with the Communists invading South Korea, Jinjoo could only look at them as brave men willing to fight for a country that wasn't even theirs.

"They were so nice! Look, they gave us all these sweets!"

"I want!" Junsoo shouted. "I want! I want!"

"Me too, me too!" Junha chimed in.

Jinjoo plopped down on the ground and sorted through the pile.

"Let's try this one," she said, opening the brown-and-gold rectangle that had smelled so sweet. Inside was a hard brown block that had a design of six squares. When she tried to break it apart, it was actually squishy and left a big smudge of brown on her finger. Junha reached over, licked it off, and crooned, "Mmmm."

Jinjoo laughed and broke off the pieces, popping one in everyone's mouth before eating it herself. The taste was like nothing she'd ever had before. She heard her sister gasp in delight while Junsoo was now running in circles shouting "Wow!" at the top of his lungs. Junha copied him exactly. Soon her brothers came back and opened their little mouths for more.

"Ah," they both said, looking expectantly at the two remaining pieces in the wrapper.

Part of her wanted to eat them both herself, but Jinjoo counted three more of the brown candies in her pile. Feeling generous, she popped the last pieces into their mouths.

She then opened the chewing gum package and gave them all a piece.

"This is for chewing only. You can chew it, you can suck it, but you can't swallow it! Understand?"

Her brothers nodded and put out their hands, but Jinjoo wasn't convinced they understood.

"Listen, you like this brown candy, right? You want more, right?"

They nodded their heads eagerly. "Yes, Noona!"

"Then you chew this, and when I put my hand out, you spit it out, okay? And if you don't spit it out, if you swallowed it, then no brown candy for you, understand?"

"Yes, Noona!" they shouted.

She then opened a piece for all of them and stuck it in the little boys' mouths. In her candy pile, she counted ten packs of the chewing gum. She then gave one whole pack to Eunjoo.

"Try it, Eonni, you'll like it."

As she listened to the little sounds of pleasure her brothers made, she wrapped the rest of the candy in the cloth that they had used for their food.

"If we walk faster and farther today, I'll give you more candy," she said to her brothers.

They clapped their hands in delight and both began to walk, holding their sisters' hands.

On the road, the children kept a faster pace than before. The boys were energized by the thought of more candy and didn't stop as much. Whenever they wanted to get picked up, Jinjoo would trade their old gum for a new piece and they would walk again.

Finally, they were too tired, and the sisters carried the

little boys on their backs until the evening sun began to set and the girls were near collapse. With very few trees on the road, they moved out into the field and plopped down under the leafy branches of a large, solitary oak tree. The boys dropped onto the soft grass and fell asleep.

Jinjoo could see that her sister was still marveling at the chewing gum.

"How did you know what this was, Jinjoo?"

"From Abeoji's store," Jinjoo said. "You would have known, too, if you had gone to his store more often."

Eunjoo shook her head. "Strangers frighten me."

Jinjoo put her arm around her sister. "It's okay, Eonni. You have me! I won't let any stranger near you!"

Her sister smiled and then frowned again. "Sometimes I think you should have been the big sister," she said. "You're not as scared of things as I am. And you're stronger than me. . . ."

"No way!" Jinjoo said. "I'm just a big bully! You're the best big sister! You take care of our brothers and are always patient, even when I want to hit them. You can cook and you are so kind. I could never be as good a big sister as you."

Eunjoo wiped away her tears and hugged Jinjoo. "I'm so glad you're my little sister."

"Hey, who are you calling little?" Jinjoo puffed out her chest, causing her sister to laugh.

They looked at where the little boys had passed out asleep on the ground. Junha had used Junsoo's stomach as a pillow.

"They're so tired, they didn't even ask for dinner," Eunjoo sighed. "I guess it's a good thing, since we have no food."

"We have to save the little that we have," Jinjoo agreed.

"Go to sleep then, little sister," Eunjoo said, cuddling next to Jinjoo.

Jinjoo closed her eyes and fell fast asleep.

Junie

"Grandma, when did you find out that the candy was chocolate?" I ask in curiosity.

"I think it was after the war," Grandma replies. "My father went to the store and bought it as a treat. I recognized it right away and loved it. So he would buy lots of chocolate for us all the time."

I look at Grandma in wonderment. "But you don't even like chocolate."

Grandma laughs. "It's because I ate too much of it and I got seven cavities!" She shudders. "Getting seven teeth drilled for cavities made me never want to eat candy again!"

Chapter
36

"WE SHOULD WAKE THEM," JINJOO said, anxious to be on the road again.

Eunjoo shook her head. "Let them sleep some more. And we should be more rested so we can carry them longer."

Since Eunjoo was her older sister, Jinjoo had no choice but to listen to her, no matter how it chafed at her. Only after thirty minutes had passed did Eunjoo allow her to wake the boys up. Junsoo woke up crying of hunger. With nothing else to give them, Jinjoo broke open another brown candy bar and gave two pieces each to her sister and brothers, only allowing herself to lick her fingers where the candy melted. There were now only two brown candies left. Jinjoo needed to save them, as they were the most filling of the treats.

"What about you, Jinjoo?" Eunjoo asked. "You'll be hungry."

Shaking her head, Jinjoo opened another pack of chewing gum. "We have plenty of this! It will keep me going!"

They carried the boys for almost an hour before they gave up and had to put them down. The American candy worked extremely well as bribes to keep the little boys going. There had been another candy that was like a soft but chewy fruit snack that was covered in sugar. Neither Jinjoo nor her sister liked it very much, but the boys loved it. Jinjoo was so grateful to the soldier for giving them such a wonderful gift.

"Eonni," Jinjoo said as they walked the empty road, "when I grow up, I want to move to America."

"Why?" Eunjoo asked in alarm. "Why would you want to move so far away? And to such a foreign place?"

"Just think of it! America is a land so powerful and rich that they can throw wonderful food like this into the street. I want to live there and never be hungry again."

"I would miss you," Eunjoo responded. "Wouldn't you miss all of us?"

"Yes, but I'll be so rich that you will be able to come visit me anytime you want!"

"You are a big dreamer, Jinjoo."

Jinjoo looked up at the bright blue sky above them. "If you don't dream, it can never come true."

She looked back at her sister and grabbed her hand. "Come on, Eonni! We have to go faster if we are to meet our parents!"

* * *

From a distance, they could see smoke rising high into the sky. As they walked farther, they saw it was a farmhouse that had been completely destroyed. Beyond it, an entire village was on fire.

Earlier in the day they'd seen a few airplanes flying ahead. Jinjoo wondered if they were the ones that had destroyed the village. She didn't know what side the planes were on. They could have been American or North Korean. All she knew was that an entire village had been burned to the ground, and to the villagers, it probably didn't matter who had done it.

A few kilometers later, they reached a crossroads. There was a sign with arrows pointing in each direction, but the words were written in English, not Korean. And there was no one around to ask which way to go.

"What happened to the Korean signs?"

Eunjoo pointed to a pile of blackened rubble nearby.

"What do we do?" Eunjoo asked.

Jinjoo looked down at the dirt road. The one to the left was heavily crossed with large wheel tracks. The one to the right was not as marked.

"We go left," she said with absolute conviction.

"How do you know?" her sister asked. "Are you just guessing?"

"Look at the tire tracks," Jinjoo said. "Remember all the American soldiers in trucks yesterday? Must have been twenty trucks that drove by us. They definitely took that road."

Her sister looked confused. "But how do you know they are going to Seoul?"

"It's our capital," Jinjoo said simply. "The North Koreans captured it, so the Americans must be here to help us win it back."

"You don't know that," Eunjoo said, fear widening her eyes. "Maybe they were running away! Maybe they're going back to their ships and going home!"

Jinjoo thought of the faces of the soldiers she'd seen. They'd been smiling. Those were not the faces of men who had been defeated or were running away.

"No way," she said with absolute confidence. "They're here to help us."

With that, she picked up Junha and quickly started walking to the road on the left.

"Wait for me, Noona!" Junsoo cried as he ran after her.

Junie

"Is that why you wanted to come to America so much?" I ask. "Because the Americans saved Korea?"

Grandma hesitates. "That's a very complicated question. Yes, America helped save South Korea from the North. But it's also true that Americans killed a lot of innocent Korean civilians during the war—stories that were suppressed by decades of terrible South Korean presidents who brutalized our people."

I nod my head. I remember Grandpa telling me about how bad it was.

"So you wanted to come here because of the South Korean government."

"That's more accurate," Grandma says. "My childish desire to go to America was based on this idea of it being a rich country. But as an adult, I wanted to get away from the corruption of the Korean government. Americans might have put President Rhee in power, but it was his corruption, and that of his military successors, that hurt the people. I wanted a fresh start. Back then, America represented hope for a better future."

Chapter 37

THERE WERE MORE PEOPLE ON this stretch of the road. But most were heading south and looked in terrible shape. They seemed too dazed to notice anything around them.

Jinjoo and her siblings just kept walking. They stopped midday for a long rest under the shade of a row of camellia trees. Eunjoo carefully gave them water to drink, and then they napped because of the dust and heat.

It was Jinjoo who woke them up again and pushed them back onto the road. But the heat and the walking had taken a terrible toll on Eunjoo and the boys. They were dragging their feet, and their pace had fallen significantly. Jinjoo coaxed and bribed them all the way to mid-afternoon, when they reached another crossroads. This one had no sign. Both roads were heading north; however, one was in an easterly direction while the other one veered sharply to the west.

Eunjoo and the boys collapsed in the grass.

Eunjoo whimpered that she could not walk any farther.

As Jinjoo tried to figure out which way to go, an old man in a horse-drawn wagon appeared.

"Harabeoji, please excuse me, but could you tell us which is the way to Seoul?" Jinjoo asked.

The man scratched his head. "Well, they both head north toward the Han River. One will take you to the east side and the other will take you to the west side."

"Thank you," Eunjoo chimed in. "Which road is shorter?"

He pointed to the right. "The way I'm going," he said. He looked at them. "Do you want a ride?"

"Yes!" Eunjoo replied. Gathering the boys, she headed toward the wagon. "Come on, Jinjoo! We don't have to walk anymore."

The thought of a ride was such a tremendous relief that Jinjoo took a step toward the wagon, but then something made her stop. She placed her hands on her chest. There was a tightening, like a warning. This was not right.

"Eonni, I don't think we should go that way," Jinjoo said.

"What are you talking about? They both go toward Seoul. What can be wrong?"

Jinjoo shook her head. "It's this feeling. I know we have to go to the west." Jinjoo pointed. "If we don't go this way, we might never meet our parents."

Eunjoo had already put Junha in the wagon and was lifting Junsoo up.

"Jinjoo, I can't walk any more. And Junsoo and Junha can't either—we're too tired. We're going to ride in the wagon." With that, she began to climb up, when suddenly Jinjoo raced forward and pulled her down.

"No, Eonni, we have to go west." Jinjoo hauled both boys out at once. "Thank you, Harabeoji, but we are going the other way."

"Suit yourself," he said as he clicked his teeth, and his horse slowly plodded away.

"No!" Eunjoo screamed. She hit Jinjoo hard on the head and shoved her to the ground "Why did you do that? I told you, I'm too tired. I can't walk any more. You're supposed to listen to me! I'm your eonni!"

Eunjoo dropped to the dirt road, sobbing wildly. Even though it was Jinjoo who'd gotten hit, the little boys crowded around their older sister and cried with her.

Jinjoo wiped away the tears that had sprung to her eyes. For a moment she fought the urge to yell at her sister and hit her back. To tell her she was tired too. And scared, so scared that maybe she was wrong. That all she wanted was for her older sister to be a true eonni and tell her that everything was going to be all right. Jinjoo closed her eyes and thought of what her father always told her to do when she was about to lose her temper.

"Jinjoo, when you lose your temper, you lose control of your tongue. Things you'll wish you'd never said will come flying out."

"Like Eomma?"

He nodded. "Instead of losing your temper, count backward from ten. Let the hotness cool down. That way you won't say things that you will regret."

"Like you?"

Her father smiled and hugged her tight. "You are the most like me, Jinjoo. And I have always struggled with my temper also. But this little trick helps me keep not only my temper, but also my friends."

Jinjoo counted backward from twenty and then pulled out the second-to-last brown candy bar and opened it. At the sound, her brothers sat up and came to her. She quietly fed them two pieces each and then gave the other two to her sister.

When she refused it, Jinjoo insisted. "Eat it, Eonni. I know you are mad, but we have to keep going. You need this more than I do."

She pushed against her sister's resistance until she finally agreed to eat the candy. Jinjoo tied Junha onto her back, and then picked Junsoo up.

"Let's go."

They walked down the westerly road, Jinjoo stubbornly holding Junsoo until her arms felt like wet noodles and she abruptly put him down.

"Junsoo, here's some chewing gum. Please can you walk for me?"

He nodded, looking tired, and held the package in his hand.

As they walked, the road they were on turned sharply to the left, and the children suddenly found themselves alongside a large field of bright orange cosmos flowers. Far ahead they could see how the road curved and bent through the field as the sun began to set to the west. The flowers blazed in the rays of the setting sun, and all around them was a sea of orange and gold. The children were enthralled by the colorful blooms and left the road to walk in the field. Junha was so little, he was hidden by the tall flowers. Jinjoo picked him up and twirled him around, to his delighted screams.

"Me too, me too!" Junsoo begged.

They laughed and frolicked in the beauty of the flowers, their cares forgotten for the moment. Even Eunjoo smiled and sat in the fragrant soft grass to make a flower crown.

Jinjoo took out the last brown candy bar and shared it with her siblings. This time Eunjoo insisted she eat one too.

"I wish I knew what this candy was called," Jinjoo said. "I'm afraid we won't find it again."

"I'm sure you will," Eunjoo replied. "You are very stubborn. If you want something, you'll get it."

Jinjoo furrowed her eyebrows as she tried to sear into her memory the look and taste of the most delicious candy she'd ever eaten.

"One day I will eat you again," she said out loud. "And I won't have to share!"

She stood up to stretch, and then noticed the dark shapes of two people far off on the road. One of them was pushing a bicycle. Something about them seemed familiar to Jinjoo.

"Come on, let's walk a little more before the sun sets completely."

They went back onto the road, holding their brothers' hands, and saw that now there were quite a lot of people who were walking in the fields and along the road. But Jinjoo's eyes were fixed on the figures in the far distance. The orange-gold flowers waved slightly in the wind as the sun set to their left, casting the entire area in a golden haze.

"Eonni, doesn't that look like our parents?" Jinjoo whispered as she gazed at the approaching forms. "Wouldn't it be wonderful if it was?"

Eunjoo squinted. "I don't know. They are too far away. But do you really think they are?"

Jinjoo didn't know, but something was making her heart beat faster. The stiff straight back of the thin male form and the way he held his head. The short height of the other person, who was just a little rounder. She couldn't be sure, and yet everything in her body seemed to know. She began to rush forward, still holding Junsoo's hand.

"Eomoni? Abeoji?"

Junsoo began to run also. "Eomma? Appa?" he repeated.

Up ahead the two figures suddenly became clear. They too began to run.

"Jinjoo! Eunjoo!"

"Eomma! Appa!" Jinjoo heard her sister scream as she ran past Jinjoo, holding Junha.

They were now all running toward each other. Their father dropped the bicycle and whisked Eunjoo and Junha into his embrace, while their mother fell to her knees and caught Junsoo. Everyone was crying; even people passing by had stopped and were moved by the reunion.

Jinjoo stood in front of her weeping family. She was so tired and yet so happy. She stood and cried. Tears of overwhelming exhaustion and fear mixed with the joy of seeing her parents. She couldn't move until her father came and pulled her into his strong embrace.

"Jinjoo, how did you come to be here on this road?"

"Appa, I was so afraid I'd never see you again."

"But you found us, my brave little girl. I don't know how, but you did," he said.

As she wept, she felt her mother come and embrace her also.

"Jinjoo-ya! Your eonni said it was because of you that we are meeting like this. I'm so proud of you!"

"Eomma!" Jinjoo sobbed.

"Don't cry, my brave girl! We are all here together now!"

The sun had set by the time they all stopped crying. Appa led them to a quiet grassy area away from the flower field, where they could rest for the night. Eomma gave them all dried squid to eat, and they told their parents of their adventures until they were finally too tired and fell asleep in a large happy heap of bodies.

In the morning, their parents got on the bicycle, their

mother wearing the podaegi with Junha strapped onto her back, Eunjoo sitting behind them holding Junsoo, and Jinjoo sitting in front of her father. They all hung on tightly as Appa pedaled his bicycle to take them as far away from the war as he could.

BOOK V

Junie

Chapter 38

"THANK YOU FOR TELLING ME your story, Grandma." I am now by my grandma's side, hugging her tight. I'm crying and feeling the warm glow of satisfaction from a happy ending.

Grandma nods and wipes her eyes. "It's been so long since I told anyone that story."

"I still can't believe you were able to find your parents like that!" I say. "It's almost unbelievable. If you hadn't insisted on taking the other road, you would have never met them."

"It was a miracle, I know," Grandma agrees. "I often think about how lucky we were. How we could have been killed, or kidnapped, or bombed. The war claimed so many innocent lives. Orphaned so many children. And yet we were able to stay together and find our parents. We were so fortunate."

"If this was anybody but you, Grandma, I don't know if I would believe it."

Grandma laughs. "Many people have said that. But miracles happen all the time."

"How far did Great-grandpa take you on the bike?"

"That bicycle got us as far as Suwon, where we found my gomo," Grandma recalls. "And then we went by car to Kunsan, where my father worked for another watchmaker until he was able to open his own shop."

Grandma shows me where Kunsan is on the map. It is almost directly south of Incheon and on the western shore.

"Did you ever go back to Incheon?"

"After the war, we went to find our house, which was still standing, although uninhabitable. I remember my mother and father digging up a hidden stash of valuables from our inner courtyard. My father used that to open his own store in Kunsan."

"What was it like living there?"

"Very different from Incheon, but we liked it because it was safer. Away from the worst of the fighting."

"Did you ever forgive Great-grandmother for abandoning you?"

"Of course," Grandma says. "She was my mother. It was wartime. And I also think she was very young. She was only sixteen when she married my father. He was just twenty. She'd been the pampered daughter of a wealthy family, and then she'd married someone who could afford to take care of her and even hire a housemaid. She'd never had to take care of anyone but herself. Then the war came and she found herself alone, with no husband and four young children. I understand why she did what she did."

I'm not sure if I understand. I think of my own mother, and I know without a doubt that she would never have done that. And as I look at my grandmother, I know that neither would she. I think she is reaching for a reason to forgive her mother. And that I can understand.

Since Grandma looks tired, I stop recording.

"I didn't have enough time with Grandpa. I wish I had recorded more of his stories," I say. "But I want to make sure I get all your stories, Grandma. Please?"

Grandma agrees. "It will be a good history lesson, maybe?"

"It will be our family history," I reply. "So, can we do this every Friday?"

"Like you did with Grandpa?" she asks.

"Yes, just like Grandpa."

She pauses and gazes at the big framed photo of Grandpa that now hangs on the living room wall. "Sure, let's do it. Grandpa would have liked that."

"He really would."

That night I find myself sketching again. Grandma's story fills my mind and I draw a field of orange flowers and a young girl carrying her little brother on her back. I can't get over how brave my grandmother was. How at such a young age she crossed a war zone looking for her parents. I admire her so much and wonder what I would have done in the same situation. I try to imagine it, but I can't. War is not something I can understand. And yet as I finish my sketch, I realize I have drawn a picture of myself in that field of flowers. Maybe, now, I can be more like my grandma.

Chapter 39

BACK AT SCHOOL, IT'S GOOD to see my friends again. They all came to my grandfather's funeral, but while I loved their warmth and sympathy, it also felt very surreal. I still catch myself thinking, *Ah, Grandpa will love this,* or *Oh, I can't wait to tell Grandpa about this.* And in those moments, the reality of him being gone cuts me so sharply, like a razor. It burns intensely and then dulls to an aching throb. But I think to myself, if it hurts this much for me, how bad must it be for Grandma?

She's the one I need to be strong for. I promised Grandpa.

And in this weird way, thinking like this helps me with my own depression. Rachel tells me it's a coping skill. Focusing on Grandma helps me not focus on my own pain. She says it's a good thing for both me and Grandma. I think she's right.

On my way to class, I bump into Esther Song.

"Hey, Junie," she says. This surprises me.

"Hi," I respond, and then just stare at her.

"Listen, I wanted to say I'm sorry about your grandfather," she says. "My grandparents were friends of his from church. They said he was a wonderful man and they'll miss him a lot."

"Thank you," I whisper. "I miss him a lot also."

She pats me awkwardly on the shoulder, and then she leaves. I watch her and think to myself, *Maybe there's still hope for her.*

During lunch, my friends start talking about the diversity assembly.

"Junie, it's okay if you can't finish the video," Patrice says. "We all understand."

"Actually, I finished it."

My friends look surprised. "Working on it helped me," I explain. "I'll bring it tomorrow."

The next day I show the video to the group and Ms. Simon. The title screen reads *What You Don't Know About Racism.*

When it's done, they all begin to clap. Patrice gets up and gives me a bear hug.

"Junie, you did it! It's so freaking good!"

"You should be a film director! It's excellent!"

"I love the background music!"

Ms. Simon pats me on the back. "That was very well done,

Junie! It is going to be perfect for the diversity assembly. It really shows people all the big and small ways racism can happen, and how hurtful they can be. I'm forty years old, and I learned so much from your video. Thank you for that."

I'm embarrassed and yet really happy from all their praise. All those long hours have paid off. They like my video. I can't wait to show it to my grandpa. My heart spasms. For a moment, I forgot that Grandpa was gone.

"Should we do the video before our speech or after?" Patrice asks.

"I think it should be first," Hena answers.

The others all agree.

"Junie, will you still introduce the video?"

I talked to Rachel about this. I asked her if I was a coward for not wanting to speak in front of the entire assembly. She told me whatever I decided was absolutely fine.

"Junie, it's okay to say no," Rachel told me. "It's okay not to do something that you will find burdensome. You don't have to push yourself into the spotlight to know your worth. You can shine from wherever you stand."

"But will Patrice be disappointed?" I worried.

Rachel shook her head. "I bet anything she will understand."

Now I take a deep breath. "What if we start the assembly by just playing the video as the introduction, and then you guys can speak?" I ask.

"That's not a bad idea," Hena says. "The video pretty

much starts with all of us anyway."

Patrice nods. "I think the video speaks for itself. It'll be perfect."

Patrice leans forward and gives me a high five, and I am both relieved and content.

As the day of the diversity assembly draws near, I can see how nervous my friends are. We've been invited to go onstage to be introduced before the professional speaker. But only Patrice and Hena will speak, so I'm not nervous at all. However, the bigger problem is that someone is still scribbling racist messages on our flyers. And as Patrice and I walk into the cafeteria, Lila and Marisol come rushing over with a Diverse Voices club flyer.

"Look at this handwriting," Lila says as she shows it to us. "It's the same person as before."

We all look at it and agree. "Yeah, it's definitely the same person," Patrice says. "I wish we'd seen the graffiti to compare this to."

"Wouldn't the police have taken photos?" I say loudly. We happen to be walking by the popular table, and I catch Stu's eye. "I bet they can do a handwriting analysis."

He smirks at me and reaches over to snatch the flyer out of Lila's hands.

"Oh, how scary these words are," he mocks. His entourage laughs.

Patrice gets in his face and grabs the flyer away. "Don't

start with me, Stu, I'm not in the mood for your nonsense."

"What're you gonna do, Patrice?" Stu smirks. "Cry about it at your stupid club meeting?"

I can see everyone in the cafeteria is starting to pay attention to their heated argument, and any minute now, the teachers will come over. But I'm not paying attention to them. I can't help but notice how upset Esther Song looks. I saw her face when she looked at the flyer, and I know she saw what it said. She sees me staring and looks away.

The teachers have come now and are dispersing everyone. My friends drag me along to our table, but I keep glancing over at Esther.

When the bell rings, I tell the others I have to do something, and I follow Esther out. She's alone and not with the Stu crew. The hallway is crowded, but I follow her into the stairwell and then I tap her arm.

"Esther," I say as I stop her.

She jumps in alarm. "What do you want?"

She is not very friendly.

"Why do you stay friends with them?" I ask.

"What do you mean?"

"They make racist comments all the time. They hate people like you and me. Why do you put up with it?"

"They may hate you, but they don't hate me," she says with a wave of her hand.

I'm shaking my head. "I don't think so," I say. "They say hateful stuff about Asians all the time. I've actually heard them make comments about Koreans eating dog in front of you. Why do you let them do that?"

"They're just joking," she says defensively.

"It's not funny. It's hurtful. You know that."

"You don't understand . . ."

"I think I do." I want to get through to her. "I know you've been friends with that group for a long time. But they don't treat you right."

"Just leave me alone!" She pulls away from me and starts to head up the stairs.

"You're Korean, too, Esther. You can't change that."

"Shut up!"

I ignore the looks from passing students and run to class.

Chapter 40

ON THE DAY OF THE diversity assembly, my friends and I meet up early at school. Everyone is dressed really nicely, but I'm in my regular school clothes. I decided that I didn't want to be introduced onstage, and they all understood.

At the assembly, I sit up front with my friends as the principal starts it off and then introduces the video as a Diverse Voices production. The auditorium darkens, and the video plays. On-screen, it reads "What it's like being a student of color at Livingston Middle School."

Then the video opens on Patrice, who says, "A microaggression is when someone says or does something that they might not even know is racist or sexist, but it is."

It then cuts to a series of students mentioning a microaggression.

An Asian student who says, "Where are you from?"

A Black student who says, "No, you cannot touch my hair."

A Latino student who says, "Yes, I speak English."

Another Asian student who says, "But where are you really from?"

Then Lila and Marisol show up on the screen together.

"I'm Lila, not Marisol," Lila says.

"And I'm Marisol, not Lila," Marisol responds.

"Stop confusing us," they both say. "And not all Latinas are from Mexico."

"You do realize that South America is actually a continent, right?" Lila asks.

"And I'm Cuban," Marisol continues. "So stop being so ignorant."

All the Latinx students in the auditorium let out a big cheer.

Patrice is back on-screen, talking about how racism causes anxiety, depression, and even physical ailments. Several Black students speak honestly on how demoralizing racism is, not just from students, but from teachers and administrators too. Hena is now on-screen sharing a story about being called a terrorist and explaining just how horrifying it is whenever anyone uses the word to describe Muslims. And then a few Asian students recount their experiences being asked if they understand English.

I'm proud of myself. I think I did a great job editing, but I tense up, knowing that my part is coming up. Toward the end of the video, I show up on-screen.

"Some of you might be watching and think that since you aren't a racist, this doesn't apply to you. But you're wrong. Every day in this school, a racist remark, a racist joke, a racist incident happens. The question is, what did you do about it at that moment? I admit that I'm one of the people who is usually silent when racism happens to me. Because I'm afraid. But my grandfather told me that silence can be a weapon. When we are silent in the face of racism, we give racism the power to continue to hurt Black people and people of color. Only by speaking up against racism can we take away that power. Our voice becomes a shield, just as our silence has always been a weapon. So I'm not going to be silent anymore. I'm going to speak up and be part of the solution, no matter how hard it might be."

The next screen is a series of students saying, "Don't be a bystander. Speak up against racism."

The video ends with Patrice thanking everyone for watching.

After the applause, Patrice and Hena go up onstage and present their speeches, and then we all watch the professional speaker walk us through the steps of what we can do to fight racism. When it's all done, I feel all the stress that was tight in my neck and shoulders suddenly relax. I am so relieved, I could melt into my seat. We did it.

For the rest of the week, we all get a lot of compliments on the presentation. It is great to hear that the message resonated so well with so many people. But the biggest surprise comes when I run into Esther Song after school. I am waiting for my mom to pick me up and she's running late. All the buses have left and there are only a few cars in the pick-up circle. I'm debating whether to wait inside when I hear someone call my name.

I turn around to see Esther Song standing behind me.

"Hey," I say in surprise. "What's up?"

She hesitates but then she shows me something on her phone. I have to look closely, but it's a video of Stu Papadopolis using a black Sharpie on a Diverse Voices flyer. I am speechless and find myself blinking at her like a confused owl.

"He posted it on his private chat app," she said. "But he's got about two hundred people following him on it, so I don't feel bad outing him."

I can't believe what I'm hearing. "He posted this on social media? What was he thinking?"

"Give me your number and I'll send this to you," she says. "But only if you promise not to tell anyone who you got it from."

"I promise!" I give her my number, and she watches as I download the video and erase her message.

"Thanks, Esther." I want to ask why, but I don't want to push her.

She smiles sadly at me. "I've been having stomach problems and anxiety since the third grade. I think it's time I found better friends."

I'm nodding. "You deserve better," I agree.

She waves goodbye and starts walking away.

"Hey, Esther," I call out.

She turns around in surprise.

"I'm bringing my grandma's mandoo to next week's club meeting," I explain. "You should come and try them out. They're the best."

"I don't know; my grandma's are pretty killer," she replies.

"What? Mandoo challenge! We should get both our grandmas to do a mandoo cook-off and we'll be the judges, cool?"

Esther is laughing. "Cool."

I watch her walk away and think that she's not that bad after all.

That night I send the video clip to my friends, and by the time I get to school in the morning, the video has made the rounds, and Stu Papadopolis is expelled. At lunch, I search the cafeteria looking for Esther, hoping to invite her to sit with us, when I spot her with a new group. It looks like she's already moved on.

Patrice nudges me and asks me who I'm looking for. I smile and point at Esther. "I'm glad she's found new friends."

We both look at her. "She looks more comfortable," Patrice says.

I agree.

"So, I bet you were really surprised it was Stu," Patrice

says, with a knowing look. "You thought it was Tobias, right?"

I nod, a little ashamed.

"I did too," she admits. "He's almost too obvious a choice, you know?"

"Yeah."

"You were probably hoping it was him so he would get expelled, right?"

I look at my friend and nod sheepishly.

"Don't feel bad. I was praying for the same thing." Patrice puts an arm around my shoulders. "Although I'm pretty happy about Stu being gone too. I wonder if his little crew will continue to be jerks."

"I vote jerks."

"Yeah, probably," Patrice says. "But this doesn't solve your Tobias problem."

I think about my grandpa and my grandma and all they had to go through in life. Tobias doesn't seem like such a big problem after all.

Nudging Patrice back, I give her a big smile. "I think I know what to do. I'll be fine."

"Are you sure? Because I got your back."

"I'm good," I say. "I'm strong."

Patrice gives me a hug. "Love you, Junie!"

"Love you too, Patrice."

Chapter
41

Monday morning my mom wakes me up super early. She's wearing her suit already and an apologetic look on her face.

"Honey, I'm so sorry to do this to you, but I got called into an emergency meeting, and your dad already left for work. Would you mind taking the bus today?"

I'm still a little groggy, but her words make my heart pound unpleasantly.

"Or do you want me to ask Grandma if she can drive you?"

I want to say yes, but it would be such a pain for Grandma. I don't want to bother her. So I say what I know my mom wants to hear.

"It's okay, Mom, I can take the bus."

"Are you sure, honey?"

No, I'm not sure. But I nod. "I'm fine."

She smiles, but I can see the worry on her face. I tell my

mom not to stress about it, which is basically useless to say, and I promise to text her when I get to school.

As I leave my house to walk to the bus stop, I have a serious talk with myself.

"Remember what you told Patrice! You're strong, you can handle this."

I don't believe myself. Argh.

I can stand up to my nemesis. He is the tiger of Grandpa's story. If I don't stop him now, I will never be free. I take deep calming breaths with every step, until I find myself at the corner across from the bus stop. I spot Tobias right away. He lurks behind the others, sneering at them all.

I am not afraid of him. He is just a mean kid. He is a terrible person who always picks on me. He is a racist. He doesn't like me. I can feel myself starting to get angry.

I don't like him either. In fact, I despise him. My blood is starting to boil. I let out an angry puff and march across the street. I will no longer be silent.

"Well, well, well, look who finally crawled out of the sewers! It's the dog eater!"

My anger erupts. "Tobias Thornton, why do you always pick on me?"

Tobias is startled. He's not used to me standing up to him.

"Whoa, point your kimchee breath somewhere else, commie!"

"Shut it! I'm tired of your meanness! What did I ever do to you?"

He stands there blinking his narrow eyes at me for a long moment.

"I don't like you," he finally replies.

"And I don't like you either," I shout right back at him. "But that doesn't mean we have to be nasty. Why can't you just leave me alone?"

"Yeah, leave her alone!" Andre chimes in, which surprises the heck out of me. "I'm so sick of you bullying her all the time!"

I'm staring in shock at Andre, but he just nods at me as if to say *I got your back*. And I feel this rush of energy through me. I'm no longer alone.

I can hear Tobias yelling at Andre to mind his business. But I also notice Andre's friends have stepped up next to him. In fact, I look around to see that many of the kids at the bus stop have stepped closer to me, as if to give me silent support. And it feels so good. So maybe the diversity assembly really did make a change. Maybe it reminded people to speak up when they see something that's wrong. The exact message we'd hoped for. To let those who feel powerless know that they are not alone.

This time, I know what to do. "Shut up, Tobias. This is everyone's business!"

"What did you say to me?" He walks right up to my face, trying to intimidate me with his size and bulk and terrible bad breath.

"You heard me," I say. I keep a tight lid on my temper but

let my voice become as loud and ringing as my soul wants it to be. "When you say racist words, it is everyone's business, because it hurts all of us. And it hurts you too, Tobias."

He looks so surprised and then scoffs. "What the hell are you talking about? It don't hurt me none."

"Yes it does, because those words are ugly and hurtful. And if you believe those words, then you will become just as horrible on the inside. Nobody is born hateful; you turn hateful. Those racist words and beliefs are making you ugly inside. But you don't have to be."

"Shut up, commie! I don't need to listen to you."

"Shut up, Junie," I reply evenly. "Use my name, not a slur."

"What?" He can't believe I'm still talking to him.

"I said, use my name. It's Junie," I reply. "It's not that hard. Instead of seeing us as these horrible words, see us as people. My name is not commie or chink or dog eater or North Korean spy. My name is Junie."

"I know what your name is . . ."

"Then use it!" I've finally lost my temper. "You want to be mean? Fine, be mean. You want to be rude? Then be rude. But don't use racist words ever again."

"What are you gonna do about it, *Junie?*" He sneers my name in an elaborate, condescending manner. But I feel like I've won, because he didn't use a slur.

"Then we'll keep having this conversation every single day, over and over again until you are sick to death of hearing it. Until you finally stop."

I can see the thoughts in his head churning, and he clearly doesn't like it.

"And don't you ever call me a commie ever again. My great-uncle and his pregnant wife were murdered by Communists during the Korean War. My great-grandfather was imprisoned and tortured by the North Koreans. My family comes from a country where a false accusation of being a Communist would get you and your entire family imprisoned or killed. So don't ever use those words again."

"Yeah, whatever," Tobias sneers at me as the bus comes. He pushes everyone aside and gets on the bus first, stomping to the back.

I've won. At least that's how I feel. I don't think I've changed him, but I can feel the change in myself. My back is straighter. I am standing taller. I've definitely won.

Grandpa, you'd be so proud of me! I fought my tiger, and I won't let him bully me ever again!

I would give anything in the world to hear him say *Good girl!*

As we line up, Andre stands next to me.

"So, was all that about your great-uncle and stuff true?"

I'm surprised he's asking me, but I nod. "Yeah, it's all true."

"Wow," he says in admiration. "Do you mind telling me what happened?"

He sits next to me on the bus, and I find myself relaying some of the stories my grandparents told me. As we pull into

347

school, he turns to me and says, "Junie, I hope you write these stories into a book one day."

A book.

Yeah, I think Grandpa would like that.

~Epilogue~

"JUNIE-AH!"

Grandma is calling me because I've wandered too far away. But it's because Incheon Airport is amazing. The ceilings are really high and beautiful with tons of natural light, and I see actual trees and lush greenery in the terminal right next to luxury-brand cosmetic stores. It might be the nicest airport in the world. Although I've only seen Dulles Airport back home, where we flew out of. I thought Dulles was nice. But Incheon is on another level.

"Junie-ah!"

"Coming!"

There's so much to see, but I hurry after Grandma and my family. My dad's trying to rent a car and Mom's getting us all SIM cards for our phones. And Justin is making a beeline for a convenience store to look for food. I don't know how he thinks he's going to buy anything since we haven't exchanged any money yet.

"Grandma, are you tired?"

"A little bit, but I slept a lot on the plane," she says. She grabs my hand and pats it. "You look so excited."

I nod enthusiastically. "I just wish Grandpa were here."

Grandma's hand tightens on mine. "He is here with us." She pats her chest. "He is always here with us."

Justin comes running back to us. "Grandma, can you buy me snacks? I'm starving, and they got triangle kimbap in the store!"

We load up the big minivan Dad rented, and we pile in for the drive. Our itinerary is full—we are going to stay in Incheon for a few days so Grandma can see how much it has changed since she left so long ago. Next we're going to Seoul to visit Grandma's friends and do a lot of sightseeing, and then Seosan to visit Grandpa's relatives who still live there. One of the suitcases we brought is filled entirely with presents for them.

I look up at the blue sky and I can't help but think of Grandpa. I touch my phone and I can see a photo of me and Grandpa on my lock screen. We were sitting together on his armchair before he got sick. I see his smiling face, and I feel the pain in my chest again. I'm getting used to it. I know I'll be thinking of him a lot during this entire trip. He's the reason we all came. To see Korea like he wanted.

"I'm here, Grandpa," I say out loud.

I can almost hear his voice saying, *Good girl, Junie. Good girl.*

Author's Note

WHEN I WAS YOUNG, MY mom would always tell me this story about how she and her siblings were separated from their parents during the Korean War. Sometimes she would say they were lost for weeks, sometimes a month, sometimes it would be raining in her story, sometimes it was just really hot, but the premise of the story remained the same. Four little kids walking night and day on the roads of South Korea, looking for their parents. I have to admit, it was always more of a tall tale to me—the long, difficult journey, the miraculous reunion. It was a family legend, kind of like the magic fish myth my father would tell me, how our Ha ancestors were turned into golden carp to save them from evil invaders. Or how my parents loved to tell me supposedly "true" scary stories about evil Korean monsters who like to eat naughty children named Ellen. So, you can understand why I might have been a bit skeptical about the lost children story.

But then nearly ten years ago, my aunt came from South Korea to visit my mother in New York City, and after dinner the two sisters became nostalgic. I listened in fascination as they reminisced about a memory that was over sixty years old. My aunt, who is the eldest, would correct my mother's version of this epic story and just like that, what had once been an unbelievable tale became a historical family truth. I suddenly realized that this miraculous journey was real, and I was overwhelmed with a burning desire to write about it and memorialize it.

I began my own journey into researching the Korean War, and soon it became clear to me that I couldn't only write my mom's story. The subject matter was too complex and too emotional. And as I puzzled over this dilemma, I became aware of what was happening in my own community. Swastikas and racist graffiti were being found in schools all over my city and my children were suffering. But how to tie this all in with a story about the Korean War? What I found myself doing was listening to my father's voice. He passed away several years ago, but I still talk to him in my heart. I can hear him telling me his stories. I can hear his voice and his wise words that remind me of how important it is to pass on the stories of our elders. So that we will always remember where we come from. And suddenly the story began to form.

Without a doubt, this has been the hardest of my books to write, the most deeply personal. In many ways, I feel very exposed by what I share in this book. But I am also proud of this story. It is both truth and fiction, historical and contemporary. It is my family's story and the story of my motherland.

I hope that you enjoy Junie's journey, and I thank you for reading.

With deep gratitude,

Ellen Oh

Glossary

abeoji — father

abeonim — father (formal)

appa — dad (informal)

aga — baby

ahjumma — middle-aged married woman

ahjussi — middle-aged man or married man

aigo — oh dear

banchan — small side dishes given at meals

bap — rice or food

boricha — barley tea

chama — to endure

chibi — Japanese slang for something short

chon — 1/100 of 1 won, the official currency of South Korea

emo — aunt on mother's side

eomeoni — mother

eomeonim — mother (formal)

eomma — mom (informal)

eonni — older sister to a female

galbi jim — marinated and braised short rib dish

gomo — aunt on father's side

gwaenchana — It's okay.

halmoni — grandmother

hanbok — traditional Korean outfit

harabeoji — grandfather

hotteok — sweet pancake

hyung — older brother to a male

jeon — battered and fried dishes

jumokbap — round rice balls shaped like a fist

karaage — Japanese fried chicken

kim — seaweed squares

kimchee — fermented cabbage

kongnamul — bean sprouts

mandoo — dumplings

nado — me too

noona — older sister to a male

omo — Oh my!

oppa — older brother to a female

podaegi — quilted blanket used to secure a young child onto a person's back

sal — uncooked rice

saranghae — love you

waseo — You came.

yaksok — promise

yeobo — term of endearment, usually between a married couple

yeontan — coal briquettes to heat house

Acknowledgments

This book wouldn't be possible without my mother and my emo and the conversation that finally made me realize the truth of what happened during the Korean War. I'm so grateful to them for sharing with me their memories. And I am filled with so much admiration for these two incredibly strong women. Thanks, Mom and Emo, for letting me tell your story. I really hope I did a good job.

For me, the absolute best part of working on Junie's story was that I got to go to South Korea on a research trip with my oldest daughter, Summer. What an incredible bonding experience for us and we both ended up falling in love with our motherland. The trip will always be one of the highlights of my life for me and I'm so glad to have been able to share the experience with my dearest Summer girl!

A great big *thank-you* to my very dearest friend, Hong Soo Yeon, who is chairman of the board of directors at Pung Saeng Academy and who acted as my personal tour guide and research adviser during our trip. I can't thank Soo Yeon enough for all that she did for me. She and her husband, Lee Kyou Hong, took me everywhere and interpreted all the hard stuff for me. (My Korean is good enough to get around with, not good enough to understand complex discussions.) They introduced me to the incredibly knowledgeable Ko Hanbin, a curator at the War Memorial Museum who answered so many of my research questions. And I must thank the wonderful tour guide Park Chungkwon, who took me on a very special and thorough English tour through the entire museum and gave me so much information that I would never have discovered on my own. I learned so much!

Thank you also to the awesome group of first year students at Pung Saeng Academy, who were so smart and so insightful. And thank you to Director Kim Joong Chan, who introduced me to the best jajangmyeon in Seoul over a lively and informative conversation about Korean society and history.

A very special and important thank-you to Professor Hong Sah-Myung of Hankuk University of Foreign Studies, who answered all of my endless questions, both in person and over email for months! I honestly could not have written this book without his help and guidance. It was Professor Hong's childhood experiences during the war that was the basis of Doha's story. I am so grateful to Professor Hong for helping me bring balance to this book by including his stories. And because he is Soo Yeon's uncle, I owe my dear friend Soo so much! Thank you, Soo, for everything you did for me! I could not have written this book without you! I just wish we were not so far apart! Miss you, dear friend!

To Linda Sue Park, you saved me!! When I got lost in the

deep abyss of endless research, you introduced me to the brilliant author of *Ghost Flames*, Charles J. Hanley, who put into my hands the one essential piece of historical evidence I needed to finalize this book. Dear Charlie, when I was absolutely stuck and in despair of finding the facts I was seeking, your email saved me. I'm so grateful to you and Linda Sue. Otherwise, I'd still be stuck in research hell forever and this book would have never been finished and I would have scratched my head bald. It would not be a pretty sight.

To my brilliant editing team, of Alyson Day and Eva Lynch-Comer: Thank you both for believing in me and Junie!

Dear Eva, your comments always challenged me to think really hard about how to tell a better, richer, deeper story.

Dear Aly, thank you for helping me write this book. To be honest, there were many moments when I didn't know if I could write it. I doubted myself the whole way. But you never doubted me and gave me so much support and guidance. This was the hardest book to write and I would not have been able to survive the writing and revision process if it wasn't for your unwavering support. Thank you so much for helping me tell my mother's story.

To my copy editors, Kathryn Silsand, Maya Myers, and Caitlin Lonning, you are so good at making me look good!!

To my Harper art team, how is it possible for each gorgeous cover to keep blowing me away? I always say this, but Joel Tippie is a *genius*! I'm always so amazed that my vague ideas of what a cover might look like are then translated into a cover that is so very perfect. Thank you to the incredible illustrator Alex Cho for bringing my vision alive with his beautiful art. I could never have imagined it and yet it was absolutely perfect in every way.

I would also like to thank the rest of my Harper team— Emily Zhu, Vaishali Nayak, Jacquelynn Burke, Aubrey Churchward, and Vanessa Nuttry. Thank you for bringing *Finding Junie Kim* to life!

Special thanks to my wonderful agent, Marietta Zacker of Gallt & Zacker agency, who heard me pitch this idea and said an enthusiastic *yes* before I knew how I was going to even tell this story. You really get me and I'm so, so, so grateful!!

I owe a lot of meals to my wonderful friends who have read for me, brainstormed with me, supported me, and been there for me in so many ways—Olugbemisola Rhuday Perkovich, Lamar Giles, Dhonielle Clayton, Hena Khan, Minh Le, Christina Soontornvat, Caroline Richmond, Sarah Park Dahlen, Mike Jung, and Terry Hong. These people are the very best people and I adore them.

To my besties Anna Hong and Jen Choi Um—Love you ladies!! I'm still waiting for our world-tour trip!

To my sister, Janet, who is such an enthusiastic supporter of my writing. Thank you for always being a light in my life.

I need to have another big shout-out for my oldest child, Summer. Not only did she go to Korea with me, but she was my research assistant and was deeply involved in helping me write and revise this book. Summer, thank you for all of your help and for all the enthusiastic love! You were the first person to cry reading Junie's story and that will always mean so much to me. Most specifically, thank you for letting me write about your special relationship with Grandpa. I know we both miss him so much. But now he will live in the pages of this book. His memory will always be there for us.

To Skye and Graysin, my two beautiful younger children, thank you for allowing me to include your experiences in this book, as difficult as they were. Thank you for helping me tell your stories through Junie.

To my husband, Sonny, thank you for buying a lot of takeout food and feeding the family whenever I've been on deadline. Okay, even when I'm not on deadline. Thank you for understanding how much I hate to cook. Thank you for always taking care of me and being my one and only.

And lastly to the memory of my father. Thank you for being my dad. I really miss you.